Peep Show

USA TODAY BESTSELLING AUTHOR

ISABELLA STARLING

Copyright © 2018 by Isabella Starling

Text set in Dante.

Book design by Inkstain Design Studio

All rights reserved. No part of this book may be reproduced or transmitted in any form or by any means whatsoever without express written permission from the author, except for the use of brief quotations in a book review

*To the part of me that found itself in Miles and became
a better person because of him. And to anyone who's ever felt it. The panic.
The fear. The anxiety. I'm here to tell you it gets better. YOU will get better.*

WITH ALL MY LOVE,
ISA xx

Playlist

Laidback Luke, Steve Angello, Robin S - Show Me Love
Oliver Heldens, Becky Hill - Gecko (Overdrive)
Bebe Rexha, Ty Dolla $ign - Bad Bitch
Tove Lo - Disco Tits
Vice, Jon Bellion - Obsession
Marshmello - Alone
M A E S T R O - What U Wanna
Flume, kai - Never Be Like You
Jack Ü, Skrillex, Diplo, kai - Mind
Bebe Rexha - Atmosphere
Lauv - I Like Me Better
ZAYN, PARTYNEXTDOOR - Still Got Time
Syn Cole, Miss Buttons, Lucas Silow - Miami 82
Camila Cabello, Quavo - OMG
Mike Perry, The Vamps, Sabrina Carpenter - Hands
Dua Lipa - IDGAF
Snakehips, MØ - Don't Leave
Xuitcasecity, No Sleep - Criminals

Full playlist on *Spotify:* goo.gl/xDsYsK

Peep Show

Chapter 1

·BEBE·

VOYEUR, NOUN
A person who gains sexual pleasure from watching others when they are naked or engaged in sexual activity.

I stumbled into my bedroom, giggling to myself and shaking on too-high heels and too much vodka.

A glance in the huge mirror on the wall reminded me of what I mess I was when I had too much to drink. My silver sequined dress was riding up, revealing a hint of my ass under the shiny fabric. My hair was wild, the dark brown locks a halo around my head, and my brown eyes glowed with excitement. At least my makeup was still in place, the perfect smoky cat-eye enhancing my looks, making me appear demure yet sexy. I'd perfected the art of it, making sure I always had someone eager to buy me a drink.

I sank down on my bed and pulled off the murderous black heels that had been torturing me all night. But it was okay – I'd learned to handle the pain, and when I was dancing, it never mattered anyway.

I lay back and I stared at my ceiling, letting myself think about what my life had become, but only for a short while.

The key was never to focus on it for too long. I had to forget, and drinking, dancing and partying, was the only way I could do it. I could never stop. If I stopped twirling, stopped tipping back glass after glass, I risked stopping long enough to think about what I was doing. And that was the last thing I wanted.

I needed to forget about Posy. She was long gone, and there was no bringing her back.

I pushed myself off the bed shakily, and went to the window to let some fresh air in. There's nothing quite like a nice fall breeze to clear your head, and God, I needed some fucking clarity.

I opened the blinds and looked outside, the street below me illuminated by the streetlights. It was gone four a.m., and most of the lights in the apartment building next door were off. I lived in a nice neighborhood of townhouses, about three apartments per floor and three floors total. It was a good place to live, and, of course, I wouldn't have been able to afford it if it hadn't been for my parents' stack of cash in my bank account.

Being a trust-fund baby definitely had its benefits.

My eyes traveled upwards and focused on the only illuminated apartment across the street from me. I could see right into their home, but the minimalistic apartment seemed to be empty, even though it was lit up.

I opened the window wide, enjoying the breeze on my face, slowly bringing me to my senses once again.

A thumping noise interrupted my reverie, and I looked up again, right into the apartment opposite mine. Except now, it wasn't empty anymore.

Peep Show

Now, there was a dark, impossibly tall figure pressing a naked woman against the window, fucking her savagely, mashing her tits against the glass, her mouth opened in an endless gasp as he took her from behind.

My mouth gaped in surprise, and I moved a little to the side, hiding in the darkness and watching the show they were putting on with a smirk on my face.

The woman had small but perky tits. Her skin was dark, almost ebony, a sharp contrast to the pale man standing behind her, towering over her. She was tiny and curvy, and he was fucking enormous.

He was all toned muscle and dark, slicked-back hair. His strong, muscular arm was wrapped around her neck in a chokehold, strangling the screams right out of her. And his skin was covered in dark, menacing ink, the black color stark against his light skin.

I wanted more.

I wanted to keep watching.

I shifted on my feet to get a better view of what was going on before me.

He fucked her like an animal. I could see his hips working, pushing, thrusting inside her from behind, claiming her petite body and making her mouth open in a silent scream. He fucked like a beast, and he looked like a monster. I'm sure I fell in love with him right then and there.

My fingers shook as I reached for my purse, scrambling to find it on the bed and trying not to look away from the scene in front of me at the same time. I wanted to watch. I wanted to see his face when he filled her up. I wanted to see if he'd pull her hair back like I imagined he would.

I managed to get my phone out of my handbag, bringing it in front of my face and quickly snapping a picture of them. Suddenly, I felt awake and sober, staring into the cold night outside and wishing I could swap places with the ebony beauty. I wanted him inside me.

A burst of inexplicable jealousy bubbled in the pit of my stomach, but I did my best to ignore it. Instead, I kept snapping pictures of them. Of him.

Wishing I could see him better, I moved from behind the curtain a little bit closer to the window. My breath made foggy circles on the glass and my hands shook as I put my phone down and reached under the hem of my dress.

The silver sequins felt cold and exciting against my fingertips, and I touched them gently before spreading my own trembling legs apart, slowly outlining the wet, dripping shape of my pussy lips between my thighs.

I was so damn wet.

In fact, I was fucking leaking all over my panties, the image across the street making my pussy drool so much I flushed with embarrassment.

But I couldn't help myself. Couldn't resist slipping my fingers under the sodden satin fabric of my panties, outlining my perfectly waxed pussy as I shivered under my own touch. It felt so strange, voyeuristic, to be watching them do this on the other side of the street. And it was horny as hell.

My fingers worked their magic between my legs, slowly teasing my cunt open and finding my clit. I'd let someone kiss me at the club that night, but I didn't bring anyone back with me, which was unusual for me. I liked having someone to go home with. It made me feel wanted.

I remembered his hot, needy lips. He was a nice guy, not one I'd usually go for, which was probably the reason I hadn't brought him back home with me. He had a buzzcut, and his face was clean-shaven too, and I loved the prickly feeling of his features under my fingertips, and the push of his bulge against my tummy. But I didn't let myself have it. I really didn't do nice guys, because I wasn't a very nice girl.

Lips parting in a gasp, I braced myself against the windowsill as I stroked myself towards an orgasm. His hand was squeezing her throat so tightly, she looked like she was out of breath, her chest heaving and her mouth open so wide.

She was crying.

He was fucking her so hard, so savagely, with so little mercy, that the poor girl was crying her eyes out, all the while coming all over his dick.

Fuck!

A moan escaped me, my fingers working in fast, messy circles to get myself off. I came with a desperate cry, my pussy making a creamy mess all over my fingers. I'd always been such an easy comer, ever since I learned how to get off by myself.

My eyes felt strained as I looked back up, and then opened as wide as they possibly could as I stared at them. He was still choking the girl, her eyes closed and her breathing ragged, but his own gaze was firmly fixed on *me*.

I panicked. Surely he couldn't see me – my room was barely illuminated. But I saw them both so fucking well.

He grinned at me. Two rows of perfectly straight, impossibly white teeth glaring in the darkness of the night. He ran his free hand through his dark, slicked-back hair, and carelessly scratched at the stubble growing on his chin. Then, he reached in front and twisted the girl's nipple so hard she threw her head back in a scream I couldn't hear.

He kept staring, and I couldn't look away, and my heart leapt when he knocked on the window. Two sharp raps, whispering something in his girl's ear, making her eyes fly open in panic, and she saw me.

I stared at her. I stared at them both, unable to move, my pussy juices dribbling down my thighs.

He raised a hand and waved at me, an easy smirk playing on his lips.

The devil waved and nudged the girl he was fucking, motioning for her to do the same thing. When she shook her head, his hand wrapped tighter around her throat.

And she looked at me sheepishly, and waved, just like he had.

I'd never wanted to be someone else until that moment, when I wished with absolute desperation that I was the beautiful petite girl next door getting her pussy slammed by a stranger.

He thrust inside her one last time and my own fingers repeated his motion. His eyes remained locked on me as he came, the girl crumpling in his arms, only him holding her up as he spurted inside her. My fingers fell away from my body, my poor cunt spasming by itself, leaking down my thighs, ruining the sequins of my dress and covering them in my own pussy juice.

My legs shook and my cunt clenched as I came again.

I watched him let go of the girl, gently laying her down on the floor. I could only see her naked back against the glass, her shoulders hunched as she cried her release out, her whole body shaking.

And then he stepped up to the window, in all his glory. He must've been over 6 feet 5. He was fucking enormous, so tall she looked like a child at his feet.

And he was completely naked, save for the condom on his dick.

His fucking cock matched his height, making my mouth water at the sight of it. He was ripped, muscles everywhere, looking not just like he worked out regularly but like he made it his mission to keep his body in perfect shape.

His cock was still hard as he took the condom off, discarded it on the floor and stroked slowly.

He grinned at me, and stroked his cock lazily with one hand as he wrote on the steamed-up window with the other.

Peep Show

My eyes danced across the words and I stepped forward, letting the light of the streetlights illuminate me. I knew he saw me now, because he jerked his dick faster, and it made me fucking ecstatic. He liked what he saw. And how couldn't he? I was always sure to be groomed to 5 feet and 10 inches of polished, manicured and slutty perfection.

I followed his fingers writing on the window and lifted my dress up, showing him my ruined panties.

His eyebrows shot up and he smirked at me, licking his fingers and palming his shaft with fast, needy motions.

I stared at his words on the glass, written clumsily, some of them fucked up because he'd tried to write their mirror reflection so I could read it.

My pussy tingled at his crudeness.

My heart thumped in anticipation.

And my mind reeled with the possibilities.

I DARE YOU TO GO NEXT.

Chapter 2

·MILES·

THANTOPHOBIA, NOUN
The phobia of losing someone you love.

I winked at the girl and clicked a button next to the window. The electric blinds came down in a flash, shielding us from any unwanted, prying eyes.

I shifted my attention to the beauty on my floor and kneeled down next to her, my fingers gentle as I tucked a stray strand of hair behind her ear.

She looked up at me, those dark eyes filled with nothing but adoration and the desperate need to please.

"Did I do g-good?" she stuttered, her full bottom lip jutting out, her eyes begging me to answer in the affirmative. "P-please tell me I was a good girl for you, Miles... P-please, I need to hear it."

I took her chin in my fingers and gently lifted it, staring into her eyes.

They looked endless in the dimly-lit room, the chocolate brown of her irises almost black in this light.

"I need you to cry," I told her plainly. "Cry some more for me, you pretty little thing. I want to taste your beautiful tears."

She blinked against the tears brimming in her eyes, and a single, fat drop of salty liquid slid down her cheek. I leaned closer to her, my mouth parting and my tongue dipping out between my lips, licking at her cheeks and tasting her. Desperation and fear mixed with lust in a delicious cocktail I just couldn't resist.

She looked back up at me as I smiled down at her.

"Will you do it now?" she whispered. "Will you do it, Miles? Please, you promised you'd do it if I cried…"

I let her stew, waiting to answer until she was so damn desperate a soft little whimper escaped her lips. I loved torturing them this way. Loved seeing them so desperate for me they would do anything in the world for my approval.

The girl in front of me was fucking ripe for it.

She would do anything, and gladly fucking so.

"Come with me," I said, offering her my hand. "Let me capture it."

She raised a shaky hand into mine and I helped her to her feet, slowly leading her trembling body out of the room. I admired the sway of her full hips, the way her tiny body was still so feminine despite its petiteness. She was a fucking stunner, and now, with my cum dripping down her thighs, she was finally ready.

I led her into a perfectly plain room with white furniture. A simple white bed, a white chair, and a white dresser.

"Where do you want me?" she asked shakily, turning to face me.

"On the chair," I said, walking to the dresser and rummaging in its drawers.

She seemed disappointed, but I didn't have time to think about that. All I could imagine was how the stark contrast of her dark skin would look against the white room. I wanted it immortalized. I wanted her, in this moment, forever.

I already knew which picture I was going to pair her with.

An image of candles burning bright in a church my mother used to go to. Her innocence, her wishful eyes, would be the perfect pairing for the whispered prayers spoken when the candles were lit and placed at the altar. Today's girl was demure naïveté mixed with an almost palpable need to please.

She wasn't a girl who enjoyed pain.

She was a woman who loved to please, and in her desire to do so, she'd gotten me off so fucking good my balls felt drained.

But the beautiful girl in front of me wasn't the reason my dick was still twitching.

No, my mind was firmly on the girl next door, the silhouette in the window across the street.

I'd never seen her that clearly before.

Glimpses here and there, when I glanced out the window, remembering there was a life outside of my four walls. I knew she was a woman, and I knew she lived alone. But I'd never seen her this clearly. The streetlights had illuminated her body more than I think she realized, and in the moonlight, she looked like a dream.

She got me curious. The memory of her fingers dipping into wet panties made me twitch as I took my camera out of the dresser and pointed it at the girl I'd filled up not moments ago.

She tried to smile for me, and I sighed in exasperation.

"Don't smile," I told her, and her expression faltered. So easily hurt. So perfectly timid. "Just look at me. Remember what I did to you. Let me see you open up like your pussy just did. Let me see you pull back the curtain, just like you did your knees, sweetheart."

She gasped and I took the shot.

I didn't need to look at it to know it was fucking perfection.

The first ones often were.

I took a few more to calm her nerves, and once she was done, immortalized on my camera, I set it aside.

"Thank you for playing with me," I told her, offering her my hand.

Now came the hard part.

"Thank you," she whispered. "Thank you for choosing me."

I kissed the top of her head and she shivered beneath my touch.

"I'll call a cab," I said gently, and she stiffened under my fingertips.

I pulled back and reached for my phone, knowing it would be the first and last night I ever touched her.

The girl had left in a mess of tears and whispered promises I didn't want her to keep.

I didn't remember her name by the time she was gone. I didn't need to, knowing I'd remember her, the night we'd spent together, by looking at her photograph. It was enough for me, even though it wasn't enough for her.

I remembered her whispered words, telling me how much she'd admired my work for years beforehand. How she'd dreamed of being my muse before she was even fucking legal.

But if she really knew of my work, she must've been aware that my subjects changed daily.

She was one of many, a number in a long line of women at my door, a muse for an hour, a fuck for a night.

It didn't mean I didn't give a shit. I did, for as long as she was in my arms. For a few hours that night, the girl had been my world, my everything. I saw the possibilities of a relationship, of a future, of waking up with her in my bed, her eager lips on mine.

But I put it all into a photograph, and then added her to my portfolio like so many girls before.

I wasn't capable of more.

Never had been.

Never would be.

After getting her in the cab, I pulled my gray Henley off, pushing my tracksuit down my hips. I stared at my reflection in the bathroom mirror that took up the whole wall. I had to work hard to look the way I did. I had a fully equipped gym on the second floor, making sure I was in the best shape, even though I never left my apartment.

My muscles were toned and defined, my skin covered in ink that told my story. I let my hands glide over it, down over my stomach and locking their grip around my thick cock, throbbing at the thought of *her*.

My mystery neighbor, the shadow behind the curtain, the girl who fucked her pussy at the sight of me ravaging another woman.

She intrigued me, the veil of mystery around her making me want to break my own rules.

I never saw the girls I fucked beyond the night they spent bouncing on my cock.

If I fucked this one, she'd be right across the street – forever.

And I didn't even know what she really looked like; her face had been shrouded in darkness.

I stepped into my shower, the marble cool beneath my feet and the cold water beating down my back. It felt fucking good.

I washed the girl's cunt off my cock, off my fingers. I cleaned my body expertly, washing and scrubbing and taking extra care to remove every trace of her off me. I knew I wouldn't be able to sleep if I could still smell her. I needed to be clean. Pristine. Scrubbed raw before I laid down to sleep.

Fingers… dipping into wet panties.

The shine of a silver sequin, almost blinding in the night.

The way she put her palm on the window, as if she was trying to touch me.

Her body silhouetted.

A stranger.

My fist wrapped around my cock and I tugged on the tip.

I was hard. Painfully fucking hard, my dick throbbing desperately, begging me to relieve it of another load of hot cum, squeeze it out, dump it all over the Italian marble, drain myself of the filthy thoughts that seemed to reside inside my head permanently.

I worked my cock with fast, mechanic motions. I let my mind wander, never to the shy girl I'd made cry, always back to the mysterious girl next door, who'd been so eager to pleasure herself at the sight of me.

I thought of my life beyond the apartment.

The fact my name was getting bigger and bigger.

My photography, the words critics used in their reviews feeling nasty and cheap when I thought of them, even though they were meant as praise.

The way I took my photos, joining two images in one using double exposure, coupling stunning naked women in their most vulnerable state with the item, the scene that reminded me of them the most. Today's girl had gotten candles, her wishful thinking coupled perfectly with the candles' glow. My agent would be pleased.

In my fucked-up head, riddled with thoughts of keeping things in order, with ways to rid my skin of the scent of the shy girl, my neighbor didn't have a picture I wanted to couple her with.

She wasn't a pairing, she was a silhouette, nothing but a shadow, a stark dark cutout on white paper.

It felt oddly calming. Strangely clean. It calmed me down, and it got me so worked up I placed my palm against the shower wall and exhaled roughly, my palm working, pulling, tugging, getting ready to blow another load all over the glass and marble.

Fuck her, I wanted to fuck her. Right here, in the sterile shower where a woman had never been, push her against the stone and take her pussy with my fingers first, my cock second, and my mouth third. I wanted to know what she tasted like with me inside her. I wanted to know how sweet that cunt was after I'd forced orgasm after orgasm out of it.

I jerked faster. My cock felt impossibly hard, throbbing in my fist, desperate to unload. Desperate for my mystery girl.

Her pussy.

Her mouth.

Her tight little ass.

My doctor always told me not to focus on these little obsessions. That I should let them go. That they weren't healthy.

But god-fucking-damnit, they made me feel alive.

The thought of her. Shit, the thought of her playing in her bed, hoping

I'd open the blinds again, taunt her, dare her again.

She could've been anyone, I wouldn't have cared. I wanted that tight cunt wrapped around my dick.

And then I was coming.

Coming for *her*.

Hot cum mixed with the cold water beating off my chest as I groaned my release and palmed my dick into a fucking frenzy.

She used her dainty little fingers to fuck that pussy.

I was going to use a whole damn fist.

After I was done, I cleaned myself off meticulously. I didn't use bleach that night. I didn't feel like I had to.

As I lay in my bed, the pristine Egyptian cotton sheets atop my skin, I let myself think about her.

Don't obsess.

Don't get attached.

Don't think you need her.

Don't make it into a problem.

By the time dawn rolled around, I knew it was too late for any of that crap.

Mystery girl was now firmly rooted in my mind, my heart, and my fucking dick.

And I wouldn't rest until I'd had a taste.

Chapter 3

·BEBE·

WONDERWALL, NOUN
*Someone you find yourself thinking about all the time;
a person you are completely infatuated with.*

Lights flashed in my eyes, the drinks I'd had making my body numb. I swayed to the music, my fingers in my hair and running down over my face and my curves seductively. I kept my eyes closed as I danced, knowing I had everybody's attention on me. It felt fucking good.

I loved nothing more than dancing like this after I'd had some shots. I loved the music they played in the clubs, too; loud and boisterous, perfect for blocking out anything and everything else.

"Bebe!"

I heard someone shouting my name over the sound of the music, but I pretended not to notice.

I needed to drown it all out. The noise helped me replace the endless pain in my head, the horrible memories that made me feel sick, the knowledge that I was heading down the same path Posy had taken, even though I'd sworn to myself I wouldn't do it.

"BEBE!"

I opened my eyes, anger flooding my body as they locked with my friend Arden's.

"What do you want?" I hissed at her, but instead of answering me, she grabbed my arm and pulled me to the side, leaning against the wall and staring into my eyes with determination.

The music thumped through my body as I waited for Arden to explain herself.

"That guy over there," she told me over the sound of the bass. "He asked me if you were Bebe when I went to get us drinks. I think he's into you."

She motioned to one side of me, and I looked over to see if he was of any interest to me.

The guy she was talking about had a stocky build. He was taller than me, but not that tall, wearing a varsity jacket over a V-neck shirt and distressed jeans. His hair was long on top and short at the sides and he wore biker boots with the outfit.

He was handsome.

Sexy.

But painfully boring.

I guess he would do for the night.

I looked back at Arden with a smile playing on my lips and winked at her. She smiled wide.

"So who have you got your eye on tonight?" I asked her, and she shrugged with a grimace.

"I don't know. I'm not really into anyone here. I guess I'll just call Nick again…" she sighed.

"That guy is boring as shit," I reminded her.

"But he adores me," she said, and I nodded thoughtfully.

I couldn't see myself with anyone like Arden's Nick. He was her oldest friend, blinded with love for her since she'd been a little girl. He was always following her around, trying to convince her he was worth her time. But the thing was, neither Arden nor I were interested in good guys like Nicholas Mackey.

They didn't get me wet like the ones who choked me and spat in my face while they fucked me. And if they called me a slut on top of it all, I was fucking guaranteed to squirt all over their dicks.

"I guess I'll see you soon?" I asked Arden, and she shrugged again, miserably this time.

I felt sorry for her, but my pity didn't last long because as soon as I walked away from her, the guy who'd been checking me out came up to me.

He wore a sexy smirk on his face and a look of determination passed through his eyes as they locked with mine.

"Hello, trouble," he said with a toothy grin, and I fluttered my lashes at him.

"Hi, handsome," I purred as he reached for my arm, gently stroking down my skin.

Once he reached my wrist, he grabbed onto it, his fingers rough and calloused against my skin.

"You wanna have some fun?" he asked, opening my palm up with his fingers.

I looked down to find a small pill in it.

Memories flooded me with the intensity of a punch to the face.

Posy.

Pretty Posy with her red hair and full lips, laughing, smiling, chattering away.

Promiscuous Posy in a sexy hot pink dress that clashed with her hair spectacularly, dancing, always dancing.

Sad Posy, crying, telling me about her fucked-up family, about everything she'd been through.

Sexy Posy, leaning into me, capturing my lips in a kiss that told me all her secrets.

Dead Posy. Her face unnaturally white, her lips blue.

She was *gone gone gone* – and I was *here here here*.

I smiled weakly at the guy, raised my palm to my lips and licked up the pill with the tip of my tongue. I showed it to him and he leaned into me, taking my mouth in a rough kiss. I swallowed it before he could get a taste, the drug disintegrating inside me and showing me how to have *fun fun fun*.

Like Posy never would again.

He moved away from me and I opened my mouth wide, sticking my tongue out to show him I'd swallowed.

"Good girl," he muttered in my ear, his fingers wrapping around my waist possessively. "Come on, let's dance."

I let him lead me to the dancefloor and I let the pretty little pill work its magic.

I danced with the guy, never stopping to wonder what his name was.

The club exploded in front of my eyes in a beautiful mess of lights and sounds. I watched, mesmerized, as the whole room was transformed into a magical wonderland where I held Posy with one hand and the guy with my other. I danced and danced and danced, and drank so much I felt so dizzy, I thought I was going to be sick from the world spinning around me so very fast.

I left the wonderland and came back to earth when we stumbled out of the club, laughing loudly and making out. He tried to hail a cab and I giggled and retched over the pavement, then giggled again. I wasn't going to throw up. I didn't want to. It would mean the pretty fun pill would stop working, and then I'd have to remember.

I *hated* remembering.

We chose my apartment, and the guy pushed my legs apart in the back of the cab, trying to feel up my pussy.

I moaned for him, pretty noises meant to get him harder.

It was distracting the driver, who kept glancing back at us in the rearview mirror. I grinned at him and parted my legs wide, showing him a glimpse of my pussy because I wasn't wearing panties that day. He stared at me, his eyes harsh and unforgiving, and I laughed my ass off.

The guy whose name I still didn't know paid the cab driver, and I dragged him towards my apartment building. In the elevator, he was all over me, his mouth hungry and his fingers too daring for such a public place. He fucked my pussy carelessly, as if it meant nothing, sliding his fingers so deep inside I squealed in pain and delight.

I didn't usually come across guys who were this rough.

I unlocked the front door with shaky fingers and we fell laughing into my apartment. He poured us drinks and I wandered into the bedroom, standing next to the window and taking one last breath of fresh air. I knew in the next few minutes I wouldn't be able to breathe with his fat cock stuffed down my throat.

I reached for the curtains, feeling dizzy as fuck as I tried to force them to close. I glanced up to see what the problem was, but my eyes locked on the apartment across the street instead.

He was in his living room, his palm against the window, his grin discernible even from this distance.

Peep Show

He was staring right at me, his hand down the waistband of his pants and his fingers jerking, tugging, getting off.

I looked into his eyes, his face shrouded in darkness but still making my pussy clench at the sight of him.

Through the haze of the drugs I'd taken, the drinks I'd had, I tried to remember the night a few days ago when he'd fucked that girl while looking right at me, getting off with her as if she were nothing more than a cum-toy ready to please his dick.

He was staring at me as he jerked himself off, and I couldn't tear my eyes off him.

He tilted his head to the side, giving me a questioning look. And then I remembered it, his silly dare, the tight feeling in my pussy whenever I thought about it.

My turn.

I shook my head and smiled at him and he sighed with a big grin.

He made my heart pound, and it was only a moment later that I realized my hand had wandered between my legs and I was stroking the inside of my thighs.

He laughed at me, throwing his head back and pulling his hand out of his pants. I stared and stared and stared some more. There was something about him. Something that made me want to do everything he said.

Strong, muscular arms wrapped around me from behind, and I kept staring into my neighbor's eyes as the guy from the club kissed a line down my jaw and over my throat.

His hand went back inside those pants and I watched him get off while I moaned for the man inside my bedroom, grinding my ass all over his dick. He grunted and tore my dress off, shredding it to pieces. I gasped at the feeling of cool air on my skin, my eyes fearfully seeking out my neighbor's.

He looked like he was in pain, his muscles taut and stretched as he palmed his cock. He pushed his pants lower down his hips and showed me his fucking impressive cock, throbbing and ready to burst in his fist.

I let the guy from the club push me against the window, my tits exposed for everyone to see if only they glanced up. But there was only one person I cared about, and it was the man across the street. I wanted him to see me like this. And I was going to stare him down as I came, thinking it was *his* cock rammed all the way inside me.

The guy fucked me savagely, slapping my legs apart and pushing himself inside me, a groan leaving his lips as his cock entered my cunt. He started thrusting, long, painful and deliciously perfect movements of his hips sending my body into overdrive. I was desperate to get off.

I felt the effects of the pill loosening as I got ravaged. I felt the numbness from the alcohol going away, seeping through my pores and leaving me horribly, painfully aware of what was going on.

Another night.

Another guy.

Another meaningless fuck that got me off and left with a fleeting kiss on my mouth and a drained cock hanging limply between his legs.

So I looked at my neighbor and I came for him instead.

I looked right into his eyes as I let my body convulse with another dick in my pussy, fucking his cum inside me like his life depended on it. He was still rough, but it was painfully obvious he was using me to get off. He didn't give a shit whether I came or not. He just wanted my cunt to milk his cock dry.

And it did.

He lifted my leg when he was close, grabbed it from behind and forced my thigh up, giving my neighbor a better view of my stretched pussy. I felt him coming, his hot jizz running inside me, draining him and filling me up instead.

The whole time, my eyes were on the mystery man across the street. And I didn't move away from the window, even when the guy kissed my cheek, slapped my ass and left my apartment. Instead, I braced my palms against the glass and kept looking, kept staring at the stranger who now had his fingers covered in the hot sticky cum I'd made him spill.

I let him see everything. My shaky legs, the guy's release oozing out of my pussy and dripping slowly to the floor. My hair sticking to my forehead, my sweaty body that I hated so much, my face messy with running makeup. I let him see it all, and I let myself come apart for him.

I let myself cry for Posy, for the girl I used to be, for the girl I was. I let the tears flow freely, my body convulsing in silent shivers as the tears ran down my face. I let it happen for as long as it needed to, and by the time I was done, I was too scared to look back up, absolutely certain Mr. Neighbor had gotten sick of me and turned his back on my pathetic figure a long time ago.

But when my eyes wandered up, he was still there, his gaze firmly fixed on me.

And he was holding something up to the window.

A piece of paper with a phone number scribbled on it in big, chunky numbers.

I looked at him and saw something in his eyes that scared me.

Desperation.

The same ugly, bad, broken desperation that looked back at me every time I passed a mirror.

With shaky fingers, I took my phone from my purse lying on the floor and sent him a message.

Dare you to call me.

Chapter 4

·MILES·

BROKEN, ADJECTIVE
*Having been fractured or damaged,
no longer in one piece or working order.*

I stared at her message blinking at me from my phone and wondered whether I should do it.

There was no question that I wanted to. I wanted to know what her voice sounded like and whether it matched the idea I had of it in my head. But it also meant making this way more real than it really was.

Because as of now, she was just a silhouette in the window across the street. And if I called her, I'd know so much more. Did I want that? Was I even ready for that?

And more importantly, was she ready for my kind of fucked up?

My phone pinged with another message and I looked down to find a photo waiting for me. My fingers shook as I opened the message and her face stared back at me from the screen.

I hadn't been able to see her properly from the other side of the street, but now my mystery girl was looking right into my eyes in all her glory. And she *was* fucking glorious.

Dark hair, falling in rich ebony waves down her shoulders and over her tits, her lips painted Barbie pink and smeared from what that prick had done to her. Her eyes, her beautiful blue eyes, were open wide and needy, staring up at me, her mascara smeared, and her look was one of desperation that sent blood rushing to my dick.

She was naked, her hair the only thing covering her tits, with a hint of a rosy pink nipple between the dark strands.

My dick went hard fucking instantly, standing to attention at the sight of her, desperate to bury itself in her, desperate to fuck the enchanting space between her tits where my dick would fit so perfectly.

Even though she was right across the street, she'd never felt farther away.

I called her number.

She picked up after the second ring, letting me know she'd been holding her phone.

"He-Hello?" she stuttered, and my cock swelled so painfully I groaned.

She let out the sweetest little moan at the sound of it, and it made me want her so much I clenched my fist around my throbbing cock.

"Your name," I growled into the phone. "Tell me your name."

"Bebe," she whispered. "My name is Bebe Hall. What's yours?"

"Miles," I said roughly, the letters forming her sweet name dancing before my eyes.

I didn't give her my last name deliberately, quickly changing the topic before she could figure out the game I was playing.

"Bebe, you're going to touch yourself for me now," I told her, and she let out a panicked little breath that made me chuckle. "Why are you acting shy, sugar? We both know you're fingering that tight little cunt at the sound of my voice."

She caught her breath and I fucking heard it. Heard her pull her fingers out of that cunt with a delicious squelch.

"I'm not," she protested.

"Okay, you're not," I groaned. "Now stop fucking lying and taste your fingers for me, sweetie. I want to know what *my* cunt tastes like."

I could practically feel her shaking.

"Don't act fucking coy," I reprimanded her. "Fingers. In. Your. Fucking. Mouth. NOW."

I heard her sucking, and my balls tingled for her. Jesus fucking Christ, she was getting me off like a pro. I could only imagine what that pussy would feel like stretched around my dick. For now, my imagination would have to do, but sooner or later, I was going to have her bent every which way around my cock.

"Tell me," I said, and she whimpered at the sound of my voice. "Tell me what I'm going to be tasting once you're ripe for my tongue."

"I… I can taste his cum," she whispered, and it all came back to me.

The guy fucking her brains out. The little trickle of cum from her legs to the floor. Fuck, I'd forgotten all about that. It made me fucking angry.

"Eat him out of your pussy," I demanded. "I don't want someone else's cum in my toy tonight."

"How?" she asked, her voice breathless.

She'd liked that I called her my toy. I smirked at the thought.

"How?" I repeated. "By fucking that pussy until every last trace of him is on your fingers and down your throat. And only then will I let you come."

"You think you get to decide that?" she asked, sounding offended.

"If you want to keep talking," I said easily. "Come on, sugar. Clean up for me."

I listened to the enchanting sounds of her cleaning that cunt and palmed my dick while she did it. Her voice wasn't like I'd imagined it would be. I thought it would be husky, needy, the voice of a seductress.

But instead, it was sweet and innocent, a sharp contrast to the image in my head of her getting used like a fuck-doll.

"Tell me once you're done, sweetheart," I said roughly, my cock growing harder and harder as I stroked it. "Tell me when my pussy's empty."

"Now," she whispered, the wet sound of her smacking her lips together making me ready to blow. "All gone now… Miles."

I fucking loved hearing my name on her lips. It was hot as sin, and I was ready to make her into my next subject when she did something I wasn't expecting.

"I don't want to come," she said simply. "I want to make you blow."

"Why?" I asked distractedly.

"I just do." Her voice was harsh but desperate. "Let me make you. You won't regret it, I promise. I'll be a very, very good girl for you."

I considered it for a second and finally smiled to myself before walking into my living room and opening the blinds.

She was on her bed, turned away from the window. I could see a hint of her round, tight little ass and her hair falling down her back. I sat in front of my window and watched her as my thumb slid over the tip of my dick.

"Okay, sugar," I said. "Let's see what you got. Let's see if you can make me come with your words."

Her voice changed in a second. From poor little horny girl to a seductive vixen that had me jerking in seconds.

"I want you inside me," she whispered. "I want to know what you feel like in my pussy. I want you to pin me down, listen to me begging for you to use a condom, and tell me you don't give a shit... Then plunge your fat cock inside me."

"Raw?" I asked.

"Raw," she repeated huskily. "With nothing between us. Stretch me out. Make me yours. Make me whisper in your ear that I always want you to fuck me raw. Always, always, always."

I groaned and fisted my cock.

"Let me have something inside," she begged. "Please, I need to... You pick the hole, I'll pick the finger."

"Ass," I said right away. "In your fucking asshole, sugar."

It was a test. I wanted to see how well she responded to orders, and she shocked me by letting out a little whimper and then a long moan of satisfaction as a finger found its way into her ass. I could see her from where I was sitting, see her reach behind and push a finger into that tight little hole.

"Fuck it," I ordered. "Fuck that asshole until you fucking weep, sugar."

"Okay," she whispered and my cock swelled for her.

She whined for me with her mouth closed, trying to hold back, and I nearly lost it.

"Open that fucking mouth," I ordered her. "Moan for me, finger that sweet little hole and moan yourself into an orgasm for me."

She moaned. God, how she fucking moaned.

My fingers worked my dick faster. I was desperate for her to be making those noises with me inside her instead of her own fingers, fucking, ravaging, taking, groping. I wanted her on my dick. I wanted her helpless. I wanted her coming fucking hard.

"Come with me," I told her breathlessly. "Count down from ten and fucking come with me."

"T-ten," she whimpered. "Oh God… nine…"

I watched her fucking that ass as she counted, getting harder until it was impossible not to come. And I only spoke again once she'd reached three.

"Three," she whispered helplessly.

"Turn towards the window," I ordered.

"Two," she whined, turning towards me.

Her tits, her stomach, her hair, her fucking face. So damn perfect, so addicting after just a few stolen glimpses, one naughty call. Bebe, my Bebe, fucking mine. My girl, my cunt, my ass, my mouth. I wanted her so badly.

"One," she breathed.

"Take your finger out and come," I told her, and she cried as she took it out.

My cock burst all over my fingers and I watched her body convulse in desperate little shakes as it brought itself to orgasm, twisting, trembling as she gave in and fucking came apart for me.

I palmed my dick full of sticky cum and stared at her as she got off the bed and walked to the window on shaky legs. She turned her back to me, bent down, and pushed her finger inside her asshole, holding her phone in her other hand so I could hear.

I thought I'd come again at the sound, at the sight of her.

Her phone came back up and she fucked her ass for me.

"One more time," she begged. "Let me come just one more time, just one more I promise…"

"Fucking do it," I ordered in a growl, and I listened to her do it, cry out, fall to her knees and press her face against the window, staring at me as she came down from it. "Good little girl. Sweet little girl. My favorite girl."

"Did I do good?" she asked softly.

"So good, little sugar," I told her, letting go of my still-throbbing cock. "Wish you could come over and lick this mess off me."

"Let me," she begged eagerly. "Let me do it. Please, Miles."

I thought about it, her hot little mouth on me, her sexy body inches away from me. I looked into her eyes in the window and saw the desperation in them.

Then I thought about my reality.

Bleaching my inked skin.

Scrubbing myself raw.

Doctor appointments.

Therapists.

Being my regular, fucked-up self. The side of me no one gets to see. None of the girls I fucked knew about it, and I'd done my fucking best to keep it that way.

I didn't do friends.

I didn't do relationships.

"Not tonight, sugar," I told her roughly and cut the call.

I watched her get up and angrily shut her curtains, enveloping her little world in darkness. It fucking hurt, even though it shouldn't have.

I wanted her.

On her knees, sucking me off, being a good little slut for me.

But I couldn't, not now, not ever.

Chapter 5

·BEBE·

DRAPETOMANIA, NOUN
An overwhelming urge to run away.

I decided I was going to hate him.

I didn't deal well with guys who didn't want me, and I hated the way he'd treated me the previous night. I spent hours and hours tossing and turning in my bed, unable to catch a wink of sleep.

Once I finally got out of bed, I kept my curtains firmly closed. I wasn't going to give him the satisfaction of seeing me ever again.

A look at my phone told me I had no messages, and that upset me even more. I wanted him to apologize, to find an excuse for not wanting to see me in person. God, I wanted him to find a fucking reason to speak to me. But he didn't, and that made me want him even more.

I got up and took a hot shower to get my mind out of the gutter. By the time I came out, Arden was sitting at the bar in my kitchen, groceries laid out all over the counter.

"You could have told me you were coming over," I said as I towel-dried my hair.

I walked to the window, and on an impulse, pulled the curtains open.

I didn't pause to see if he was looking.

"You never lock your door," she shrugged. "And I wanted to talk to you."

I wrapped my hair in a turban and leaned down to give her a fleeting kiss on the cheek. She smiled.

"What did you bring?" I asked.

"Donuts," she said, and I squealed with excitement.

This used to be our thing. Mine, Posy's, and Arden's. We'd all meet up at my apartment after a wild night out, and Posy and I would binge on the donuts Arden brought from our favorite bakery down town.

Arden never ate.

Or if she did, she threw it all up when she got back home.

She was starting to get better when we lost Posy, but now she was right back to her old ways. I never said anything about it, and neither did she. It was too painful to talk about, and I had no right to scold her when I was doing shitty things as well.

"How did last night go?" Arden asked me, and I shrugged.

I didn't want to tell her yet. A part of me wanted to keep my stranger to myself. I got possessive quite often, but not like this, with an intensity that made me zip my mouth shut and pretend nothing happened.

"I fucked that club guy," I said carelessly.

"Anders?" she asked, and I gave her a blank stare. "His name was Anders, Bebe. I thought you would remember."

The old me would have been embarrassed. The new me just grinned at her and took a bite of the salted caramel donut that had made my fingers all sticky and sugary.

"How was he?" Arden raised an eyebrow at me.

"Good," I replied, keeping it vague on purpose. "Did you fuck Nick?"

She looked down at her perfectly manicured fingernails and I gasped.

"You did, didn't you?" I squealed. "You freaking fucked him! Oh my God, you're finally not a virgin anymore!"

"Shut up!" She was blushing fiercely. "It doesn't matter. It wasn't that good, anyway."

"Of course it wasn't," I rolled my eyes, grabbing another donut. "The first time never is. Anyway, how come you did it? I thought you guys were just friends?"

"He came over to watch a movie," she said. "And we just… I don't know, it just happened. And I guess he was sweet. And nice. He made me drink a smoothie."

I gave her a long look and she returned my gaze, which was a good sign. It meant she didn't spend the whole night bent over the toilet, throwing up the food her new boy-toy had made her eat.

"I can't believe you've joined the slut club," I grinned at her.

It was what Posy and I used to call ourselves. The slut club, and Arden, the innocent one, was forever our wing woman. But not anymore.

It hurt to think of what Posy would have to say about this, so I just shut the thoughts out, packed them up in a tight little box in a dark corner of my mind.

"So now you can finally fuck someone else," I said. "He was your practice cock. Now you can have another one!"

"I…" She was blushing. "I don't really want to."

"What?" I gave her an incredulous look. "Oh god-fucking-damnit, don't tell me you have feelings for Nick. For real?"

"I might," she said defensively. "You know, he's a nice guy. A great guy. The kind you take home to meet your parents."

"Yeah, exactly," I rolled my eyes. "God, Arden, when did you become so traditional?"

She sulked quietly and I picked up my phone that had just pinged with a message.

"What is it?" Arden asked me as I read it. "You've gone pale. Is everything okay?"

No, everything was not okay.

I glanced towards the window and squinted against the sunlight, seeing a figure against the window across the street.

Dare you to drop your clothes in front of your friend, the text read.

"As if," I muttered to myself, just when another message arrived on my phone.

A picture.

His fucking cock, his tattooed knuckles holding it up for me, a vein throbbing on his shaft and enticing me. It was covered in cum.

I walked to the window and shook my hair out, dropping the towel holding my hair up to the floor. Arden was chatting to me from behind, but I could barely hear her. My attention was on the phantom figure across the street.

I untied the towel around my tits and let it drop to the floor slowly. I smiled to his silhouette and turned towards Arden again, flashing him a view of my toned ass.

Arden didn't take any notice, apart from glancing at me quickly. We'd been naked in front of each other before, it was no big deal. And she was too involved in her boring Nick story to notice what I was doing anyway.

I walked back to the counter and grabbed a jug of milk from the fridge. I drank it sloppily, droplets of milk running down my chin, over my neck and dribbling over my tits.

"Why do you have to be so messy?" Arden asked me once I set it down, and I grinned at the sight of a new message on my phone.

Make her lick you fucking clean.

I walked over to her, pushing my tits in her face. Arden groaned and glared at me.

"Why don't you help me with that?" I asked her, winking.

"Come on, Bee," she said with a sigh. "I thought those days were behind us."

Memories filled my mind. Memories of three bodies twisted together, getting off, licking, sucking, fucking, until each one of us had our first orgasm. Mine came from Arden, and I still remembered it so fucking well. And now she wasn't a virgin anymore, and Posy was no longer with us. Life fucking sucked balls sometimes.

"Lick me," I asked her in a soft, sweet voice.

She looked up at me, her eyes once again showing me the vulnerable girl I'd met when we were both seventeen. We'd come a long way since then.

I thought of Miles, and turned my head to the side to look through the window. I couldn't see that well with the bright sunlight, but I could tell he was standing by the window, watching us. And I wanted him to.

Arden didn't move, so I grabbed the back of her neck and forced her mouth against my hot skin.

"Lick," I said gently.

Her tongue shot out and she licked the drops of milk off my chest. I moaned when she did, so many memories coming back to me, flooding me with things we'd never do again.

"That's enough," she finally said, wiping her mouth with the back of her hand and glaring at me. "You're bad, Bebe. We aren't supposed to be doing that anymore."

"Because of Posy?" I asked her roughly. "We aren't supposed to be doing a lot of things, but it's not stopping either of us, is it?"

She looked away guiltily.

"When was the last time you ate, Arden? Not the smoothie. Before that," I said, my voice soft.

"It doesn't matter," she mumbled in reply.

I reached for her, my fingers tangling in her long honey-blonde hair.

"Tell me," I urged her, and she finally looked back up at me, her eyes filled with pain.

It was right there. The hole between us. Yet we had never, not once, talked about it.

"The day before yesterday," she said softly.

I just stared at her. I never knew what to do when she got like this. Posy was the glue that held us together. She was the girl who made sure both Arden and I were alright. But now she was fucking gone and I had no idea how to fix this, any of it.

"You have to eat," I told Arden. "Does Nick know about this?"

"He knows a bit," she said miserably, and I shook my head.

I wanted to fix her, I wanted to fix both of us. But without Posy, it wasn't possible. We needed each other, and with one missing link, the whole friendship had fallen apart.

I grabbed my robe from the back of a chair, shrugging the plum silk over my shoulders. It felt nice and cool against my skin, but I left it open in the front. Partly because I wanted to tease Miles, and partly because I was hoping he'd just fucking lose his cool and come knocking on my door.

I didn't check my phone again.

"Are you going out tonight?" I asked Arden.

She shook her head no. "I'm spending the evening at Nick's."

"Good," I said with a smile. "Make sure he makes you some food again."

I had a feeling this new relationship was going to be good for Arden. She'd get better with his help, and he'd do things for her that I wasn't capable of. Arden needed stability, and I was the last person she could turn to for that.

"Do you want to come along?" she asked me hopefully. "He has some friends you could meet, or you could bring that guy from the club with you…"

"No," I shot her down, giving her a chilly look. "Maybe you don't want to have fun, but I do."

"Bee…" she gave me a worried glance. "I know you took something last night."

"So?" I snapped. "You don't get to tell me what I can or can't do, you know."

"I know," she said, her voice trembling. "But I thought because of what happened with Posy, you'd maybe…"

"Maybe what?" I spat out. "Stop living my fucking life? Well, I won't. And neither should you. Now please get the fuck out so I can finish getting ready."

She got off her chair and didn't even look at me again as she walked out. The front door slammed after her, and the second she was gone, I felt fucking miserable.

Instead of letting myself think about it, I picked up my phone again.

A new text was waiting.

Call me once she leaves.

I didn't want to, but there was a part of me that couldn't resist. I slid behind the counter, in a spot where he couldn't see me at all, so he wouldn't know there were tears streaming down my cheeks. I called his number.

"Bebe," he said in that deep voice that sent shivers down my spine.

"Miles," I replied, keeping my voice as level as I could possibly manage. "Why did you want me to call you?"

"What are you doing tonight?" he asked me.

His voice was fucking divine. All dark roughness and rugged need. God, I wanted him so bad.

"Probably going out," I said. "Why, you want to come?"

A long pause followed and my heartbeat quickened at the thought of him somewhere outside with me, touching me as we danced to a heavy bass. I'd come for him right there on the dancefloor if he let me.

"How about you watch a little show instead?" he asked me with a dark chuckle.

He sent my blood pumping through my veins.

I thought of Arden, her implied warning that I should sort my life out.

I thought of going out, having mindless sex with a faceless stranger once again.

I thought of Miles.

"What kind of show?" I asked him, feeling my pussy clench under the silk of my robe.

"A peep show, of course," he laughed, sending chills through my body.

Chapter 6

·MILES·

PHILOPHOBIA, NOUN
The fear of falling or being in love.

I had something special planned for my sweet little toy.

I'd promised her a show, and by the time 10 p.m. rolled around, I was ready to give her one.

The blinds opened slowly, showing me her illuminated silhouette in her own window, waiting, ready for me. She was wearing a sexy little nightie that sent my pulse racing, complete with black lacy stockings and a killer pair of heels. I'd told her to dress up. Maybe if she was dressed to fuck, I could imagine it was *her* cunt hugging my dick.

I didn't acknowledge her, not giving her so much as a wave. I barely glanced at her, and the next second, the doorbell rang.

I felt Bebe's eyes on me as I walked to the door, opening it wide and regarding the couple before me.

The girl was nervous, her hands twisted in front of her. She wore a little black dress that left nothing to the imagination and sexy heels that matched her daring outfit. Her lips were painted a dark shade of red and her long blonde hair was styled perfectly. She wore thick false lashes, fluttering open for me and revealing her pretty brown eyes.

It was really a shame because all her efforts were in fucking vain. She was going to be a perfect little mess in no time.

Her man stood to the side, regarding me with something between hatred and admiration.

He wasn't as tall as me. His hair was light brown and cropped close to his head, his eyes a murky shade of blue. He didn't like me, I could tell.

But why would he? I was about to fuck his little girlfriend into pieces, and he was going to watch.

No man in his right mind would like that. Not until they saw me in action. Not until I handed them their woman back, fucked so well she'd worship their cock for the rest of their time together.

I wanted to tell him he should be grateful, but I knew I shouldn't.

Instead, I just smiled wide and moved aside to let them in.

As soon as they stepped inside, my brow furrowed with worry.

"Shoes off, please," I said roughly, and they gave me incredulous looks, but slipped their footwear off.

The girl was much shorter now, and I towered over her. Her discarded Louboutins were the last remnants of her confidence. Now, she was shaking and scared, holding on to her boyfriend's hand for support.

What a sweet little whore. I loved them scared.

"It's okay, babe," he told her in a strained voice.

Of course, it wasn't okay. It was never going to be okay again. It was going to be so much better they'd beg me to come back and make me fuck her again. But of course, I would say no.

I knew my rules, and I never broke them.

I never wanted to, either.

Not until Bebe.

"It is okay," I repeated after him, giving them both glowing smiles. "Let's get you both something to drink. Relax your nerves, okay?"

The girl nodded timidly and her man stared me down as I led them into the living room where the bar was.

"What's your drink?" I asked him first, trying to make him more comfortable with the whole arrangement.

"I'll take a whisky," he said, looking at my collection of bottles.

"On the rocks?" I asked easily, and he shook his head.

He walked around my living room, his filthy hands touching every surface they passed. My fingers tightened around the glass as I poured his drink. I wanted to fucking kill him. I'd have to clean the whole place after they left.

The girl stood in the middle of the room, frozen to the spot. She looked like she was on the verge of tears and it turned me on so much I had to readjust my jeans.

I handed the guy his drink and sat down on my pristine white sofa, making myself comfortable.

"Don't you want to know our names?" the girl asked softly, and I gave her a curious look.

"No, not particularly," I said in a low voice, my eyes drinking in her sexy little body.

She had big tits, barely covered by the dress she wore. But where the decolletage was daring, the dress reached her knees in a modest length that suggested she wasn't as comfortable with the whole scenario as she wanted me to believe. I wondered whether her legs were in tights or stockings. It didn't really make a difference to me. I liked tearing things apart, be it fabric or people.

She shivered at my words and her boyfriend walked up behind her. I was curious as to what his next move might be.

He locked eyes with me and I saw it, the emotion I'd come to know so well.

Desperation.

It was what drove them to my apartment, I was fucking sure of it.

She was more beautiful than him, but he was confident where she was shy. She could probably have any man she wanted with the dose of self-confidence I was going to give her. A small, sentimental part of me hoped she wouldn't leave her guy. He seemed to genuinely care about her. I could tell from the way his hand holding the whisky shook with nerves.

He pushed her forward slightly, and she stumbled towards me. I opened my legs and stared right into her eyes.

"Go on," her boyfriend urged her, and I saw goosebumps erupt all over her skin in anticipation.

"Do you want a drink?" I asked her, and she shook her head, her gaze glued to mine.

She needed direction. She needed encouragement.

But because I was a sick fucking bastard, I wasn't going to help her, I was only going to make things worse for her.

"Walk to the window," I told her simply, and she nearly tripped over her own feet in her effort to obey. "See if you can see my friend on the other side of the street."

"I-I see her," she stuttered, and my blood pumped all the way down into my cock.

"Why don't you give her a little wave," I growled, watching the blonde wave timidly at Bebe silhouetted in the window.

I smiled to myself, motioning to her boyfriend to sit down, and getting up myself. I walked to the record player in the corner of the room and put on some music, watching their nerves loosen ever so slightly.

I winked at the guy as I walked over to the window, gently placing a palm against the spotless glass. The girl flinched when I approached her, but I didn't give it a second thought. My eyes were on Bebe as I leaned closer to the blonde, my voice a caress against her skin.

"Undress," I whispered, my fingers finding the zipper on her back, gently tugging it down until it revealed her toned, sexy body.

She shivered under my touch, and the tension in the room grew until it was almost palpable.

She reached up, peeling her dress off her body and exposing herself to my watchful eyes. The dress pooled around her feet.

I glanced at her before looking at Bebe.

I'd never thought of how ridiculously close our apartments were. I could see every little movement she made.

I lowered my head against the girl's skin, my lips brushing against her shoulder ever so slightly. She flinched at the touch.

"Shh," I told her softly. "It's okay. It's going to be okay."

She relaxed, her shoulders sagging submissively and her whole body leaning against mine. I reached up, my fingers tangling in her light mane of hair until I had them wrapped around her silky strands. It was so light compared to Bebe's. Barely a shade above white.

I pulled, hard, and her head snapped back, her lips parting in a surprised O and her eyes fearfully finding mine.

"Open your mouth wide," I said, just as gently as earlier, and she did. "Good little girl."

My thumb hooked in the corner of her mouth and I opened her up, looking at her pearly white teeth and her little tongue, her mouth gathering spit as she looked up at me with a mix of fear and adoration.

"What a pretty little mouth," I muttered. "It's going to look so good once it's full."

I pushed her down to her knees unceremoniously, and she tumbled down the rabbit hole.

Her boyfriend was long forgotten, and I didn't give a shit what he thought of me manhandling her. He might as well learn something from me – if he didn't storm out in a fit of rage, that is.

"What hole is your favorite, darling?" I asked the girl, holding her chin gently between my fingers. "What's your favorite hole to have filled to the brim?"

"P-Pussy," she muttered.

"Pussy?" I repeated, my voice sweet like I was talking to a child.

She nodded.

"You want that tight, hot little cunt full of my cum?" I asked her, rougher now. "You want a stranger to fuck you full of his steaming hot jizz while your boyfriend watches? What a nasty little slut you are."

She blanched at the realization of what she'd said, assuming I was going to fuck her raw.

I always fucked with a condom on.

I couldn't remember a time when I hadn't used one.

"Would you like to have your wish come true?" I asked her softly, even though my heart was pounding with panic at the mere thought of it.

"Y-yes," she whispered. "Please."

"Please what?"

"Please, sir," she moaned.

I was fine with 'sir'. Or Daddy. Or my name. Anything to get them wet for me. There was nothing like the feeling of a tight, hot pussy dripping with need for me as I pushed myself inside it.

"Beg," I told her sweetly, and she looked away, tightly shutting her eyes. "Aww, are you shy, little girl?"

She nodded.

"Don't be shy," I said, my voice gentle again. "Don't be shy now. Because in an hour you're going to be begging for much worse things than having your pretty pussy filled."

"Please," she whispered. "Please fuck my pussy, sir. Please fuck it full."

"Go on," I urged her, my eyes going up and locking on Bebe as I unbuckled my belt.

I fucking loved the metallic sound of the buckle as I undid it, pushing my jeans off but keeping hold of the leather belt just to scare the little slut in front of me.

Bebe was staring. She looked angry. Actually, she looked fucking pissed as hell, and I loved it. I loved getting a rise out of her. What I was doing with her felt like insanely long, drawn-out foreplay that could result in the best sex I'd ever had.

That is if I was ever brave enough to let her get close.

"Please, sir, please fuck me, please make me come, let me get you off, I'll do anything," the girl said desperately.

Her eyes kept going to her boyfriend, and it made me chuckle. So self-conscious. She didn't need to be. She'd have us both, and soon.

"I asked you to come here so my friend across the street could watch," I said simply. "I want her fucking marinating in her lust until she's ready to pop like an overblown balloon. Wouldn't that be fun, little girl?"

She nodded, desperate eyes wanting to do desperate things to have my dick inside her.

I palmed my balls through the fabric of my boxers, right in front of her needy face, and she mewled like the helpless little whore she was.

"Why don't we put on a little show for her, then?" I asked, and she nodded again, her eyes glazed over with lust. "What a good girl you are. Now come here."

She crawled closer on her knees and I wrapped my black leather belt around her neck, but not before snapping it threateningly in front of her eyes. Her face was ghostly pale as I wrapped the belt around her slender neck, twisting it in the front and bringing her lips closer to my crotch.

With my free hand, I tugged my boxers down, and the girl breathed in deeply at the sight of my cock. I didn't give her a chance to change her mind, instead squeezing the belt tighter and entering her mouth as savagely as I dared.

"Open wider," I barked at her, her teeth grazing my shaft.

She looked up at me, blinking fast, her little face so pretty and desperate.

"Don't be scared," I said, more of a warning than it was a consolation. "Come on, wide as you can. Take me in. I know you can fit me in that whore throat of yours. Just open up for me, slut."

She did, and I groaned as my cock slid deeper down her throat, all the way down. I pushed her back, the heat of her skin fogging up the window. I held the belt in my hands and ordered her to suck without saying a word, my eyes going back to Bebe.

Her hands lingered above her tits, obviously wanting to touch.

"Get me my phone," I barked at the guy sitting on the couch.

He got up as if in a trance and brought my phone to me. He didn't say a word.

"Hold the belt," I told him, handing him the thick leather, his fingers shaking as he took it from me. "Make her suck."

My fingers moved across the screen of my phone, and I typed a message to Bebe, then looked back at her, waiting for a reaction.

Don't fucking touch yourself. Don't you fucking dare.

I groaned at the feeling of the girl trying to swallow me, her boyfriend breathing heavily as she sucked me down.

Bebe's reply came back in seconds.

Come and stop me.

I wanted to fucking kill her, but instead, I sent off another text.

If you touch that whore body of yours, I'm going to make you regret it.

I looked back up in time to see her smirk at her phone and toss it on the bed behind her, her hands roaming down her tanned skin.

"Fucking get out of the way," I barked at the guy, and he stepped aside as I pulled out of his girlfriend's mouth. She let out a shocked little gasp when I pulled her to her feet and turned her around, that dripping cunt right next to the tip of my dick. I got a condom from my discarded jeans and hurriedly put it on, my cock covered in her spit and latex.

I pushed her against the window and sank my cock balls deep inside her and she howled at the sensation. But before she could come, I pulled right out of her, my coated dick dripping.

"I'm sorry, darling, but this is going to hurt," I told her gently, not giving her a chance to respond and plunging my whole length inside her asshole.

She cried out and I looked to stare at Bebe while I fucked her virgin hole. Her boyfriend had told me she hadn't had anything but a plug inside her, and I'd promised not to take it myself. But what the hell, it wasn't the first promise I'd broken, and that tight little ass felt too good to stop now.

"I can't believe you fucking did that," her boyfriend muttered next to me, holding his head with one hand and his dick with the other. "Fuck, I can't believe it, fuck, fuck, fuck..."

I didn't even glance at him, just fucked the girl until her mewls and moans turned into sexy little sobs, my eyes always on Bebe, taunting her. She was touching herself, even though I'd told her not to, and I badly wanted to fucking hurt her.

"Don't come," the girl begged me. "Please don't come, I want it in my pussy, please, I'm on the pill, I promise..."

"Shut the fuck up," I growled at her, tightening my grip on the belt around her neck and making her gargle on her own spit. "Be a good whore. Good whores just moan, they don't *want*."

I felt myself getting close with her tight ass around me, her sobs edging me. But my eyes were always on Bebe, on her furious expression and her fingers toying with what should have been mine.

"Come for me," I ordered the girl, and she let go, coming apart on my dick like it was the only thing she could do.

I'd made her boyfriend teach her how to come on command, how to be a perfect whore, before I let them come see me. And she played her role perfectly, like a good little slut.

When she came with a cry, I pulled out of her. My dick was hard as hell as I palmed it, the girl's boyfriend rushing to her help just as my phone started to ring.

"Hello, Bebe," I muttered, picking it up.

"Miles," she breathed.

"Yes, sweetie?" I asked, watching her desperate fingers fucking my pussy while my own palmed my dick. "Is there something you wanted?"

"Come fuck me," she begged. "Come here, I want you, come see me, or let me come over there, anything, just let me…"

I grinned at her before giving her my answer.

"No," I said firmly.

She seemed surprised, glaring at me through the window and being stubbornly quiet.

"Then let him," she spoke up. "It's not fair. Let him come over. Let him fuck me."

I pondered her idea.

"Please, Miles," she begged desperately. "Please, let him! I'll do anything, I'll film it for you, if you want."

"No," I finally decided. "I told you not to play. If you want treats, you better learn to fucking follow orders."

"Miles!" she cried out, her little fist banging against the window.

"I think," I went on, "what you really want is to watch us both fucking her."

"No," she begged.

"And wishing it was you," I added.

"NO!" she hissed.

"Learn to fucking follow orders, sweetheart," I told her. "Because I only fuck good girls who do."

I cut the call and turned to look at the boyfriend.

"Right," I said pleasantly. "Wipe her tears off and get her sweet cunt ready for me."

Chapter 7

·BEBE·

ENVY, NOUN
Desire to have something belonging to somebody else.

I was fucking furious. So damn angry, part of me was tempted to shut the curtains once and for all, but another, more desperate part of me, wouldn't let me do it.

I watched him fucking the girl, his cock stretching her asshole until the echoes of her screams tormented my mind, even though I couldn't even hear her. She was desperate, her poor boyfriend helpless against the hurricane that was Miles. And that phone call… After he cut the call I felt tears of frustration welling in my eyes, threatening to fall any second.

But I swallowed my pride. I walked to the living room, and after only a short second, opened the French doors leading onto my balcony.

So far, all of the games we'd played had been in the safety of my own home. But out here, with the black iron fence holding me captive, the fresh air felt as chilling as the street below me, that and the knowledge that anyone could look up to see my naked form desperately playing with myself.

But Miles didn't even glance at me. The view was even better from out here, their bodies so close I felt like I could practically smell the sweat on their skin.

I leaned back against the glass door, my palms resting on the window and my ass touching my hands.

And I just watched, because for once in my life, I wanted to fucking follow every rule. Anything, everything, just for a chance of having him touch me, fuck me.

Both men descended against the crying mess of a girl on the floor. Once she realized what was going on, her knees gave out and she dropped down onto her ass, her hands behind her, awkwardly trying to get away from them and failing.

I saw their mouths opening and my mind filled with the dialogue I wasn't hearing.

They ordered her to sit still. Miles was barking orders, making the girl undo her boyfriend's jeans with her shaky fingers. She never once looked into the face of the man she loved, always at Miles. Always seeking his approval, needy to see his dark features break into a smile, desperate to hear the words *good girl* in his menacing, deep voice.

The guy's cock sprang free and I gasped when Miles told her to suck him off. She leaned closer, her tight little mouth wrapping itself around the tip and her eyes were still always on Miles. She wanted more. She was crying, big, fat salty tears dripping down her cheeks, but even from where I was standing, I could tell how fucking much she needed this.

Miles stepped behind her as she sucked the guy off, his fingers gently wrapping in her hair and tugging on the long blonde strands. He stroked her and she looked up at him with utter adoration in her eyes. And then he started twisting her hair around his fist, rougher and rougher. I could see her panicking as he leaned down next to her, gently caressing her jaw, his fingers so close to the guy's cock in her mouth, it made me shiver, and then he was pointing towards the window. Towards me.

She looked right at me, carefully listening to every word Miles was saying without ever taking her mouth off her boyfriend's cock.

She stared at me and it scared me how vulnerable she looked. Not because she felt weak, but because she held more power in the whole situation than I ever had. I was still just the girl on the other side of the glass. I was jealous. Painfully, fucking awfully jealous of the pretty little blonde whose ruined makeup was flowing freely down her cheeks.

Miles reached for her, roughly wiping her face and smearing her makeup further.

"Please," I muttered to myself, blushing when the words left my lips.

Miles took the girl's throat in his rough, big fingers, and whispered in her ear as she took her boyfriend's dick. She kept looking at me, big, sad eyes. I couldn't pity her. All I felt was red hot, blinding fucking rage, because she was getting what was mine, what I deserved, what I'd been working for.

He was mine. And in that moment, with the freezing air kissing my shivering body, I felt like I would never have him. So, I decided then and there to do everything I possibly could, to make sure Miles was mine.

I'd always been competitive. But seeing that girl being fucked by him, being brought to her knees by his fucking dick, made me more determined than ever. Miles was fucking *mine*.

Peep Show

Now, his fingers wrapped around the girl's hair tighter than ever. He yanked her up, and I felt myself gasp as the guy's dick fell out of her mouth. He twisted her arms behind her painfully and dragged her away. The boyfriend followed meekly behind, his cock huge and angry red, his body fucking sinful. But I didn't give a shit about any of that. All my attention was on Miles, on the games he was playing with me just to fucking taunt me.

He dragged her to the couch in the living room, where her discarded clothes lay on the floor. He forced her to get on the couch on her knees, her ass turned towards the window, feeling so impossibly close yet just out of reach. He said something to her guy and walked away. My eyes followed him desperately, but the rest of his apartment was too dark for me to see a thing.

In front of my eyes, the guy started feeding his girlfriend that engorged cock, and I watched her fight him off, her tiny fists hammering his thighs as he fucked her mouth. He slapped them away every single time as if they were nothing. As if her resisting was nothing but a blip on his radar, nothing he couldn't get rid of with a smack and a sweet word whispered in her ear.

The guy was hot, there was no doubt about it. He was shorter than Miles, his shoulders broad and his body taut with muscles. His face was handsome, but constantly etched with worry, and there were two different emotions in his eyes. One, the unmistakable love he felt for the kneeling girl, and another, a savage fucking need to absolutely destroy her for what she was making him do.

The air was so cold on the balcony, I felt my teeth chattering, but I didn't give a shit anymore. I was so ready to touch myself again, my fingers trembled when my phone started ringing in my hand.

"He-Hello?" I answered shakily.

"Hello, sugar," he said with a dark chuckle. "Listen, I feel like I've been too hard on you. I'm going to send a gift to you, just for you and for me to enjoy. Would you like that?"

My blood boiled and I had to bite my tongue before I snapped at him.

"Come back," I finally whispered.

"Come back?" he repeated innocently. "But I'm just picking something out for you, sugar. You don't want your gift?"

"Please, Miles, let me watch you," I begged, feeling all the pretense of being stubborn leak out of my body. "Please, I want to watch."

"I didn't catch that, Bebe," he taunted me. "Now you want to fucking watch me with her?"

"Both of you," I whispered. "Both of you with her."

A light turned on in the room to the left of the couple, and Miles appeared next to the window. He looked like a fucking monster covered in ink and dark, evil intentions, and my pussy tingled for him, my nipples so painfully taut in the cold air.

A small moan escaped me. I'd never wanted *anyone* more.

"You want to watch, sugar?" he asked gently, his free hand going to his crotch and stroking there. But I couldn't see, the window didn't reach low enough.

"Yeah," I cried out. "Let me watch, let me watch you fucking her."

"Beg," he said easily, grinning at me.

And then he groaned, and I was a fucking goner. It was my favorite thing in the world, a man fucking forgoing words just to fill the tense silence with animalistic, needy sounds.

"Please, Miles," I whispered. "Please, let me watch you fucking her…"

"You changed your mind?" he growled. "Tell me you changed your mind, sweetheart."

"I changed my mind," I said miserably. "Please, let me watch, I want to see you inside her."

"You want me to fuck her?" he asked, his hand pumping that cock so furiously his face contorted with need. "You need to see? Tell me what to do, Bebe. Tell me exactly what you need, and if you're a good little girl for me you can have it, you can have it all…"

"Yes," I rasped. "Just fuck her, make me watch, I want you both fucking her, hurting her, fuck her like she's me, Miles, fuck her like she's a whore, make me feel it, I want to feel it in my fucking cunt."

He stormed out of the room, ignoring my desperate pleas as he sauntered back into the living room. He handed the phone to the girl and she held it up to her ear with shaky hands. Her boyfriend pulled out of her and the two naked men stared her down as she whispered into the phone.

"Hello," she said. "My name is Lana…"

"Please," I begged her. "Let them fuck you."

She looked at me over her shoulder. I saw the same desperation that filled my own eyes in her gaze.

"Okay," she whispered, lowering her hand.

"No!" I cried out. "Stay on the phone, fucking stay, let me listen…"

Her hand went back up, and the little bitch smiled.

"Okay," she purred.

They approached her, two large, intimidating bodies with their hands on their cocks and her holes on their minds.

I could hear them, and the girl put the phone on speaker, setting it down and grinning at me over her shoulder before she turned towards them. They walked up to her from behind the couch, two huge cocks suddenly in her face as she tried to swallow them both.

The sound of it was fucking divine, and my hand roamed between my thighs, shyly outlining the shape of my pussy as I watched and listened to her face getting fucked.

She was a good girl, but she wasn't as good as I was. She had a gag reflex that made her cough and splutter, something I'd gotten rid of years ago. But she was desperate, and she worked their cocks with so much need, so much desire to conform completely, the room filled with their joined grunts as she took them both in her mouth.

I'd never wanted to be someone else this fucking bad. I wanted to feel what she was feeling instead of the constant, painful ache between my legs reminding me that I hadn't felt Miles' cock inside me yet.

"Bebe," he barked over the speaker. "Look at me, you little slut."

My hazy eyes went to his and he grabbed Lana's mouth, driving into her with incredible force and forcing her boyfriend out. He stared at me as the girl gagged and choked, and I shivered uncontrollably, barely resisting the urge to plunge my fingers into the wetness of my cunt. God, it was unbearably hot, and I wanted them to do so much more.

I watched them fuck her mouth.

I watched her boyfriend sit and I watched her sink down on his cock while she kept sucking Miles off.

I watched until my skin was prickled with goosebumps and my body felt fucking frozen solid until she got the first load of jizz all over her pretty tits.

Her boyfriend blew all over her skin, too soon for my liking, and judging by Miles' groan, too soon for him as well.

The boyfriend dropped down on the couch like a stone, but Miles wasn't fucking done.

He pulled a condom over his dick, dragged the girl to the window by her hair, and opened the window wide.

My blood froze in my veins. This was the closest we'd ever been to one another.

"Hi, sweetheart," he growled at me, the girl moaning helplessly as he pushed her head out of the window, her upper body dangling over the street below.

My palms felt sweaty against the glass window despite how cold I was, and I swallowed thickly as I watched him dangle her over the windowsill.

"H-Hi," I whispered.

He was so close, and I'd never been more terrified.

"Look at Bebe," he told the girl, and she raised her ruined, pale face to meet mine. "Look into her eyes and ask her what I should do to you."

"Please," she begged pathetically.

I watched a drop of cum slowly fall from her tits... down, down, down.

"What s-should he do to me?" Lana asked, her big eyes needing so much more than I was willing to give her.

"Fuck you," I said, my voice scared. "Fuck your pussy. You want that?"

"Y-yeah," she whispered. "Please, I want it, I need it, please."

"Beg," Miles told her, pulling on her hair and making her look up at me.

She whimpered and I took a step towards them, my feet unsteady as I gripped the railing.

"I said fuck her," I growled at Miles, and he laughed at me before grabbing the girl by her cheeks and making her look down at the street.

She moaned when he entered her, and I felt so fucking jealous my knuckles turned white.

"Please Miles," I begged as he grunted. "Please, can I touch myself now?"

"Sit the fuck down!" he barked, and I followed his command, shivering more when my ass touched the cold stone floor. "Open your legs!"

I parted them, fully aware he could see everything through the railing.

"Wider," he panted, fucking the whimpering mess he'd made of Lana. "Fucking WIDER, Bebe!"

"I can't do it wider," I cried out.

"Fucking do it," he growled, and I did.

I forced my legs wide and I felt so stretched out, my gaping pussy on full display, his cock buried inside Lana's cunt. I could hear her boyfriend cursing in the living room through the phone as he saw them like that.

"Touch it," Miles ordered me. "Touch *my* cunt, play with it for me, sugar."

My fingers shook, finding my clit and touching, teasing, tickling myself into a desperate little orgasm I tried to hide.

"Fucking bitch," Miles spat out. "Did you just come without permission?"

I looked away, blushing fiercely, just as he pushed the girl farther out the window. She screeched, and I wasn't sure whether it was from getting her cunt pounded or from being so scared. I felt so jealous, wanted it to be me. Wanted to be fucked just like that.

"The more you disobey," Miles growled. "The worse it gets for her. You don't want her to get hurt, do you?"

"No!" I cried out.

"Why not?" he grinned, fucking himself deeper inside Lana.

"Hurt *me*," I begged. "Choose *me*, make me, fuck me, give it all to *me*!"

He groaned and fucked her harder. Her eyes were on mine, wide and scared and needy at the same time.

"Tell her to come," Miles barked at me. "Tell her to come instead of you, because you don't fucking get to anymore."

"Come," I begged her. "Come, please, come, you have to…"

She dissolved in a fit of tears and whispered words, and he grabbed her waist and fucked her with desperate, fucking insanely hard thrusts that I could feel all the way over the street.

"Tell her to come on my dick," Miles growled, and I did.

Lana came apart. Desperate cries, fucking desperate. She was a fucking mess.

"Bebe!" Miles called out, and I looked up at him.

Brown eyes on brown. Fucking desperation. Absolute desperation between us, longing to touch as he fucked someone else and I lost my mind staring at him, lost myself to my filthy fucking neighbor.

"Tell me to come," he said.

"Come," I whispered.

"Inside?" he asked. "Inside her?"

"Inside her," I begged. "Yes, come inside her."

But he didn't. He slipped his cock from her, grabbed her throat and made her look up at him while he kept his eyes on me. He ripped the condom away and came with a curse and a growl like a fucking predator, his cum splashing her face over and over. I pulled my knees up and crawled back, curling up, crying for no reason.

"Fucking look at me, Bebe!" he shouted, and I did.

He held her crying, broken body in his arms. His cock was still leaking cum as he pulled her back in and handed her off to her boyfriend, his eyes dark and holding a promise as he stared me down. He'd just fucked me into a mess without ever laying a finger on me.

He was an animal.

And I was completely and utterly addicted.

Chapter 8

·MILES·

NEFELIBATA, NOUN
Cloud walker.

I started every morning by staring through the window – into Bebe's apartment.

She wasn't a morning person, often getting up later than noon, and grumpily walking around until she had her first dose of caffeine. The girl was addicted to her coffee, making cup after cup. The worst thing though was that she drank a horrible, cheap instant mix. I made a mental note to tell her she was better off not having any at all if she wasn't ready to splurge on the good stuff.

Despite her horrific coffee habit, she was a mesmerizing sight in the morning. A completely different woman to the dressed-up party girl who left the apartment in the evenings. Morning Bebe wore thick, fuzzy socks and a fluffy black and white robe wi

alcohol, morning Bebe nursed the hangover.

Partygirl Bebe made my cock twitch, and the vulnerable morning Bebe made my heart hurt because I fucking wanted her, yet I knew I could never have her.

It had been two days since I'd given Bebe the show she hadn't wanted, and my gift for her was almost ready. I'd successfully kept my distance, knowing I was getting unreasonably attached to something that wasn't even mine in the first place. I didn't seek her out, didn't call her, and she stubbornly didn't even text. She was sulking, I could tell. She barely glanced out the window, and she kept her curtains shut a lot of the time, only opening them to tease me

She would wear the sluttiest lingerie, waltzing around her apartment and making damn sure I saw every lace-covered inch of that tight little body. And it only made me want her more, of course.

My life without Bebe collapsed back into its routine, though I hadn't had a new girl over since the couple left. I carefully hid every broken, corrupted part of me from Bebe's prying eyes. Because the little slut still fucking looked, as I knew she would. She'd look through the window hastily, hoping I wouldn't notice, or watch me out of her peripheral vision, making sure she had the effect on me she wanted. And I couldn't help myself. Not just because she was a hot piece of ass, but because she was somehow irresistible in all her sarcastic, bitchy glory.

I had a Skype call with my psychiatrist that morning, just like I did every Thursday.

I stared into Dr. Halen's eyes and lied to her as smoothly as I always did.

"Are you sure, Miles?" she asked me gently. "Are you sure you've been out this week?"

"Yes," I lied. "I went to the corner store two days ago to pick up some bread."

"How come?" she asked, scribbling something on her notepad, her wise gray eyes inspecting mine.

This was our routine. Dr. Halen knew I was lying, of-fucking-course she did. But she never called me out on it, apart from posing questions that I dodged like bullets. Part of me wished she would catch me in a lie, but I was too good a bullshitter to let that happen. So, we played our little game of cat and mouse week after week, and I never admitted the truth.

"The housekeeper wasn't here," I said. "I gave her the day off."

Dr. Halen stared at me before pushing her glasses higher up on her nose.

"How many bleach baths this week, Miles?" she asked me gently, and my skin prickled at the memory of the tingling sensation still left over from when I'd scrubbed myself dry after the couple left.

"Only three," I said, almost feeling proud.

Usually, it was five or six.

On bad weeks, it was over eight. More than one a day.

I'd never tell Dr. Halen that, though.

She'd get me fucking admitted.

Again.

I knew better than to tell her the truth, and she knew better than to pry. It was the real reason we lied to one another. We both knew I needed to be in an institution. Staying out here, fucking up my life and my body, meant me going against the advice of every single doctor I'd ever met.

"Has anything happened?" Dr. Halen went on, peering at me over her glasses.

I adjusted myself in front of the camera, my eyes glancing behind the computer and towards the window. Bebe's curtains were shut.

"Not that I can think of," I said lamely, and the doctor smiled at me. She didn't smile often.

"Something has," she said. "Your number of baths is down. You seem restless. Have you met someone?"

Dr. Halen knew about the visitors I entertained. She knew about my job, and she was discreet about it, which was the main reason I'd decided to work with her. I liked her.

She was a kind woman in her forties, with a pinched face and a calm, friendly manner. She never pried, and she did her best to help. Whether she actually gave a shit about me or not, I still wasn't sure. I had a feeling she was one of those people who turned off her brain after her work hours were over.

I tried to imagine Dr. Halen being a party animal like Bebe, and a small chuckle escaped my lips.

I looked back into her knowing eyes and smiled.

"Yeah," I finally admitted. "There might be someone. I'm not ready to talk about her yet, though."

A hint of a smile played on the doctor's lips as she muttered, "There always is someone."

She looked back up. "I'm afraid our time is up, Miles," she said softly. "I have to get to my next client. But please keep track of your bleach baths and monitor your activities. And, Miles…"

"Yes?" I asked, my attention already shifting back to the girl across the street.

"This girl, whoever she is," Dr. Halen went on. "Does she… does she know?"

I stared at her on my screen.

No, she didn't know.

And it wasn't like everyone did. It wasn't like 'head case' was tattooed on my forehead.

But the women, the men who came to my apartment, could tell I was fucked up. They didn't know exactly how or why, but they sure as fuck knew something was going on.

As for Bebe, she was completely cut off from my reality. She only saw the bits I wanted her to see, and I didn't let her see much. It was for the best, really, because nothing could ever happen between us.

"No," I said simply and cut the Skype call.

I stared at my blank screen for a second, looking at my own reflection in it.

There was nothing wrong with me at first sight, and there was no reason Bebe would know how fucked up I really was. And I didn't want her to know. As badly as I wanted her in my fucking arms, bouncing up and down on my cock, this was more important. This semblance of normality, this pretense that everything was going to be okay.

I needed Bebe to believe it, because if she did, maybe I could too.

If only for a night.

I texted her that afternoon because I was getting way too fucking restless. I'd spent all day doing work stuff, trying to ignore her presence right across the street. But she was like an itch I couldn't scratch – omnipresent and gnawing away at me until I finally gave her the attention she so badly craved.

She'd been walking around the apartment sulkily in a silky robe, not giving me a single look, pretending we didn't share a history anymore. My text would see to that right away.

Hope you've had enough time to rest, sugar. Your new toy arrives today.

She didn't text back. The little slut left me waiting for two hours before she graced me with a reply.

What makes you think I still want you to play with me?

I grinned to myself and my fingers worked on the screen to send her a reply right away.

Because the second you got my text, your little fingers went straight to those panties. Don't lie. I saw it.

She got up to her feet furiously and I laughed in her angry little face as she shut the curtains. She knew I was right, but she wasn't ready to admit it just yet. She was also in a bit of a mood, but I didn't give a shit. The online tracking number for what I'd ordered her showed me the delivery man was only 10 deliveries away. Soon, she'd have my gift, and we'd be able to play again.

I watched the tracking number like a hawk, and once her delivery was up next, I looked down on the street to find the van parked on the pavement.

A middle-aged man rang her doorbell and a minute later, she opened the front door, shivering in the cool evening air. She signed for the package, completely oblivious of the man's stares. I wanted to fucking throat punch him but I convinced myself to keep my cool. Instead, I watched impatiently as Bebe went back to her apartment. I waited until my phone rang. She was calling.

"Hello, sweetness," I greeted her.

My cock was painfully hard before she even opened her mouth, but the second I heard her speak, it twitched for more.

"Why did you get me a camera?" she asked.

"I want you to take some photos for me," I told her. "I'll text you a connection code to input into the camera for sending direct to my computer, so whatever you film or shoot will come straight to me."

She was silent for a second, making my heard pound nervously. I could hear the shakiness in her voice when she spoke up again.

"What do you want me to take photos of?"

"Everything," I told her. "I want to watch you live your life. I want to watch you go out. Come home. Strip down. Get dressed. I want to see it all."

I kept staring at her window, watching her pull the curtains open slowly. She stood in front of the glass, her body illuminated by a streetlight and her face curiously beautiful. God, she was fucking incredible. A mystery, a precious little whore who was going to do my bidding, whatever the fuck it was. I was in deep, probably too fucking deep, but it was too late to get out now.

"But won't that be boring?" she asked me.

I thought of the alternative.

Empty fucking days in my apartment.

Cleaning myself, and everything that surrounded me with vigor.

Finding new girls to abuse, new men to break. Fucking with my head, fucking with theirs, fucking everything that moved.

And I thought of her.

Sweet, broken Bebe.

Morning Bebe.

Partygirl Bebe.

My Bebe.

"It won't be boring for me," I told her.

She didn't need to know the whole truth.

She didn't need to know I hadn't been outside in fucking weeks. That the last time I left my apartment I had such a bad panic attack I clawed at my own wrists, and I still bore the slashes and red scars I'd made. That I was so fucking terrified of it all it was easier to stay in my safe, pristine, clinical apartment, and live my life between four walls.

"Are you sure?" she asked.

There was a hint in her voice, an opportunity to explain, to tell her how fucked up I really was.

And I deliberately ignored it.

"Yeah, sugar," I muttered instead. "Now turn it the fuck on."

Chapter 9

·BEBE·

SCINTILLATE, VERB
To emit sparks, to twinkle as the stars.

I fiddled with the camera, finding the power button after a few seconds of searching.

"You sure you want to see me?" I asked him, feeling self-conscious. "I don't have any makeup on."

"I don't give a shit," Miles growled. "I've seen you without plenty of times."

My heart swelled. I'd always made an effort to wear something nice for him, to wear nice clothes and pretty makeup. Which meant he'd been looking at me when I wasn't ready for him. I should have known, really.

"Been stalking me, Miles?" I asked him playfully, and he growled into the phone, sending shivers down my spine.

"You wish I was," he said. "You wish I'd come up behind you and drag you into an empty fucking alley. Fuck your brains out in there and toss you aside like you meant nothing."

It hurt to hear him talk that way, but I didn't care, because it made me impossibly, unbearably wet.

"You want to use me?" I asked, my voice shaking.

"Don't you want me to?" His voice was gentle and sweet, calming.

It was a sharp contrast to the words coming out of his mouth, yet I found it fucking irresistible. His whole demeanor, the way he was condescending yet dominant, caring but cruel. It was a delicious cocktail and I needed another sip.

But the whole time, there was a nagging voice in the back of my head, whispering nasty things in my ear and making me think I wasn't good enough.

I really wasn't. I was a poor little rich girl, abandoned by most of her friends and family. I had all the money in the world but I had fucking nothing to show for it. An empty life filled with thousand-dollar handbags and smudged designer lipstick, a pussy forever dripping with cum, and lips that tasted like whatever drink was trending.

"Bebe," he interrupted my thoughts. "Where did you go, my pretty little slut?"

My hands shook as I switched the camera on and turned it towards my face. I heard him groan in seconds, and a sheen of cold sweat covered my skin, nerves getting the better of me.

Not. Fucking. Good. Enough.

Never was, never would be.

"I'm here," I whispered, my eyes darting between the camera and the window. I couldn't see him anymore and it made me feel alone. "Can you see me?"

"Yeah," he muttered. "I can see you."

An awkward silence followed, and finally, he spoke again.

"Put your phone down and put it on speaker," he said.

I was so fucking scared my legs barely carried me over to the living room area. I placed my phone on the coffee table, following his instructions. His deep, booming voice filled the room.

"Good girl."

God, he got me so fucking wet. Just two little words in that sinful voice of his and I was putty in his hands. I had to bite my tongue before I gave him more. Before I fucking humiliated myself and promised him anything and everything he ever wanted. Because I was already fucking ready to give it to him. But I'd never let him know that. Never ever.

"Hold the camera out so I can see you," Miles said, and I stretched my arms out, giving him a good look.

I panned the lens over my body, the little silk nightie I was wearing and the kimono robe on top of it. I deliberately ended the shot just above my lips.

"Your face," Miles rasped. "Let me see your fucking face, sugar."

"I don't want to," I whispered.

"Why?" He didn't sound angry, or disappointed, and it almost scared me more.

"I'm..." I swallowed thickly, the embarrassing weight of the truth heavy on the tip of my tongue. "I'm not ready, I... I'm worried you won't like me like this."

"Like what?" he wanted to know.

He was making me blush, tears gathering in my eyes, even though I was too stubborn to let them fall. I hated it, and I didn't want him to know.

"The way I am," I explained. "The way I look."

"Why wouldn't I like it?" There was a hint of anger in his voice.

"Because you like beautiful girls," I whispered. "Beautiful, thin, sexy, flawless dolls."

He was quiet for a second too long, and it killed me inside. I was just about ready to end the call when he spoke, gentler this time.

"Look over here," he said, and I moved towards the window, my palms landing on the cool glass, my eyes finding him.

There was a message scribbled on the window, the letters clumsy and fucked up from where he'd tried to make them face me. The words were written in thick slashes of pink lipstick, probably something the girl from a few days ago had left in his apartment.

YOU'RE SO BEAUTIFUL IT HURTS

My fingers slid down the glass and I looked at him, so fucking far away, feeling closer and yet farther away than ever.

I was falling for him. Slowly slowly slowly falling, feeling my body getting pulled by the current, sinking, sinking deep.

Miles was in my head.

In my pussy.

He was in the shivers down my spine.

In the tremble of my fingers.

Miles was in my body without ever being inside me.

Thank you, I mouthed. His face contorted in a grin that looked almost painful, and I let myself fall because I knew it was inevitable.

I already belonged to him.

"Now, sugar," he said gently through the speaker. "Back to your little task, don't be a bad girl."

I took the camera and panned it over my face, my eyes downcast, my lashes resting against my cheeks.

"Beautiful…" Miles' voice was gentle yet firm on the speaker. "You're so beautiful. Show me more. I fucking want more."

I held the camera in front of me, slowly opening my eyes, my lashes going up and up and up until he could see my eyes, still filled with a few tears and sparkling with emotion. I heard him take a sharp intake of breath when I looked at him through the lens, and I smiled shyly at the camera.

I stared at the camera, feeling like I was looking straight into his eyes. Then, I slowly panned the camera down over my body. I arched my back and my tits jutted out for him, so desperate to have him take me, to feel something special other than meaningless cocks and the numb emptiness that had filled my days since we lost Posy.

"Strip," Miles ordered me, and it was my turn to gasp. "Come on, sugar, be a good girl for me and strip. I want to see you."

With shaky hands, I placed the camera down on the side table; it seemed to be around the right height to capture all of me. I stood back, smiled at the camera, and slowly peeled off my kimono.

The silk felt cool and pleasant against my skin as I slid it off, the pretty fabric pooling around my feet. I loved having this power over him, hearing him gasp over the speaker on my phone, his voice a low rumble and his words demanding more as I teased him. I didn't understand why he didn't just come over. I had never met a guy who was as patient as Miles was.

Because we both knew how this was going to end.

With his cock all the way inside me and his hands around my throat.

With my pussy spasming around him and Miles filling me up like I wanted him to.

It would be the best sex I'd ever have, I was already certain of it.

But what scared me was that I already wanted so much more.

I blocked the dangerous thought as soon as it entered my mind, instead focusing on taunting him, making sure he saw every inch of me exposed for him.

"Do you want more?" I asked, my body swaying to the rhythm of the music playing in my mind.

"Fuck yes," Miles growled. "Of course I want more, sugar. Get naked for me. Everything off. I want to see every gorgeous inch of you."

I felt my nipples tighten at his words; felt the rush of heat to my pussy as I slipped the straps of my nightie down my shoulders, revealing inch after inch of my tanned skin. He growled at the sight of it, but it only served to encourage me, and I slid the silk off, over my tits, exposing myself to the camera.

"Do you like me?" I asked softly, my hands touching my pebbled nipples and tweaking them into hard buds desperate for Miles' lips locking around them, biting down until I had tears in my eyes. "Do you like what you see? Doesn't it make you want me, Miles? Doesn't it make you want to come over here… and just… fucking… take me?"

I mewled when I pinched my own nipples, and the low growl that came over the speaker made my legs go weak. I backed up against the window without looking over my shoulder, my back leaning against the cool glass, my ass pushed against it so he could see me from all sides – my front with the camera, my ass with a look through the window.

"Don't fucking tempt me," he said as I took hold of the hem of my nightie, lifting it slowly, revealing my tanned thighs.

"Or what?" I asked, and peeled it all the way off.

I stood in front of him in nothing but a lacy black thong, and I could feel the tension coming off him from all the way over the street. He wanted me just as much as I wanted him, but for some reason, he was staying the fuck away. And an evil little part of me wanted him to break, wanted him to say fuck it and just come over and feed me his cock until I choked on his hot cum.

But he wouldn't. He groaned and growled and cursed but he didn't break, and it made me feel so fucking useless I had to blink the tears away.

"Please," I said in my softest voice.

He didn't hear it. He couldn't, I was too far away from my phone. But then he spoke again, and hearing his voice again made it all okay.

"Bebe… sugar," he said, his voice torn. "I want you. I want you too much."

"I know," I whispered, my thumbs hooking under my thong, toying with it. "I know you do, Miles, I want you too…"

"You don't get it," he said, his voice strained. "I fucking *want* you."

I slid the thong off, over my hips, onto the floor. I'd had a fresh wax only a day ago and he groaned at the sight of my bare pussy as my fingers slid over the lips, opening them up for him, offering him a look inside me.

"Tell me what to do," I rasped. "Tell me what you want me to do to *your* pussy, Miles."

"Move the camera closer," he said. "I want to see close up."

I did as I was told, moved the camera to the low coffee table and then I sat on the sofa in front of it, opening my legs for him.

"Like this?" I asked him.

"Perfect," he said, "Now, open for me," he growled. "Open your pretty slit for me, sugar, I want to see you fucking exposed."

My fingers trembled as I pulled the lips of my pussy back, showing him my clit, shivering from the cool air of the room hitting it in a way that almost felt like a tickle.

"Do you like me like this?" I asked gently. "Do you like that I'd let you do anything to me, Miles?"

"Yes," he said. "I love it. I fucking love it. The way you are. What you want. This fucking… need to…"

"To what?" I whispered, my finger dipping inside me for just a second.

Miles cursed as I brought it out and licked at the juice on the tip of it.

"The need to fuck you," he went on. "I'm not like this. I'm not some fucking animal. It's you, you make me this way. I fucking need it. Need to take you. Need to hold you down. Need to take it all away from you."

"Let me fuck your pussy for you," I said, my mind spinning from his words. "Let me do it, please."

"Fuck it," he ordered. "But don't you dare fucking come. Remember, you always need permission for that."

"Y-yes," I whispered.

"Yes what?" he demanded.

"Yes… Thank you, Miles."

A silence followed, and I wondered whether he thought I'd call him a name that suited his dominant nature. But I couldn't – didn't want to. Miles felt too perfect on my lips, so fucking intimate and special.

"Fuck it," he growled. "Fuck. It. Now."

I did. Hitched my ass forward and sunk two fingers deep.

I heard him breathing, shallow and desperate, and I could tell he was palming his dick. I fingered my needy cunt and brought myself so close I thought I was going to pass out from the sensation of having only my fingers inside me, and then I dropped to my knees and looked into the camera on the coffee table.

"Want to see something?" I asked him shakily, and his answer came back right away.

"Show me."

"Let me come," I begged, placing the camera between my legs so he had a perfect view of my cunt. "Let it come for you, Miles. See how desperate I am? See how fucking wet I am?"

I pulled my pussy open, making it leak all over the hardwood floor beneath my ass.

"Jesus fuck," he said. "Fucking come, Bebe. Count to five and come with me."

"One," I whispered, slipping three fingers inside myself. "Two…"

"Faster," he said, his voice needier than I'd ever heard it. "Fucking faster, Bebe!"

"Three."

I fucked myself so hard my legs kept spasming and my pussy made wet squelchy sounds.

"Four, please, Miles, fuck, please…"

"Five," he grunted, and I came for him, spraying the camera when my pussy squirted and my fingers came out.

I fucking howled and he laughed at me, laughed with a desperate edge.

"You fucking dirty little slut," he said, and I fell back on the floor, raising the camera over me and licking the lens. "Jesus, Bebe, you're something fucking else."

I stared at him, my breaths slowing and my pussy starting to ache.

"Thank you, Miles," I whispered. "Did I make you come?"

"Yeah," he grunted. "All over my fucking fist."

"Let me lick it off," I said softly.

He went silent.

And it took me a minute to realize he'd ended the call.

Chapter 10

·MILES·

SILLAGE, NOUN
The scent that lingers in the air, the trace of someone's perfume.

I was addicted to her, and there was no point in denying it anymore.

That morning, I called a man who I worked with on occasion. Flint Meyers used to be a journalist, but now he spent his days finding out shit for rich people. Mostly women trying to find out whether their husband was having an affair. But I used him for background checks on the girls I fucked, and now, I had a new task for him.

"Good morning, Miles," he answered his phone cheerily. "Another background check?"

"Not this time," I replied, running a hand through my hair.

I risked a look through the window towards Bebe's apartment, but she was nowhere in sight. Probably still asleep from the late night she'd had.

"I want you to follow someone around," I said, letting the words hang out there in the open. "It's a woman. She lives across the street from me. Her name is Bebe Hall…"

"Got it," Meyers said simply. "What should I watch out for? Anything specific you need info on?"

"No," I said curtly. "I just want to know what she does. Everything. And bring me some shit to look at. Photos – plenty of photos, and anything discarded, like receipts she left behind, that kind of thing."

"You've got a deal." I could see Meyers smiling in my head.

All he saw was the hefty sum of money I'd let him have for helping me, but all I saw was the opportunity to get more of her. More of Bebe. I needed so much more.

"I'll see you tonight," I said, ending the call.

I got off the sofa I was sitting on, pacing the room. The way Flint worked, he usually came to meet me in the evening to give me a roundup of everything he'd found. But he also sent me updates throughout the day, so I decided to keep my phone close, so I could see exactly what my Sleeping Beauty was up to.

But now, the day stretched out in front of me with nothing to do. I felt jittery and nervous in a way I wasn't used to, and it worried me.

Usually, a bleach bath would help, but weirdly, I had no desire to damage my skin that day. I just wanted information, I wanted to know what she was doing, what filled her days. I needed it like a fucking addict needed their drug, and I resented myself for not being able to track her myself. But there was no way I'd be able to go outside, no way I could follow her around with every thought focused on germs, on the fucking disgusting people around her, when all I wanted to focus on was Bebe.

What she ate for breakfast.

What kind of outfit she wore when she left her house.

Whether her hair was up, exposing that slender neck I wanted to bite into, or down, falling down her back.

How she held herself when she walked; how her tits bounced.

How she smiled at others.

What she ate for lunch. How often she pissed.

I wanted to know every fucking thing about her.

I paced the room restlessly, finally deciding I might as well do some work while I waited for Meyers' first find of the day.

Leaving the living room, I walked into the all-white room I used as a studio. There was a hidden door in the wall behind the bed, and it led into the room no one knew about. The room of shame. The one space in the whole apartment I couldn't let anyone see because they would finally know just how badly fucked up I really was.

I opened the hidden door, stared into the fucking mess, and retched at the awful stink.

It was a tiny room, used for storage by the previous owners. There was only one small window to the outside, but that was grubby with grime, and the ceiling was so low I had to crouch to get in there.

And it was a fucking mess.

A terrible mess.

Trash everywhere. Not things I'd used, actual trash I'd collected on rare trips outside. Trash from a garbage can, ranging from soiled newspaper clippings to tissues, some food well past its prime, just anything I could get my hands on. The tiny room stank so badly. It was disgusting. Fucking gross, fucking unbelievable for a man of my stature.

I walked inside calmly, to the small wooden desk that stood against the wall. I sat on the stool in front of it and leaned against the wall because the room was so small I could do that. And then I started thinking, with the trash surrounding me, the oppressive stink of the room making me want to gag.

It was the only way I could work. The only way I could clear out the constant buzz inside my head. And I was fucking ashamed of it. I'd never let anyone see this part of me. My parents made me ashamed of what I did in there, and they made sure I kept it my dirty little secret.

I heard flies buzzing in the pile of trash on the floor. The stench was overwhelming, but I made myself take it because it was the only way I knew how to function.

My phone vibrated, and I grabbed it from my pocket, desperately checking for a message.

It was from Bebe, and the moment I saw her name on my screen, my heart thumped a little louder in my chest.

I wish you'd talk to me when you weren't just trying to make me come.

My fingers ached from wanting to reply so badly, but I made myself wait. Couldn't look too eager, could I? Couldn't let her know how badly I wanted her, how much I craved her.

The phone buzzed with another message, this one from Meyers.

She's been out for brunch. Three mimosas with it. She had Eggs Benedict.

It fucking hurt to read it, because it was the most normal thing in the world, and I knew I'd never be able to do it with her. Simple things like grabbing food at her favorite place or going out shopping seemed insurmountable to me. They were like a mountain I had to climb without the proper gear and equipment, and the mere thought of it sent me into a panic. I needed to breathe.

I broke out of the room, cold sweat running down my back, and only just made it to the bathroom before I finally gagged and retched up a whole load of puke into the sink. I felt disgusted. Mostly with myself. With what I'd let myself become.

Thoughts filled my head, dirty, horrible thoughts that reminded me of my childhood, of what I'd ran away from, of what I'd left behind.

My parents. Rough, hardened faces, staring down at me, always with that faraway look in their eyes. They rarely spoke to me. The only person who bothered to do that was my grandmother.

Nana. Where are you, Nana? Are you still out there? Are you wondering where I went? Did I take a piece of your heart with me? Do you wonder if I've fallen down the same hole as your son and his wife? Do you wonder if I'm okay? Or have you turned into a rotting pile of flesh just like them? Is there nothing left of you but decaying meat and fucking bones? Are you cremated? Are you a pile of ash and regret, Nana? Where are you? WHERE THE FUCK ARE YOU? WHY WON'T YOU HELP ME?

I collapsed on the floor. Shaky limbs, beating heart, a pile of shit, a diamond in the rough. Fuck, fuck, fuck, not this, not again, not now, not right now. Please make it stop. Make it go away.

I slammed my fists on the floor, trying to break out of the vicious cycle. But it held its grip on me, its talons harsh against my skin, digging, fucking digging into my flesh, making me submit, making me fall *down down down*. I couldn't fight it. Couldn't break away from the madness. It was fucking clawing at me. Tearing me apart.

I could handle pain.

Emotional, physical, what the fuck ever.

But I couldn't handle this.

This fucking numbness, the panic, the crazy, the fucking insanity of my life; what I'd gotten myself into.

Fear and adrenaline pumped through my veins, and I managed to pick myself up on shaky feet. I wanted to call Bebe, ask for help. Something I hadn't done in fucking years… But I couldn't reach for my phone. Couldn't muster up enough strength to take my damn phone and call her number and beg her to come and help me. I couldn't do a thing. Just stand there, shaking and utterly broken.

I didn't know how long it lasted, I never did. The helplessness started to go away, slowly leaking out of my body, along with the sweat that seeped from my pores.

I dragged myself to the sofa and made myself sit down, slowly relaxing, my muscles cramping up from being in such a rigid position. Slowly, I came back to my senses. Back into my own body.

I'd been having panic attacks for years, but the anxiety was something I wasn't as used to.

Back when I still lived with Nana, she was used to the manic episodes – screaming, thrashing, trying to get away. She'd worked out how to help me and she knew exactly what to do. I hadn't had them in years, but now that I was alone the anxiety got the better of me too often for my liking. A bone-deep anxiety that made me double over and retch bile and venom. I hated it. Hated that I couldn't call for help, couldn't do much of anything until it passed.

Paralyzed.

I was fucking paralyzed.

I sat on the sofa in my rigid position and watched the sun go down. My phone kept buzzing but I couldn't pick it up. Couldn't even go to the bathroom, even though I had to go badly. Couldn't get a glass of water despite my mouth being parched, feeling like it was filled with cotton.

I sat there until it got dark, so dark I couldn't make out the objects in the room. Bebe's room was dark, too.

And then my doorbell rang.

I couldn't get up. I just fucking sat there.

"It's open," I croaked, and it took all I had in me to say it.

I could barely turn my head to the direction of the door to see Meyers walk in. The light from the hallway illuminated the room, and I shrank away from it.

When he saw me, his mouth set in a thin line and he approached me cautiously.

"Come on," he said, his voice dark. "Bathroom."

Meyers had seen this before. Too many fucking times for my liking, because it was fucking embarrassing.

I let him help me up, feeling ashamed. So fucking ashamed.

He helped me to the bathroom and I had to lean my head against the wall, just so I could fucking piss. He didn't even close the door. Kept watching me trying to stand, my hands shaking so badly I sprayed the tile. I knew I'd spend the night cleaning that up, once this went away. This fucking part of me that I hated so badly I wanted to rip it, cut it out of my flesh, and feed it to a stray fucking dog.

I washed my hands vigorously, slowly coming back to my senses. Meyers stood there, averting his eyes.

I knew he felt sorry for me.

Everyone did.

I felt my strength coming back, and I walked out of the bathroom with my back straight and my chin held high.

"What do you have for me?" I asked him, flipping on a switch in the living room as if I hadn't been sitting in the darkness for what was probably hours. "Anything interesting happen?"

"Well, she's a party girl alright," Meyers chuckled, handing me a brown paper envelope.

My fingers shook as I got the contents out of it. A bunch of photos. I always asked for photos. I loved seeing my girls like that.

But she wasn't my girl. Not like the others, not like any of them.

She was *the* girl, the only girl, the one I wanted to keep.

Too bad I couldn't, not now, not ever.

"She's had more drinks in the span of a few hours than I have in a month," Meyers muttered, shaking his head.

I appreciated him pretending my meltdown hadn't happened. He knew there was a good tip in it for him, but I didn't give a shit, I was still grateful.

"She likes booze," I muttered, going through the photos.

Bebe in a sweet little dress that was much too short to be modest despite the cute style. It made me smile to myself. Her hair was up, just like I'd hoped. Her neck was slender and very pale, and it made blood pulse towards my cock. She was a fucking vision, and in several photos, I noticed men in the street or the cafe she was in fucking staring at her. I wanted to strangle each and every one of them while she watched.

"What else did she do?" I asked, going through the photos.

"She was out most of the day," Meyers went on, handing me a bigger envelope. "I saved you the receipts like you asked. She went to brunch, then shopping. Dropped her stuff at home and got changed, then went out again with another girl. I think her name was Arden? Does that ring a bell?"

"Her friend, I think," I said. "Did she notice you?"

"No, not once," Meyers smiled. "You'd be proud of me. I stayed in the shadows."

I looked at all the receipts, grinning at her choice of groceries.

A shit ton of chocolate and energy drinks. And a head of lettuce. Such a weird girl.

"Oh, one more thing," Meyers said, reaching into his briefcase. "She dropped this at the brunch place. Thought you might want it."

He handed me a piece of fabric.

A cardigan.

I palmed the fabric as he handed it to me, the soft cashmere pleasant under my fingertips.

"Get out," I growled at Meyers.

He gave me an incredulous look.

"Don't make me repeat myself," I said, glaring at him. "Get the fuck out!"

He backed away and closed the door behind him.

I was left sitting on the couch, staring at the cashmere cardigan in my hands. It was light pink, and the buttons were little pearls. It was cute. It was hers. It smelled like her.

I raised it to my face and inhaled her sweet scent, groaning out loud. It was almost enough to make me fucking spill.

But through it all, I had to remember…

This was the closest I was ever going to get to having Bebe in my arms.

Chapter 11

·BEBE·

NEPENTHE, NOUN
Something that can make you forget your grief and suffering.

"How's the club life?"
I squinted and pressed my hand against my ear, trying to block out the sound of the blaring music.

"It's good," I shouted back. "How's the married life?"

A guy in his late twenties approached me, and I gave him a distracted smile as he grinned at me. Arden was sighing on the other end of the line, and I tore my attention away from the hottie.

"I'm bored," she said restlessly.

"Bored of?" I asked, moving outside until the cool night air enveloped me in a thick hug smelling of autumn.

"Everything." She sounded sulky. "I just want to get out of here."

"You're not missing anything," I tried to convince her, but she'd already cut the call.

Suddenly, I felt very alone on that club balcony, like I had absolutely no one in the world who would want to take care of me. Not that I needed anyone. I was a fucking grown-up, and I could take care of myself, couldn't I?

With that new thought in mind, I marched back inside the club with my head held high proudly.

The music blasted through my body like a gust of wind, the heavy bass reverberating in my core. My nose was assaulted with the smell of alcohol and sweaty bodies, and my eyes watered when someone blew smoke right past me. I glared at the guy smoking a blunt right there, but he just laughed in my face when I motioned for him to put it out. He wasn't having any of it.

I pouted and made for our VIP table, located a few steps up from the dancefloor and sectioned off from the masses with a red velvet rope.

"Where did you get off to?"

I looked at my friend Billy who'd spoken to me, offering him a weak little smile.

"Just a phone call," I shrugged.

"Arden?" he guessed, and I nodded, sliding into the booth with him and the rest of the gang.

They were fast friends I'd made in the city, people I'd known for a maximum of six months.

Six months since we lost Posy. Six months since I felt the need to replace every familiar face in my life with a new one. Six months since I decided Arden was the only person from my past I'd keep around because I loved her too much to let her go.

"Don't worry about her," Billy winked at me. "We got a new bottle of champagne and we're ready for more if you are."

"Sure," I shrugged, plastering on a fake smile that told him I was a good girl, the Bebe he liked, the Bebe who danced on tables until the morning and threw up in the alley behind the club after getting fingered a few feet away. "Let's get this party started, why don't we?"

He handed me a glass, but I pushed him out of the way and went straight for the ice bucket. The whole crew cheered me on as I grabbed the frosty bottle of Möet and started chugging straight from it. The champagne felt cool and fizzy in my mouth, and it went down my throat almost too easily. So easily I drained half the bottle before someone pried it out of my hands.

"Leave some for the rest of us, girl," a girl in the booth giggled, and I rolled my eyes as she glugged the rest of the bottle down.

It wasn't a problem anyway. Each and every one of us had enough cash – or loaded parents – to cover the bill for as many bottles as we wanted. It was just a competition for attention, just like most of the things in my life were. I didn't mind it though.

Because I always fucking won.

I drank and drank until someone at the table shrieked and ran off to the dancefloor to hug someone. Through the girl's embrace, I noticed Arden standing there, being enveloped in a bear hug and wearing a smirk on her pretty lips.

"Come to join the party?" I called out to her as she approached the table, waving at our friends, or whatever the fuck they were.

"Fashionably late," she winked at me and sat down on the sofa next to me.

I air kissed her, but she surprised me by pulling me in for a hug.

Surprised me so much I just sat there, rigid and stiff as she wrapped her arms around my body.

We never hugged, we weren't huggers. Posy was. But Posy was gone, gone, gone.

"What's going on with Nick?" I asked her once she moved away, and she gave me a guilty look before shrugging. "Babe, talk to me. Is everything okay?"

"Yeah," she sighed miserably. "I guess it's just… moving a little fast. I'm not used to this relationship shit."

"You'll be fine," I yelled over the sound of the music. "You deserve a good guy, Arden."

"I guess," she shrugged again, and I giggled at her, tugging on her long honey blonde hair.

She was wearing it down that night, along with the silver-sequined dress I'd worn a few weeks ago and I'd let her borrow. She looked fucking amazing, filling my head with memories I'd be better off forgetting. Posy was the center of all of them, giggling, laughing in that loud, obnoxious way of hers. She was always the life of the party, it was all about her. And now here we were, lost without our leader.

"I promise," I told her again, nudging her bony ribs. "Nick's okay in my book."

She gave me a sideways look. "I thought you hated him."

I made a face. "Because I knew he was a keeper," I said. "I knew you'd end up with him, and I was scared of losing my friend."

"Bebe…" She looked at me, cracking a tiny smile. "You can't be serious."

"Well, I am," I replied, my voice strained now.

I'd told her the truth. I couldn't cope with losing Arden too, not on top of Posy. I couldn't handle the world alone.

Arden leaned over to me, taking my chin between her fingers and looking into my eyes. I let her, remembering all those games we'd played, the things Posy had made us do. Things Arden and I never talked about, because they were too taboo, too off limits to even mention.

She leaned closer and pressed her lips to mine. No tongue, no show for the guys in the club.

This kiss was just for me.

When she pulled back, we smiled at each other.

"I know I'm selfish," I muttered, and she laughed out loud, making me scowl at her.

"That's the understatement of the year," Arden said, and I stuck my tongue out at her.

"I want the best for you, though," I told her, putting a hand on her lap. "I'm just jealous…"

"Jealous?" Arden rolled her eyes. "Every guy in here knows who you are, Bebe. You're the *it* girl. Everyone wants a piece of you. I'm just tagging along."

I wanted to answer when we were interrupted by Billy, pulled to our feet and dragged to the dancefloor. My moping was replaced by raucous laughter, and I let myself be dragged to the center of the room. The music was loud in my ears and Arden's smile burned brightly. I danced with her. I danced with them all, my body moving to the rhythm of the music, dancing my heart out.

I felt the booze pumping through my veins, and for once, I let myself forget. Not just about Posy, but about the mess my life was. I even forgot about Miles, even though he was constantly at the back of my mind, clawing angrily to be let out, to let him play with me.

Hands touched my body, and I wasn't sure whether they were mine or someone else's. I let them touch me, roam my skin, tug my dress up, slide over my tits. I just cared about dancing the stress away, pretending it was all going to go away, as long as I kept dancing, all night, all day.

A girl appeared in front of me, her eyes wide and drugged out. She was laughing, laughing so much.

I tugged on the bell sleeve of her plum-colored dress, and she turned to face me. I opened my mouth, sticking my tongue out, and she laughed, reaching into her bag and bringing out a small plastic container. She took out a small piece of paper and placed it on my tongue, but I grabbed her wrist and held up two fingers. The girl rolled her eyes, but complied, placing another piece on my tongue.

And then I really danced.

And it felt so fucking good.

I felt sweat dripping down my back, but I didn't give a shit. It felt too good to be in the moment, to watch my surroundings changing from the shit I was used to seeing every day into an exciting wonderland where I was the reigning queen.

I wasn't in my favorite club anymore. I watched it turn into a whole new world, where the dancers became caricatures of themselves, moving slowly in tune with the music. The DJ was the caterpillar, Billy was the Mad Hatter. Arden, where was Arden?

I wasn't the queen anymore, I was Alice, utterly lost in Wonderland, starting to grow scared but not scared enough to stop. I needed to keep dancing, keep fucking going. So I danced. Danced and danced and danced until I felt like I was trapped inside the club, trapped and made to dance to the music blasting through the speakers. But I still danced, my feet moving of their own volition, my body swaying to the music that was starting to turn into growls and laughter that scared me, scared me so fucking much.

Someone tugged on my arm and I spun round.

"Arden," I whispered, my tongue heavy in my mouth, my lips trembling, my eyes crazed.

"Bebe," she growled.

Her voice was menacing. She was a monster. She was out to get me. Everyone was.

"What did you take?" she asked, shaking my shoulders. "What did you fucking take?"

I started screaming but no sound came out. I just covered my eyes and screamed in silence, where the only person who could hear me wailing was sitting in my head on their throne, fucking *laughing laughing laughing*, and it was Posy, sitting there, laughing at me, making me fall down the same rabbit hole, *down down down*.

"I don't want to fall," I whispered. "Don't let me fall, I don't want to go, I don't want to go down, let me go, let me fucking go, I don't want to be like you, I want to live, I want to smile, I want to fucking survive!"

But that's not what came out of my mouth.

All that I heard was my own manic laughter, loud, crazy, drugged-up laughter, and I realized how Arden was hearing it, what she thought, that it looked like I was mocking her.

"No, Arden," I tried to say, but it came out muffled. "I need help, help me, help me please, don't let this happen, don't let me go, don't let this happen to me, save me, Arden, get Miles, get me away from Posy, can't you see? She's evil, she's dragging me down, she wants me to suffer, she wants the same thing to happen to me, don't let her, don't fucking let her, Arden please, Miles, please, don't let her!"

All she heard was my laughing and my sobs mixing together, and she wasn't inside my head like I was, she couldn't hear what was happening. It was too much, and she didn't… Even. Fucking. Know.

She was crying now, little sad tears falling down her cheeks as she pulled me against her, held me tight.

"Bebe," she whispered in my ear as I laughed, fucking trapped, cursed by the evil queen to laugh, laugh and fucking laugh when I really wanted to cry. "It's okay, Bebe, I understand, come on, I'll get you home, I'll make sure you're alright."

I howled. Like a wolf, like a wounded animal. I howled for her to help me.

But all that came out… Was. Fucking. Laughter.

She dragged me out into the cold night and slapped me across the face, hard, making me stumble back. And then she was holding me up, supporting me, making sure I was alright.

"Arden," I whispered. "Arden, please."

"Please tell me what you took," she begged me. "So I can help you. I need to know what you took."

"I fell," I explained. "I fell down the rabbit hole. Someone pushed me, someone pulled me down, and I fell."

"Bebe…" She looked into my eyes, and I saw the despair in her own. "Fuck, Bebe, this has to fucking stop."

She dragged me down the street, with people watching us in wonder. Some of them were good but most of them were *evil evil evil*.

I decided to hide in a corner. The corner I knew so well. In the back of my mind, in the tiny dark alley that no one knew about. Where I could mourn, where I could be the fucking broken little mess Posy had made me into. I hid there, and I pulled the darkness around me like a blanket of nightmares. And I stayed there, made my legs work so I could follow Arden, but kept my mind in that fucked-up little corner where I could scream as much as I wanted to.

And no one could hear it.

Chapter 12

·MILES·

AGORAPHOBIA, NOUN
Extreme, irrational fear of open and public places.

It was late, and I couldn't sleep.

I'd been awake all night, too shaken up by the events of the day to let myself have some rest. But another thing distracting me was her cardigan, the sweet scent of Bebe permeating my nostrils every time I raised it to my nose. I couldn't fucking sleep with that thing in the house. All I wanted to do was have the girl who owned it in my arms, and not having her made me more fucking anxious than ever.

I kept my eyes on her apartment that whole night, but nothing happened. I needed her to come home. I needed to talk to her.

No text messages all evening, no calls, no nothing. She was out somewhere meeting people who were so much better than me, much less broken, much less fucked-up. And I was jealous as hell, the green-eyed monster rearing its head and threatening to eat me up whole. God, I fucking wanted her to come home. I wanted to see her strip and climb into bed, even if it was with some guy she didn't even know. I just needed her to be alright, to make sure she made her way home okay, to know she was in one piece.

It was eating me up, and I kept pacing the apartment trying to clear my head unsuccessfully. Her cardigan felt soft in my hands, but not as soft as her skin would feel when I bit into it.

It was almost five a.m. when I got a horrible feeling of dread, raced to the window and stared down at the street below me.

I lived in a good neighborhood where apartments were stupidly expensive and vandalism was unheard of. The residents of my apartment building were private and didn't give a shit about what I was doing in my own home. I liked it that way.

So, hearing the commotion below me was something rare, something that made my skin crawl with worry.

I looked down at the scene unfolding before my eyes. There were two girls, one dragging the other along. I watched her dig in the stumbling girl's purse for keys, and I watched them walk into the building with my shoulders tense and my knuckles white. I waited for the light to come on in Bebe's apartment, and I watched her friend drag her to the bed. Bebe collapsed on the mattress, asleep or unconscious within moments.

I watched the other girl – Arden – slam her back against the door and slowly slide down, her face etched with worry, tears falling down her cheeks. She cried like a girl who was completely lost in the whirlwind of her life, and watching her felt so fucking wrong I almost turned my back to the scene in front of me.

Almost.

I couldn't. I was too addicted to it, to watching Bebe's life unfold right in front of me. God, I wanted to be there. I wanted to be part of the mess, part of the people she knew, the ones who could touch her, feel her, see her laugh. I'd never wanted anything more.

I watched Arden come apart in front of my eyes, and I watched her gather herself, stroke Bebe's cheek, and slowly let herself out of her friend's apartment.

But when she was leaving, I noticed she forgot to lock the door, and worry filled my body, making me dig my nails into my palms. She forgot to lock the fucking door. What if some maniac, some fucking lunatic, went into Bebe's apartment and took advantage of her while she was sleeping? I couldn't let that happen, I fucking couldn't. I needed to lock the door for her.

But how? I'd have to take her keys and lock the door from the outside, and she'd panic in the morning.

But I couldn't just leave it like that, with the door open for anyone to walk in and take advantage of her.

I needed to go over there. Make sure she was alright. Make sure she was breathing, that she wasn't fucking unconscious, wasn't choking on her own fucking puke – SHIT! I needed to go there, and I couldn't even step foot outside my apartment. What the hell was I supposed to do?

I walked to the other side of my living room, grabbed a decorative vase and smashed it against the wall. I breathed in deeply, trying to calm myself down, but I couldn't fucking do it. I was too anxious, too nervous, too fucking desperate to do something, help my girl, make sure she was alright. I needed to go over there, there was no way around it. Needed to make sure my Bebe was alright, even if it fucking killed me.

Peep Show

I stared at my own reflection in the mirror on the wall, breathing slowly, looking at the shards of the vase around my feet. I needed to get the fuck over there.

It was cold outside, and I was only wearing a tank top and sweatpants, but I couldn't muster up the energy to change. I knew as soon as I stepped foot out of my apartment, I'd have to fight battles bigger than the need for warmth.

I made myself walk briskly to the front door. I opened it wide and stared at the hallway in front of me. It had never seemed huge – so menacing.

I closed the door carefully. Made myself step on the doormat. Breathed in, breathed out. Tried to survive, tried to fight my demons for her.

I walked down the hallway and the demons made way for me, clawing, laughing, biting at my skin.

I couldn't face the elevator. I took the stairs instead, practically running down them until I reached the lobby.

The doorman was asleep in his chair, snoring loudly as I fought another mental battle right in front of his eyes. Slowly walking towards the revolving doors, I let my panic take the front seat because I knew adrenaline would come rushing right after it.

I slipped inside the revolving glass panel, walked with it until I was suddenly, mind-bogglingly, outside.

The air was cold. The sounds were almost too much. The smell of the fresh night air was oppressive. I wanted to fucking strangle the woman laughing a few feet away, walking home with her boyfriend.

I felt like an animal let out of its cage. Like a fucking monster, finally freed to do what I wanted, but blinded by the night, by the possibilities of everything I could do now that I was unleashed.

My steps made me stumble, stumble in the street like a fucking drunk. I made myself walk, reminding myself to do what Dr. Halen had told me – focus on something else, not something that makes you panic.

Not the fact that I was outside.

Not the oppressive voices.

Not the demons snapping at my heels.

Just putting one foot in front of the other. Moving slowly towards my destination. Just across the street. Just a few more steps. So fucking close, almost there... almost. I kept walking, stumbling, almost falling, forcing myself to keep going, keep going towards her.

Towards Bebe, my Bebe, my pretty little girl, passed out on her bed, fucking left to fend for herself when she couldn't even move.

I forced myself to keep going until I reached the door. I grabbed it like a fucking life jacket and practically dragged myself into the lobby.

"Can I help you?"

I looked down at the voice, a small man with glasses, looking more scared than inquisitive. He wore the uniform of a doorman, and I did my best to push my demons back to speak to him.

"My friend," I rasped. "Bebe Hall. Floor three. I need to help her, she just c-called me."

"Bebe?" he asked, licking his lips. "I know Bebe."

I wanted to fucking smack him. Fucking choke him. Fucking kill him, if I had to.

"She's passed out," I went on. "L-let me go up there."

"Do you need help?" he asked with a hunger to his voice.

"NO," I practically growled at him, making him take a step back. "No. Let me g-go."

"Alright," he said sceptically. "Floor three. Elevator's there."

"S-stairs?" I stuttered. "Can I take the stairs?"

"Sure." He gave me a strange look. "To your left."

I stumbled towards them, trying my best to keep walking upright, to not freak out like my body was telling me to. I reached the stairs and started going up, feeling a little better because at least I was inside. But still, it was unknown territory, a building I wasn't familiar with, crawling with germs and disgusting shit I didn't want to touch. But I fought against it and climbed the stairs until I reached her floor. I stared at her door that Arden had left ajar. Was I really going to do this? It felt so fucking wrong to go into her apartment, but I knew I had no choice.

Slowly, I approached the door, pushed it open and entered Bebe's home.

Her scent assaulted my nostrils the second I stepped inside. The smell of her cardigan back at my place, amplified a thousand times until it was all over me. All over my skin, in my pores, in my nose, in my fucking mouth. And fuck, did she smell good. I couldn't understand how someone could smell so sweet. Sugary enough for me to sink my teeth into her skin, sweet enough to wonder how many licks it would take to get to her molten center.

I found her bedroom, the scent of sugar stronger here than anywhere else.

My Bebe lay on the bed, on her stomach. She wasn't moving, just lying there, either asleep or unconscious.

My hands formed fists at my sides. Was I going to be able to touch her? Would I be able to touch her unmoving body to make sure she was alright? I had to try. I had to see if she was okay, at least.

I approached her with slow, unsure steps, the hardwood creaking under my feet. I gazed down at her.

She was beautiful, painfully beautiful, just like I'd told her she was. But up close, she was so much more, her face a map of freckles and tanned skin, each lash a stark contrast to the cheeks they lay upon. Her pouty mouth was smeared with red lipstick and she looked so vulnerable as she slept, the perfect victim for me to do anything I wanted to. I reached out for her, unable to stop my hands from touching her, something that didn't come easily to me.

I brushed a hand against her cheek, her beautiful, soft skin tight under my fingertips. Her skin was cold, but I could feel her breathing against my palm. Thank fucking God for that.

"Bebe," I murmured, my voice barely above a whisper.

I wanted to kiss her so badly it shocked me. Physical contact wasn't easy, and kissing was something I was really cautious with. But with her lying there, her hair fanned out on the bed and her breathing barely there, I wanted nothing more than to touch my lips to hers, to feel her breath on mine.

I knew I wouldn't be able to stay for long. Already, my skin was itching, itching horribly and demanding I go back to a safe place. But I couldn't make myself leave just yet.

I managed to get my hands under her lithe body, and I lifted her up gently to get her in a better position. She sighed when I moved her, the sweetest little sound, just letting me know she was still there, not gone completely, not yet. I placed a fluffy pillow behind her head, making sure she was sitting semi-upright just in case she puked. Her body was limp and powerless compared to mine. I could have done anything in the world to her in that position, and my skin crawled with the possibilities.

I let my fingers wander down her skin gently, teasing her arms into goosebumps, making her sigh and fidget restlessly as she slept. It was like a fucking miracle, like a dream, finally having her in front of me. She was perfectly vulnerable, but she was still my sweet, headstrong, bitchy girl. I'd never wanted her more.

My head was pounding though. Fucking hurting with everything in her apartment, everything new around me, fucking me up because I needed to get back to my place where at least I didn't feel like I was dying every second. I looked around Bebe's bedroom and found a thick faux fur throw, grabbing it off her recliner and gently covering her with the fabric. She stirred in her sleep and I tucked her in, pretending just for a minute that she was my girl, that I'd get to do this every night. That I owned her, that she was all. Fucking. Mine.

I moved away from her, taking two steps back and watching her breathe more easily now, fast asleep. Why was she so perfect? Why couldn't I have her? Just for one night. Just maybe, one night would be enough to make me better. Maybe one night with her would make me a better man, a good man, a normal man. Maybe one night with Bebe would cure me.

My bottom lip trembled at the little fantasy I'd built for myself. Of course it wouldn't be okay. I was a mess, and Bebe would never want me. But it was okay. I could exist without her. Not live, but exist at the very least.

I walked out to the front door and put all the bolts and locks in place, making sure she was locked inside safely. One last look at my sleeping beauty, and I climbed out of the window onto the fire escape.

The cold night air hit me straight to the core, chilling me and reawakening my instincts. I figured the faster I moved, the faster all of this would be over, and I could get back inside, pretend nothing had happened. Maybe after a few baths, I really would be okay.

I took the stairs two at a time, practically jumping down them in an effort to get away from her apartment. I raced all my fears and insecurities to the bottom of the stairs and jumped off onto the ground. My legs were shaking, barely able to carry me the distance to the other side of the street.

I staggered into my apartment like a fucking drunk.

And then I sat on the floor, and cried for the first time in twenty-five years.

Chapter 13

·BEBE·

DAREDEVIL, NOUN
A reckless person who enjoys doing dangerous things.

I woke up with a pounding headache, rolled off the bed and vomited all over the floor.

With a groan, I picked myself up and dragged myself to the kitchen to get some cleaning supplies. I managed to get the floor clean before tumbling into my bathroom and showering the remains of last night off my body. The cold shower woke me up a little but did nothing to help my head that was begging for painkillers.

I had just gotten out of the shower and wrapped my hair up in a towel turban when the doorbell rang.

"Coming!" I yelled, grabbing a fluffy robe and wrapping it around my still wet body.

Running towards the door, I nearly tripped on the piece of fabric that held my robe in place. I cursed out loud and opened the door totally out of breath.

A huge bouquet stood in front of me, red roses, so many of them it blocked the whole entryway and my view of the delivery man.

"What the f–" I started, but the person behind the flowers cut me off.

"A delivery for Bebe Hall?"

The man handed me the enormous bouquet and I nearly fell over with the weight of it.

"Let me just put this inside," I mumbled, carrying the flowers into the apartment and putting them down on my dining table.

They dominated the room, the scent so heady it made me smile. I returned to the delivery man and signed for my flowers, then closed the front door and went to search for a card to go with the flowers.

There was a thick envelope between the roses, and I took it out, slowly opening it and taking out the contents. I loved prolonging the moment of mystery, hope filling my whole body. Maybe it was Miles. Maybe, just maybe, he wanted me to have something this beautiful. Maybe he did something traditional just to make my day…

A Polaroid photo fell out of the envelope, and I bent down to pick it up. It was face down, and I held it in my hand as I read the note attached to the flowers.

They smell like you.

My skin erupted in goosebumps and I bit my bottom lip nervously as I set the card down and turned the photo around in my hand. The photo was taken from his apartment, but my bedroom window was open. I was lying on the bed, propped up with a pillow and covered with a blanket I never used.

I ran back into my room. The blanket was on the bed, and the window was open, a breeze billowing the curtains. I felt a shiver go down my spine.

Peep Show

He'd been in my room.

No... he'd been in my room while I was there. Last night, when I was passed out, too messed up to remember him being there, taking care of me.

I felt my pussy leak all over my thigh. He'd really been here, with me, touching me, smelling me. The mere thought made me whimper out loud. Why hadn't he woke me up? How had he gotten in? The door was locked from the inside when I greeted the deliveryman, and Arden couldn't have done that. Miles must have and left on the fire escape – that was why the window had been open.

I swallowed thickly, my heart pounding in my chest. *Should I be scared?* I thought to myself, but even though every basic instinct in my body was telling me to run, I couldn't. I wanted more, so much more. I wanted him in my room every night, holding me, putting the blanket over me. I shook my head to get the thoughts out. But I couldn't – the thought of Miles in my apartment was firmly planted inside my mind now, and I wanted it so badly, it made my fingers curl up with need.

He was a stalker.

A fucking stalker that came into my room while I slept and touched me.

And I was horny as hell for him.

I walked away from the roses, the scent too overwhelming and making me forget about what I was supposed to be doing. I went into the bedroom and sat down in front of my vanity, undoing the towel on my hair and letting the wet strands fall down my shoulders. I couldn't even bring myself to close the window or look across the street to see if he was watching. Instead, I just started doing my makeup. It was already half past one, and I had a day to get ready for.

Staying in the apartment didn't seem like an option. Instead, I called

Arden, wanting to meet up for a drink. But she didn't answer.

"Thanks for picking up," I said bitterly into her voicemail. "I'm glad you checked to see if I was okay."

Worry and guilt swept through my body in a second, and I sighed heavily.

"I'm sorry, Arden," I went on. "Okay? I'm really sorry. I know I'm a mess. I'm a train wreck–"

I let out a little whimper. It was one thing to know I was fucked up, but a whole different one to admit it out loud like that.

"I'm sorry," I repeated. "I just want things to go back to how–"

The voicemail clicked off and I glared at my phone before throwing it on the couch. Fuck that, then.

I turned on the TV, sulking as I watched show after mindless show, not even remembering what the storylines were. The hours passed, and the room grew dimmer and dimmer around me as the clock started moving towards evening.

My phone remained silent. Not a call, not a single text – neither from Arden nor Miles. When it vibrated, I jumped at it, fumbling with the screen to see the message waiting for me.

Bored. Want to hit a club?

I didn't have the number saved, but my fingers were already busy texting back whoever it was.

Frenzy. Meet u outside at 11?

I waited for a reply, my heart beating too fast. I didn't want to admit to myself how sad I was. A fucking bitch with no friends and no boyfriend, getting excited about going out with someone I didn't even have saved in my phone. But then again, my life was always like that. The only people I'd kept around me for years were Posy and Arden, and now one half of the pair was gone, and the other one was ignoring me for reasons I didn't want to admit to.

You got it, see you then.

I smirked at my phone and turned my attention back to the TV.

I guess it would be a surprise to see whoever showed up in front of Frenzy in a few hours.

I was late, but then again, whoever messaged me probably knew I would be. I was kind of infamous for it.

I'd taken my time getting ready, making sure I looked incredible. My outfit was perfect – I'd stood in front of the mirror long enough to ensure it. I was wearing a flared dress that was tight on top, black with silver studs and zippers. Two of the latter were placed strategically on my thighs, and I'd unzipped them all the way up, knowing that when I danced, I'd be flashing inches of my legs to anyone who looked at me. On my feet, I wore platform black velvet shoes with a silver heel, and I felt like a million bucks with the makeup I'd carefully applied and my hair done perfectly.

I rushed across the road to the meeting spot, and my eyes widened when I saw who was waiting for me.

It took a moment for me to recognize him, but when I did, an easy smile settled on my lips.

"Hey," I said with a grin, and he leaned in for a hug.

"Hi, gorgeous," he said, baring his teeth. "You look hot as fuck, don't you?"

"Thank you," I fluttered my lashes.

Fuck. I couldn't remember his name.

The guy who I'd brought home from the club. The one Miles watched me fuck...

"Anders!"

He turned towards the sound of the voice, and I sighed with relief. Thank God for that.

He chatted to a friend of his, a tall guy with stubble that kept eyeing me while I twirled a strand of hair around my finger and winked at him. Anders leaned in to whisper something to the dude, and they both laughed, grinning at me. I just smiled back, wishing I had some liquid courage to keep me going. I didn't exactly suffer from lack of confidence, but with these two, I felt a little out of my league.

"So, are we going in?" I asked, and Anders turned back to smile at me.

"Of course we are, darlin'. You ready?" He raised his eyebrows at me, heading towards the back of the line forming in front of the club.

I laughed at them both, hooked my arms through theirs and marched them right to the front. The bouncer grinned when he saw me.

"Hello, Bebe," he said in a deep voice, and I leaned in to kiss him on the cheek before sauntering past the red velvet rope and straight inside.

The guys stared at me, and I turned back, watching the stunned crowd. They all knew me, I bet. I was the city's it girl, at least for another year or so if I played my cards right. No one would dare say a word if I cut to the front of the line. Not the case for Anders and his friend, though.

"They're with me," I added lazily, and the bouncer nodded before opening the rope for them. The crowd groaned as they joined me on the other side, wearing big grins on their faces.

"Is this what it's like going out with Bebe Hall?" Anders whispered in my ear, his hand resting on the small of my back possessively. "Because I fucking like it, darlin'."

"Good," I smiled back. "Treat me like I want you to and you can stick around."

I left the words up to his interpretation and headed straight for the dancefloor.

This was the only way I knew how to forget, how to distract myself. Drinking, eating pretty little pills, dancing my heart out. It was the only way to block out the horrible thoughts inside my head telling me that eventually, I would have to stop spinning, and my life would come to a stop. No more dancing, no more booze, no more distractions, just me and my mess of a life, all fucking alone.

I made myself stop thinking about it and danced my heart out. Anders and his friend joined me a few moments later, and I let their hands wander all over my body while I bit back the tears in my eyes, the bile rising in my mouth. They weren't gentle, either. Their hands were demanding, wanting more and more every time a new song came up. And I let them have it all.

I kept my eyes closed for the most part, just letting my body and theirs do their thing as I swayed in time with the music. But when my lashes fluttered open again, they settled on a familiar figure across the room.

Petite. Blonde. Pretty blue eyes, long legs despite her tiny figure. A waist every girl dreamed of, a dress that screamed money. Heels that barely made her reach her boyfriend's shoulders.

I'd seen her before.

I'd seen her get fucked by two men while I watched.

"Lana," I muttered to myself as my eyes settled on her pretty mouth, laughing at something her boyfriend had whispered in her ear.

As if on cue, she turned towards me and looked right into my eyes. She obviously recognized me as well, because the color drained out of her face right away, and she just stared and stared.

I mouthed a hello and her doe-like expression changed. Slowly, her eyebrows came down and her lips quirked upwards. She waved.

Little Lana was ready to play.

And so was I.

Chapter 14

·MILES·

LATIBULE, NOUN
A hiding place, a place of safety and comfort.

I couldn't get Bebe off my mind. I knew the gift I'd sent her had been a bit over the top, but I couldn't help myself. She'd looked so perfect lying there. And I realized I was falling for her.

I recognized the warning signs as alarms went off inside my head every time I thought about her. This was dangerous, this could be the real deal. But I was getting attached – something I never let myself do. But this time it seemed inevitable, Bebe's taste, her scent, her fucking image plastered all over my thoughts, even when I tried to fight it. I couldn't resist her anymore, and the magnetic pull she had on me was getting to be too much. I needed to have her in my arms, and soon, or I knew I'd fucking lose it.

But it was impossible. How the hell was I going to do that? I couldn't have her over in my apartment, and I certainly couldn't go over to hers. When this went up in flames, and it inevitably would once she realized just how fucked up I was, I would end up hurting and alone, just like I always did.

Even though I knew all this, I found Bebe impossible to resist. And I knew that I wouldn't be able to keep my hands off her. I watched her get up, receive the flowers, and leave the apartment. I watched and watched and watched, but the place remained empty in the evening, and it made me fucking anxious. I wanted to know where she'd gone. To keep tabs on her seemed so important now, as if I was scared she'd get hurt the second she stepped out of my vision.

I had a call scheduled with Dr. Halen that day, but I hastily asked her to change it to the next day. Her assistant had replied, and I was grateful for that. I really didn't want to explain myself to my shrink, because I had no idea in hell what to say. That I was obsessed with my neighbor? Practically stalking her already? That I'd sniffed her fucking cardigan like it was my drug of choice? No, Dr. Halen would never understand this side of me. She'd just say it was another obsession and write it off as unimportant.

By the time nine p.m. rolled around, I decided I'd waited long enough. I fired off a text.

What are you doing?

Twenty-five minutes later, there was still no reply to my text, and it made me irrationally angry. She was avoiding me for some reason, even though we were both starting to realize something serious was developing between us. And here she was, just pushing me away so insistently, it had me wondering whether I really should give up.

My mouth set in a thin line as I got up from the sofa, impatiently pacing the room. Something strange filled my body, an aching desire to go back to her apartment. I'd seen one of the windows had been open earlier, and I knew I could probably get in using the fire escape.

I shook my head to get the thought out. I was acting crazy, like a damn stalker. But the need to smell her again, to go through her shit, was so strong. Without thinking, I shrugged on a dark hoodie and forced myself to stand in front of the door leading to outside.

I was shaking, the mere thought of leaving my apartment so soon after already being out made me terrified. Terrified of the outside, just like I always was.

But then my body moved of its own accord. I stepped forward, opened the door, calmly locked it behind me and took the stairs two at a time. By the time I reached the lobby, my heart was pounding in my chest and I felt bile rising in my throat.

The doorman nearly blew a coronary when he saw me, and I gave him a reassuring smile that ended up shakier than I would have liked.

"Mr. Reilly," he said, his voice shocked. "Are you alright?"

"I'm okay," I smiled. "Just need to pay someone a quick visit."

As I stepped into the night, fighting every single instinct in my body screaming at me to get back inside, I practically ran to the other side of the street. I looked around to make sure no one was around, then climbed the fire escape as fast as I possibly could.

And then I was standing outside of her window, blood pumping through my veins, and my head telling me I was fucking insane. But I couldn't stop, the thought of going back to my apartment suddenly crippling. I swung a leg inside and pulled the window up, and then I was in.

The whole damned place smelled of her: sexy fucking roses and sugar mixed into a concoction that was wreaking havoc on my senses.

Her clothes lay discarded on the floor, and I couldn't help myself. I picked up a shirt, covered in lipstick stains and smelling so much like her I could have fucking cried on the spot. I'd never wanted someone this much, craved them, unable to resist her body, everything she'd touched. I was acting like an addict and I didn't even give a shit. I would've done anything to find her sleeping in that bed. I'd take her in my arms and kiss those rosy lips, not just dream of doing it.

I walked around with her shirt clutched tightly to my chest. Every single thing in that apartment sung to me, telling Bebe's story, even if she didn't want it told. Everything spoke of her personality, of her amazing mind.

The fact that she drank the cheapest coffee, the instant variety, not out of one of those fancy espresso machines, made me grin.

Her toothbrush was a kid's one, pink and princessy and so fucking perfect I laughed out loud in the bathroom.

She had a closet full of clothes. It seemed like there were two extremes – extremely sexy, tight little dresses for going out, mixed with comfy loungewear. It was adorable.

Her fruit basket was full of too-ripe bananas, and her fridge was stocked with varieties of yogurt I didn't know existed. It looked like she lived on cheap coffee and yogurt. Ridiculous.

The urge to take care of her awoke inside of me, yearning to cook for her, to make her proper stuff to eat. To let her know she couldn't live like this, filling her belly with booze and God knows what else and eating a yogurt here and there. I could've made proper food for her… I was a good cook, and I wanted to, fuck, I wanted her to come over, so I could spoil her with fettuccine alfredo with fresh cream, make her a salad that would blow her socks off, make every kind of dessert – possibly with yogurt – to make her regret eating like this. Make her regret not being mine… Make her *want* to be mine.

I went through everything.

Her toiletries – insane amounts of hairspray – her cutlery drawer, I even looked at the brand of her toilet paper. I wanted to know every fucking thing about the gorgeous Bebe Hall.

But there was one bit I'd missed, or avoided on purpose.

I stood in front of her lingerie drawer, the one I'd skipped when I was looking through her closet. God, I wanted to see. I wanted to see everything she wore under those outfits that drove me wild.

I opened it, slowly pulling it out until her smell hit my nose hard, roses and sugar, always roses and sugar. I wanted to bury my fucking face in her underwear. I wanted to steal all of it, take it home, and drive myself wild by getting off with her panties around my dick – my dick that was now straining in my pants. I felt like a madman because she turned me into one. And fuck was I desperate for more.

I reached into the drawer with shaky fingers, bringing out a lacy pink bra. I imagined her tits in it, filling out the lace perfectly, the mere thought making my mouth water.

I pressed a lacy cup against my nose, inhaling her intoxicating scent. Fuck, it made me want her more than anything in the whole world. I would turn my life around for her. I'd stop being a mess, I'd sort my life out, I'd let her be all mine, I'd do it all, just for her… I'd do anything to call her mine.

Pressing the bra to my chest, I leaned against the chest of drawers and exhaled slowly. It was starting to hit me that I was out of my apartment, out of my safe place and out in the open.

The walls of Bebe's apartment suddenly felt threatening, like they were closing in on me and threatening to crush me.

I leaned my palm against the doorway and tried to breathe the way Dr. Halen had told me to, slow, steady breaths. It was half the fight, or so she claimed, but I couldn't bring myself to be calmer about the situation. Bebe was everywhere in her apartment, her presence cloying even without her actually being there. And suddenly it was all too much.

I stuffed the pink bra in my pocket and closed the drawer, stumbling over to the fire exit. I left the window ajar as I managed to get outside, my legs shaking and my chest heaving. I needed to get away from all this shit, away from Bebe for one second, because I couldn't think straight with her all around me. I was too consumed by lust and the need to make her mine.

I climbed the fire escape clumsily, my legs feeling heavy as fuck as I got down on the street. A group of women was passing, and one of them winked at me as I made my way back to my building with my breath coming in short, scared rasps. I was a fucking mess. I could barely even walk, and the thought of facing the doorman just so I could get back home seemed too daunting to even think about.

Instead, I chose the fire escape again, this time making my way home quicker and more efficiently. I'd left the window in the white room ajar, and I half-fell, half-climbed through it, taking deep, labored breaths as I collapsed on the hardwood floor. I tried thinking calming thoughts, but of course as always with these damn things, I failed miserably. I couldn't stop it, the fear, the panic, and the adrenaline settling in, the intoxicating mixture dizzying.

It took several excruciatingly long minutes to feel human again, and when I could finally trust myself enough, I picked myself off the floor and walked through the door into the living room.

"Hello, Miles."

I looked up with a start.

She stood in front of me, all business-like in a tight pencil skirt and a white blouse with a bow around her throat. She looked just like the photos.

"Dr. Halen," I said. "What the fuck are you doing in my apartment?"

Chapter 15

·BEBE·

WHELVE, VERB
To bury something deep, to hide.

I didn't approach her. I waited for Lana to come to me.

It didn't take too long before her curiosity got the better of her. She whispered something in her friend's ear and sauntered over to where I was standing. I pretended not to notice, chatting with Anders, even though my heart was thumping so hard.

She'd touched my Miles. She'd fucked my Miles.

Jealousy mixed with rage and genuine curiosity of my own when she tapped my shoulder, and I turned my head to look at her.

"Hello," she purred, her fingers going through her mane of light-blonde hair. "So, you do remember me."

"How could I forget?" I smiled. "Nice to see you."

She leaned down to the arm of the sofa I was sitting on, and we exchanged air kisses as my new friends watched. Lana moved away, and we gave each other the once-over. She wore too-high heels, stilettos even I would find difficult to walk in. Her dress was knee-length but so impossibly tight it hugged every curve of her petite body. She was gorgeous, a tiny little doll, perfect for throwing over a man's shoulder and fucking until she screamed for mercy.

"Where's your boyfriend?" we asked at the same time, and I gave her a long look while she giggled.

"Johnny," she said. "His name's Johnny. He's just over there."

She pointed behind her without turning around, and I saw the guy who'd watched her getting fucked by Miles, laughing easily with some friends. How could he do that? How could he share her and now act like this, as if it meant nothing? It was a mystery to me. Lana was gorgeous, and he should've clung to her for dear life. It was so fucking obvious he liked her better than she liked him, and even though I couldn't see into the future, I predicted their relationship would be over in months. She'd finally realize he could never fulfill her desires, and dump him for someone who could. Of course, Johnny would be devastated. I wished I could have spared him the hurt, but there was nothing to be done. Neither of them knew their relationship was failing yet, and I wasn't about to speed the process up.

"What are you doing here alone?" I asked next, twirling my straw between my fingers. I took a sip of my drink, my eyes focused on Lana as I slurped the boozy liquid through the straw. "Don't you think you're out of your depth?"

"It's him," she said, a note of desperation so very obvious in her voice it was almost pathetic. "Miles, that guy Miles."

"Miles?" I asked innocently, batting my lashes. She stomped her little high-heeled foot down, giving me an annoyed look. It would have been adorable if I didn't hate her guts with every cell of my being. "Miles who?"

"Miles Reilly," she said.

His last name. Oh my God.

"What about him?" I played it off, pretending the sound of his full name hadn't sent butterflies dancing through my whole body. "I don't think he wants to see you again, Lana."

"And he wants to see you?" She crossed her arms, right away looking defensive even though I hadn't so much as given her a threatening look. "You want me to back off, don't you? Just admit it."

"Back off?" I asked, raising my eyebrows. I tapped my friend on the shoulder and handed him my glass before getting off the sofa, towering over poor little Lana. "You think you're any kind of competition, little girl?"

"You seem to think so," she said with her head held high.

But I'd played these games before. I knew a scared little bitch when I saw one. I smiled in a syrupy-sweet way and leaned down against her lips.

"We better settle this somewhere else," I told her while my friends went quiet.

"Bebe, don't…" Anders muttered in my ear, but I waved him off.

"Come on, let's go," I said to Lana, and pulled her in the direction of the ladies' room.

She followed closely behind, and as we started walking, I pulled my phone out of my purse. We made our way through the crowd, the dancefloor reverberating with the sound of the bass.

I swung the doors into the luxurious ladies' room open. It was empty.

I settled on the round pink sofa in the middle of the room, the foyer of the bathroom made to look like a powder room.

"I think we have a common interest," I told Lana when she settled down next to me.

If she was surprised by the fact I wasn't about to kick her ass, the little bitch didn't show it. She just glared at me and thought of how to respond. At least her mouth wasn't as quick as her mind. It would do her a world of good when it came to dealing with me.

"Miles Reilly," she said finally, and I smiled in response. "What do you know about him?"

"Probably not much more than you do," I lied smoothly, shrugging. "But I know he's probably at home right now regretting not having either of us. So, what do you say we have some fun?"

The girl's eyes sparkled, and I thought to myself that I'd really underestimated her.

"What did you have in mind?" she asked, her voice shaking a little, and I giggled, showing her my phone.

"Want to take some selfies?" I asked her, my voice as wicked as my thoughts.

Her eyes sparked with recognition of a fellow troublemaker, and she nodded vigorously, only one question coming from her pretty pouty lips. "For Miles?"

"For Miles," I agreed, snapping a shot of us sticking our tongues out for the camera.

I fired it off to his cell phone, deciding not to check obsessively for replies. Instead, I was going to have some fun. The kind I hadn't had in years.

I fired off photo after photo.

Lana licking my ear.

Me pulling her hair back while she arched her spine.

Us, mouth to mouth, a sultry smile on our lips for the camera.

"Take your dress off," I finally told her.

"What?" she blanched right away. "But… somebody could walk in."

"This is the VIP bathroom," I told her, pointing towards the sign. "You shouldn't even be in here. But anyway, so what if they do? We give them a fucking show. Trust me, nobody is going to throw Bebe Hall out of a club. I fucking made this place what it is."

She looked back at me, her wide eyes feigning surprise.

"Oh, stop," I said simply. "Come on, show me your tits."

Her shaky fingers pulled down the straps of her dress, and her tits spilled free with no bra or even tape to hold them in place. She was gorgeous, a natural beauty with a slim body and big, sexy boobs. Our bodies weren't alike at all – she was pale where I was tanned, I was toned and she was tiny and curvy. A different kind of girl, but a beauty nonetheless.

Her nipples were pretty, a dark shade of pink. They settled into tight buds as I took pictures. She didn't need much guidance, the alcohol and whatever the fuck else she'd had that night working her up a treat and making her the slut I knew she could be.

She licked her own nipples, let me suck on them. She rubbed her cunt over a lacy black thong and moaned for me while I filmed her. Every new snapshot was sent to Miles' phone, hopefully driving him insane.

We burst out of the bathroom, laughing and holding hands, already fast friends as we made our way to the bar. We got drinks from a group of guys, Johnny and Anders long forgotten. We drank shot after shot. Downed pill after pill. I was fucking dizzy, delirious and giggling like a fool, and little Lana was being a complete slut, her mouth desperate for mine, her eyes drinking me in as I danced all over the dancefloor, a bottle of Moet in my hand and raised to the DJ.

She found a pink feather boa somewhere and had it wrapped around my neck the next moment. I threw my head back and laughed, and the world spun around me in slow-motion. If only I could get off on the right stop. The one where Posy was waiting for me patiently, ready to fix all the mistakes I'd made in the past years.

But when I looked ahead, I didn't see Posy. I saw a girl I didn't know, a girl I was using to get to a guy that wasn't even mine.

I pulled her against me and a tear slipped down my cheek as I kissed her.

I felt everyone's eyes on us as we devoured each other, tongues intertwining, pussies dripping, the scent of her strawberry shampoo heavy in my nose. I handed my phone off to someone I didn't know or care about and asked her to take photos of us. She did. Moments later, all of them ended up in Miles' inbox, because I couldn't help myself.

I was angry and jealous, bitter and upset because *she* had touched him, and I still hadn't.

I kissed her harder, sucked on her slutty tongue and filled my phone with raunchy images of us.

And with Lana's lips hot on mine, I could almost remember a different moment, a moment just like this one.

"Posy, don't be such a messy drunk!" Arden giggled as our friend sprayed a bottle of champagne all over her brand new Alexander McQueen dress. "Oh my God, you're going to ruin your outfit!"

"I don't care!" Posy climbed on the table and got everyone's attention in a matter of seconds. "Hey. HEY! Can you hear me?"

Everyone cheered her on and Arden groaned and hid her face in my shoulder as Posy shouted into the bottle, pretending it was a microphone.

"Who's ready to have some FUN tonight?" she asked at the top of her voice, and everyone cheered again.

"I'm here with my best friends," she went on, grinning at us. "We're new to the city. Oh, except for Bee. She's been here for years."

I shifted my feet uncomfortably. My glasses felt thick and uncomfortable on top of my nose, the dress they'd forced me into way too tight and way too short.

"Arden and Bebe," Posy went on dramatically. "I love you bitches. Forever!"

We helped her get off while everyone cheered. It was only the beginning of our evening, and only the start of the three years we'd spend in the city together.

I was a nobody before Arden and Posy. I was a bookish geek with her nose in a book and glasses so thick people still bullied me at eighteen. I was boring. A nice enough face, but a body I hid in baggy clothes because I was afraid of my own curves. Then, they appeared... Broke, glamorous. Spending every last cent they had on clothes and booze, and taking me under their wings. They dragged me out every night, and I let them, because for once in my life, I wanted to know what it was like to be an it girl.

I had the money. They had everything else. And slowly, as the weeks passed, I became one of them.

Someone put another pill in my hand. I stared at it for a long time.

It was shaped like a heart, a neon purplish glow making it look like it was something from another planet.

I remembered snippets of conversation.

"It was a heart-shaped pill..."

"...we don't know the name..."

"....*overdose*..."

"*Too late... we can't do anything...*"

I realized in a very small, very quiet part of my brain that this was the pill Posy had taken the night she overdosed and died.

I stared at it in my palm, the purple heart so innocent. It would never hurt me. I trusted my heart. I trusted the pill. And Miles had my back, anyway, right?

Miles. Miles. Miles.

Maybe if I did this, he would finally come to get me.

Maybe. Maybe. Maybe.

I swallowed the pill, washing it down with more champagne and letting Lana kiss me, her tongue twirling and licking up the remains of the pill on my lips.

And then I let it take over.

Chapter 16

·MILES·

UNFAMILIAR, ADJECTIVE
Not known or recognized.

She was an odd sight in my apartment, and she looked different in person than I had imagined her.

It had always been obvious Dr. Halen was an attractive woman, but seeing her in person told me just how stunning she was. She was very tall, but that didn't turn her off from wearing heels, and her feet were arched on black lacquered pumps with a red sole and a pencil-thin, staggeringly tall heel. She was blonde, her hair somehow enhanced to make for a mane of honey-blonde, tumbling in easy waves around her shoulders. She wore a lot of makeup, most of it serving to bring out her sky-blue eyes. She was a stunning woman, probably around fifty or fifty-five. I could barely take my eyes off her, but not because I was attracted.

I was concerned. She'd just seen me get into my apartment through a window. As far as Dr. Halen knew, I was crippled by the fear of outside. I didn't leave my apartment, ever. What would she think now? And what was I going to tell her? The truth, or more thinly veiled lies to shut her up?

She sighed as she moved closer to me. Her body was slim, her breasts pressed up in the décolletage of her ivory blouse. Her skirt was tight. Very attractive indeed.

"I've been worried about you, Mr. Reilly," she told me. "That's why I had to come and check up on you. Something wasn't adding up, and I knew something was going on."

My fingers gripped the doorframe as she drew closer. There was something in her attitude that didn't speak of a doctor-patient relationship. She found me attractive. Her eyes kept dancing over my inked muscles, settling on my mouth, drinking in my heavy frame.

"Dr. Halen," I repeated. "How did you get in here?"

She smiled at me, tilting her head. "Well, past the doorman, obviously. I guess that's not how you come and go, though."

She was so close now, and I moved away from the door, peeling myself away from her and approaching the bar.

"Would you like a drink?" I asked her hoarsely, and she nodded, her hand on the door. She had long red nails shaped into neat, rounded points. "What's your poison?"

"Whatever you're having," she said, waving a hand as if it didn't really matter. "You know, I was wondering how long it would take for the two of us to finally meet."

I gave her a sideways glance. She may have gotten through to our doorman, but she wasn't fooling me. There was another reason she was here, and she wasn't ready to tell me just yet. But I was going to get it out of her one way or another.

I poured us both a Scotch on the rocks.

"What are you really doing here?" I asked her once we clinked our glasses and each took a long sip of the amber liquid. "You're not fooling me, Dr. Halen."

"Agneta," she said with a smile. "You can call me Agneta. I'm not on office hours right now."

"Agneta," I confirmed, cringing the whole way through. I didn't want to call her fucking Agneta. I wanted to call her Dr. Halen, and I wanted her back on the other side of the screen where I was safe from her toxic fucking touch. "Please, explain what made you come over here tonight."

"Warning signs," she said, walking over to the sofa and sitting. When she crossed her legs, I caught a glimpse of her stockings, and my cock twitched at the sight. "We've been talking online for a couple of years, Miles. I know all your habits. I also know when you're trying to hide something from me."

"I'm not hiding anything," I insisted, and she let out a short laugh.

"Spare me the lies, Miles," she said simply. "I'm here because I was worried about you. I was convinced you were planning something. You spoke about ending your life quite often a year ago, Miles, do you remember that?"

I looked away, unable to handle the pressure of her gaze.

"You don't have to answer," she said gently, and I walked over to the window, one hand in my pocket and the other clasped around the cold glass. I needed a fucking smoke like never before in my life, even though I hadn't smoked for years. But my thoughts kept escaping to the hidden pack of cigarettes in the back of my closet. I would be desperately taking the poison from one of them in my lungs the second I got rid of Dr. Halen.

"But it seems like I needn't have been worried at all," Dr. Halen finally said thoughtfully. "Actually, Miles, you seem better than ever."

I raised my gaze to her eyes, and she smiled at me gently.

The attraction between us made the room heated, but I would never make a move.

Not now, not ever. The obvious reason was Bebe, but I'd sooner die than admit that to myself.

"What's her name?" Dr. Halen asked quietly, breaking the tense moment as if she was shattering a window. "Come on, Miles. At least tell me something, so I can leave here in peace."

"She's a girl," I said. "Just… a girl."

"Just a girl?" she pressed.

"No," I barked back. "She's… I don't know. She's everything. She's all I can think about. The only thing on my mind. I'm worried I'm getting addicted, you know, like the cigarettes."

I didn't mention my urge for a cancer stick, but it looked like she knew. In fact, it looked like she knew everything. And suddenly we were patient and therapist again as she got off the couch and grabbed her coat and gloves.

"I'm glad you're alright, Miles," she said simply. "I will admit I came here because I wasn't just worried professionally."

My heart hurt when she went on.

"You have people who care about you." Her voice was soft, but I couldn't so much as look at her. "I know you don't want or need them, Miles. But you are not alone. Remember that."

Any other time I would have ripped her clothes to shreds, choked her while I fucked her into oblivion. But not this time.

She left a fleeting squeeze on my wrist, and then she was gone in a cloud of Chanel perfume and expensive shoes clacking on my hardwood floors. The door closed behind her and locked into place.

I felt suddenly overheated, over-pressured, and overstressed.

I tore at my clothes. My T-shirt ended up on the floor and my pants followed suit until my body was exposed. I stared at my own reflection in the window, wishing Bebe was there with me. I didn't want Dr. Halen. I didn't want anyone I'd met. I wanted her, and only fucking her, and now I knew I wasn't going to stop until I tasted her.

Bleach. I needed bleach.

Intense feelings of self-hatred mixed with overwhelming emotions took over my body. I grabbed a pristine white bottle from my secret stash in the pantry, along with a packet of cancer sticks, and raced to the bathroom. My glorious, custom-made tub awaited me, offering comfort only it could bring. I emptied too much bleach into its bowels, pouring and pouring even when I knew it was too much.

Then I stopped, and I thought of her. Of Bebe.

My fingers shook as I turned the drain and watched most of the bleach leak out. I only left a little.

I got into the ice-cold bath, the bleach burning, tingling, itching. In my right hand, I held the packet of sins in a shaky hand. And my fingers shook harder as I lit one up, throwing my head back and staring at the ceiling above me as I let the smoke into my body.

My mind was swimming with her, sexy, sweet little Bebe that I would never get enough of. Fucking shit, she was messing with my head. I never got like this, and much less over a girl that was supposed to mean nothing. But I kept remembering the most basic details. The way her sheets smelled. The feel of her bra against my nose. Her hair fanning over the silk pillows.

I soaked in the bath for what felt like hours, until it was so cold my teeth were chattering despite my stinging flesh. Finally, I climbed out and dried off my damaged skin.

I felt better now. Not yet relaxed, but at least a little more in control than I had been when I'd found Dr. Halen in my living room.

I wrapped a towel around my waist and made my way into the living room, where my phone sat blinking in the darkness.

Picking it up, my eyes bulged at the sight. I had seventeen messages, all from one number that I'd come to know very well.

I clicked through to the photos, staring and staring and then staring some fucking more.

They started coming in three hours ago, probably around the time I'd been snooping around in Bebe's apartment.

And fuck, were they hot. So fucking hot.

I didn't recognize the other girl right away. My eyes were focused on Bebe, her sexy little body in that sinful dress, her eyes so desperate as she stared into the camera. She really wanted me, but I knew it was only because she hadn't discovered the horrible truth that lay behind my exterior.

And then it clicked. The other girl was Lana, my conquest from the other day. She was still just as pretty and cute, but a little less disheveled than she had been with my cum splattered all over her face. And now she was fucking working with Bebe to get me off.

I'd never hated my agoraphobia more. Every cell in my body was demanding I go right over there, put Bebe over my knee in front of all her shitty friends, and spank that tight little ass while they all watched. God, I wanted to. I wanted her to know full well what bad girls get when they misbehave.

Instead, I was left with a tented towel, and wondering why I wasn't fucking man enough to just get over my damn irrational fear. But I couldn't move, couldn't even take a single step to the front door. I was glued to the spot, fucking doomed. I would never be able to get a girl like Bebe.

A girl who needed friends, parties, people. A girl who lived for the thrill.

Who was I to even try and satisfy her? I was a piece of shit that used girls with daddy issues to fix my own problems. I wasn't worthy. I would never fucking deserve her.

In the midst of my pity party, my phone started ringing shrilly with a number I didn't recognize. I furrowed my brow and raised my phone to my ear, answering the call.

"Hello?"

"Hi, I just, I didn't know who to call," a frantic female voice said.

"Lana?" I asked gruffly, and a small pause followed.

"What?" she asked. "No, who is that?"

I was about to answer when she cut me off again.

"You, you are in Bebe's phone, you're all over her messages," she said with a pleading voice. "If you care about her at all – whoever you are – you will come help."

"Who is this?" I barked down the line.

"Arden," she said, her voice heavy with tears. "I'm Arden."

"What's wrong, Arden?"

"It's Bebe," she sniffled. "She's… she's not breathing."

Chapter 17

·BEBE·

AXIS, NOUN
An imaginary line about which a body rotates.

The world was spinning and I was its axis.

I danced with the blurry people around me. I hugged bodies I didn't know, kissed lips that felt too soft to be a man's. I danced and danced and danced until I was so dizzy I could barely move anymore. And then I collapsed on a sofa and felt my feet twitching in time with the music. I laughed to myself, not giving a shit what anyone thought because all that mattered was my blurry dizzy world where there were no threatening voices and no angry faces.

Someone pulled me up a while after, and I danced again. Then, I started to feel my trip going from amazing to fucked-up beyond belief.

The blurry faces turned into monsters, their features mashing together in grotesque masks of pain and rage, all snarling at me, demanding things, asking for things I could never give them. They wanted answers, they wanted apologies, they wanted me to feel like shit, but all I wanted was to keep dancing forever. I didn't have time for worry, or for pain. I didn't have time for fucking Posy and her overdose and the mess she'd made of us when she left.

The monsters screamed for justice, but I couldn't give it to them. I danced and danced, and now my feet felt like they were touching hot coals, burning the soles of my feet while I cried desperately for someone, anyone, to save me.

Then I saw his beautiful face through the ashes and the night, his ink-covered muscles and his tall frame towering over me. I made a desperate grab for the man in front of me, but stumbled into thin air. And I knew it couldn't be real. Miles didn't care about me enough to show up and save me. If I was lucky enough, maybe Arden would come. Arden still cared about me. She had to. We'd both had our hearts ripped apart by the same hurricane named Posy.

Arden appeared through the curtain of nightmares, her eyes as disappointed as ever. She stared at me and I cried and held out my arms, hoping she would be the one to help me. She shouted through the fog, screamed and demanded answers, but the only thing I could do was laugh and cry at the same time.

I could tell Arden was crying too, but I couldn't help her. The fog was too thick to reach her, and I struggled to keep up with her words. To my ears, they sounded slurred and helpless, and they only made me panic more. There was only one person I wanted, only one man who could make it all better. But now I couldn't remember his name. All I remembered was his voice, whispering my name, telling me I was a good girl, begging me to come for him and come apart in his arms. I begged Arden to call him, kept pushing my phone into her hands between sobs and soft pleading whispers.

She raised the phone to her ear and I saw her calling someone, but I didn't understand the words coming out of her mouth. She was trying to help me, but I wasn't sure whether I was too far gone to be helped. I needed him. Needed to see his lips open when he said my name, and needed to fall asleep in his arms, where I would finally feel safe.

The haze from the drugs and alcohol was mind-numbing, at the same time making me weak yet energetic as hell. But every time I tried to get up, I ended up tumbling back down. Arden was gone, the fog too thick to reach her. I screamed for her to help me, but no sound came out, and now I was lost, utterly lost, without a single soul to help me.

And then, suddenly, I felt his presence like an electric current in the room. I shakily got off the sofa I was lying on, and looked towards the place where the sparks flew the strongest. His eyes connected with mine, and I tried to stop the whimper that left my lips the next second. I was hooked the second I saw him. He made me feel like I was the only person in the packed room that reeked of sweat and spilled alcohol. I was all that mattered, and he was going to make it all better. He was going to fix me.

I reached out to him, and he came to me.

He looked like a god up close, and I shivered in fear and anticipation. He was so huge, towering over me, his body a mass of muscle and ink I wanted to taste with my tongue. He wore a white Henley shirt, the ink beneath the fabric peeking out at his sleeves and collar. His hair was dark and closely cropped, his eyes just as dark. He was handsome as hell and built like the devil. He could crush me with a single move of his strong, inked fingers.

"Miles," I breathed, his name coming to me easily now, as if I'd never forgotten it at all. "Help me, Miles, please help me."

He reached for me, wincing when his fingertips made contact with my skin, and I stared at him like he was my only salvation. I understood, despite my condition, how special this moment was. I knew it would change everything between us the second sparks flew from his arms to my naked flesh. It only took me a second to understand that after that first touch – I belonged to this monster of a man completely, and there would be absolutely no going back.

I watched him speak to Arden who appeared out of nowhere, but I didn't hear the words. I just wanted him to take me home. I wanted to be alone with him, so I could explore the lines of his tattoos with my fingertips, so I could kiss the vein in his forehead and find out if he had more throbbing parts like it underneath his clothes. Pure childlike curiosity hooked me in its grasp as I stared at the man, the monster. I wanted to leave with him. I wanted to lay all my worries and troubles on his broad, capable shoulders, and beg him to carry me right along with them. And I was sure he would let me, because when he looked at me, I saw exactly how he felt about me. The same way I felt about him.

Once their conversation was over, he came back towards me, my eyes deceiving me and making him dance before them. He grabbed me, and it all happened in slow motion, so painfully slow I wanted to scream and beg him to hold me, save me, fuck me, but my mouth wouldn't open, and the words wouldn't come.

"Let's go," he muttered in my ear and held me close in his arms.

I inhaled his scent, leather and musk and pine, and I wanted to cry. Something in my fucked-up head, a tiny little voice of reason, was telling me I'd been waiting for this for so, so long, and now that it was finally here, I was too drugged-up to make sense of it. But I couldn't stop my fingers flying up, tearing at the fabric of his shirt, sending buttons everywhere. My mouth latched onto his throat and he groaned as I sucked him, desperate for more, to drink down the unique scent of him that was making my head spin.

We stepped outside and the cold hit me like a fucking slap in the face, but I couldn't stop, gasping around his skin and leaving red and blue marks all over his flesh. He told me to stop but I couldn't.

"I can't," I cried out, "I need to taste you because you won't be here tomorrow."

I could feel his eyes on me as he carried me down the street. I knew where I'd been at some point, but now our surroundings didn't look familiar at all. It was a dark forest, the branches of evil trees reaching for us, strangers standing behind the curtains of the broken windows in the buildings that lined the forest. I felt them staring, felt their gazes trying to hurt me, so I dug my face into Miles' chest and cried like a little girl afraid of the dark.

Time was passing in ways I couldn't understand, and he was my only anchor. I clung to his clothes, his skin, his body like it was my lifeline. I'd never been more afraid than that night.

I murmured things neither of us understood against his skin when my body started rebelling against the shit I'd put into it. Convulsing, shaking, sweating and swearing, he had to stop and put me down because I'd started scratching and biting, so fucking scared of him letting go I tried to do it for him.

"Don't," I screamed at him, my fists pummeling against his chest. "Don't let go, you bastard!"

He grabbed my wrists and pinned them behind my back against a streetlight.

"Stop," he growled at me, his voice all molten honey and dark intent. "Stop fucking fighting me, sugar."

Sugar, sugar, sugar, it was so sweet, it made me melt for him, and I stopped fighting, stood there feeling everything and nothing and let him pull me back into the safe haven of his arms.

"Beautiful girl," he whispered into my hair, his lips so close to mine but so far away, as if there was a whole galaxy separating us. "My beautiful broken girl."

This time, he just threw me over his shoulder and carried me away, his hand dangerously close to my ass. The nightmares kicked back in as we kept walking. I saw my apartment building in the distance, but we didn't go there. Miles carried me to the building next door, past a grumpy old doorman whose mouth hung open when he saw us, and up so many flights of stairs I wondered how he didn't collapse under my weight.

But he didn't let me go, didn't stop holding me as he unlocked the front door.

The scent of his apartment was clean, sterile like a hospital with a faint hint of his own perfume. He carried me inside, kicking the door closed behind him, past the pristine living room and into a sparse, barren bedroom that contained nothing but an enormous bed and a framed painting of the color white on the white wall in a white frame. I felt like I was in a dream, my heart pounding and thumping with fear and expectations.

He let me down on the bed, and took a step back, taking deep breaths as he stared at me. I sat up on my knees and stared back, my head cocked to the side and the drugs making my vision spin.

"Miles," I breathed. "Miles, you saved me."

"No," he said roughly, his breaths so ragged I was afraid something was very, very wrong.

"Come closer," I begged him.

"No," he said again, looking at his hands as if they had betrayed him. "No, I can't be near you. Can't stand it, can't take it, can't fucking deal."

"Miles," I whispered, the darkness reaching for me and trying to pull me under yet again. "Miles, I need you."

He looked up from his shaking hands, this mountain of a man reduced to trembling wreck as he stared at me.

"You have me," he said softly, and I crawled closer on the bed.

"I love you, Miles," I whispered again. "I love you so much, Miles Reilly, anything for you, anything for this, anything for *us*."

My arms gave out and I fell down, tendrils of darkness pulling at my consciousness. I was so close to passing out, but I needed him to know.

"Tell me you heard me," I begged him.

"I heard you," came the strangled answer. "I heard you, Bebe."

"Closer," I begged, and he dropped to his knees, came to me slowly and brokenly, his legs scraping the hardwood floor. "I need you to know. I need you to understand."

"I do," he promised. "I do, Bebe, I do."

I reached for his beautiful face and he shook uncontrollably when I touched him.

"Not like with the others," I whispered. "Just me."

"Just you," he nodded. "Just you, fucked up and just with you."

"It's okay," I promised, my mind drifting. "Because I love you."

"You do?" he asked, his eyes big and scared. A broken soul in the body of a monster. Of a god.

"I do," I promised, and let my eyes close. "I love you, Miles Reilly."

Chapter 18

·MILES·

TRISTFUL, ADJECTIVE
Deeply yet romantically melancholy.

I stared at her face, finally finding peace as she drifted off to sleep. I was worried fucking sick, wondering whether my instincts had been wrong, that I should have taken her to the hospital despite the warnings from her friend. She was beyond fucked-up, her eyes telling me as much as they flitted open and closed before she fell asleep. I was scared for her and scared of her, my body trembling and making me think I wasn't the man I'd seen myself as for years if a tiny woman like her could bring me to my knees.

The need to touch her was overwhelming. The simplest of touches, feeling her lashes against my lips, feeling her eyelids fluttering with dreams beneath my mouth. I wanted to kiss her, taste her, have her, but it was an ordeal just being in the same room as her. I was fucking struggling, fighting two conflicting urges in my head – one telling me to run as far away as possible, and the other demanding I wake Bebe up and make her finally submit like she should have a long time ago.

When I'd gotten the call, I didn't even think twice. I rushed out of there the next second, and I felt like I'd been transported to a new world when I walked into that club and saw Bebe passed out on the couch. A world where beautiful girls drank too much and took questionable drugs; a world where Bebe and I could be together, where it was the easiest thing in the world to throw her over my shoulder and at the same time, throw caution to the wind and take her home with me, where she belonged.

Seeing her on my bed, her hair fanned out over my pillow, made my heart ache. I couldn't bring myself to put her in the white room. She belonged here, in my bedroom, on the sheets that smelled of me. She was so stunning, so vulnerable lying there. My heart pounded with a pain I didn't understand, and as badly as I wanted to touch her, I couldn't bring myself to do it.

I watched her fall asleep, her eyelids heavy as sleep took her away from me. I got up from the floor and took a step backward to the door. I needed to get away. I couldn't be this close to her, couldn't afford to lose my cool when she was just a few inches away. There was nothing I wanted more than to touch her, have her in my arms again and inhale her sweet scent. But I couldn't handle it, the pressure so strong I thought my head would explode. I needed to get the fuck away from her.

Stumbling out of the bedroom, I held onto the doorframe for dear life. I was dizzy, feeling nausea take over as I half-walked, half-fell into the living room. When it came down to it, I couldn't be near her, couldn't stand her being so close because I was terrified of her hurting me or me hurting her.

Nothing in my head made sense. The only thing that was prevalent and so very clear was the fact that I needed to get away. Being outside, alone in the cold streets, would be better than being alone with her in my apartment.

I took the stairs one by one, shaking with each step that brought me closer to my cold destination. The doorman didn't say a word this time, though he seemed worried about my sudden departures when I hadn't left the apartment for at least a year beforehand. I walked away from him, from the confines of the apartment building. I needed to get away from it all.

The cold air hit me hard, chilly and threatening with its frozen fingers wrapping around my throat. I stumbled down the street, only realizing then I'd forgotten my jacket. The cold was biting my skin, desperately trying to get through the thin fabric of my shirt and making my heart freeze under my skin. I was afraid, more afraid than I'd been in years.

Stopping meant thinking about her in my bed, so I kept going. Step after step, one moment blending into another until I started to breathe lighter, without the panicked gasps that could barely get any air down my throat. I followed the street, away from the center of the city and towards a park I'd been to before, back when I still thought my agoraphobia was something I'd get rid of.

The park was closed with a wrought iron gate, but I climbed it easily. And then I was inside. The small ponds were frozen, the park still and quiet in the midnight hour. It wasn't time for dawn yet, but if I stuck around for long enough, I would see the sun rise above the peaceful park.

I sat down on a stone bench, my heart pounding and my head hurting from the thoughts trying desperately to claw their way into the worried part of my brain. Bebe was first and foremost on my mind, the image of her sleeping body on my bed wreaking havoc on my mind. I was upset with myself for walking away, but there was no way my body would let me stay in the apartment.

The shock of seeing her in person, feeling her tight body under my fingertips and almost – fucking almost – tasting her was too much. I'd never wanted anything more, yet I couldn't even bring myself to stay in the same building as her. Real fear settled in, deep and crippling in the marrow of my bones. I was afraid of her. Me, Miles Reilly, torn to fucking shreds over a little party girl that had gotten the better of me.

"Bebe," I muttered to myself, letting my head settle into my hands.

For once in my life, I let the outside forces take over. I listened, I felt. I was quiet, stunned by all the sounds that made the silence so overwhelming.

Birds chirping. Leaves blowing in the wind. The sound of cars in the distance. All of it made for a perfect chaos that I'd been missing out on for years. And in a way, a strange, alien way, it was oddly calming.

Making myself sit through an hour of it seemed like a nightmare at first, and I counted every second of it, my lips wrapping around the numbers as they escaped my lips. I couldn't leave just yet. I needed to stay here, let my body calm down and my mind stop reeling. Maybe after an hour, I would be ready to face Bebe again. Maybe after an hour, I'd be able to hold her again.

Maybe I would be able to tell her how I really felt. Maybe, just maybe, I could say those three little words back.

Because I felt it, too. And I knew exactly what she was talking about when she muttered them to me in her drugged state. I knew exactly what she meant because the same fire burned inside me. The embers that had ignited her own spark burned brightly inside my soul and for once, I wasn't afraid of my feelings. No, I was afraid of her.

My Bebe.

Because she was beautiful.

Because she was broken.

Because she was just like me, and yet, unlike anyone I'd ever met before.

The pull I felt towards the girl was magnetic, the fire a passionate one, consuming me like nothing I'd ever felt before, not even my own panic and fear. I'd never wanted anyone this much, never craved another person the way I craved her. And that's why I was afraid.

I would lose her.

Undoubtedly.

She would leave when she found out what I did – what I had to keep doing to keep my business going. Yes, she would leave when she found out the truth about me.

How obsessive I was. The shameful bleach baths. The hidden cigarettes. The dark, smelly room in the back of the apartment. She wouldn't stick around for that kind of crazy, not beautiful, talented, stunning Bebe. Not her. When I lost her, I would finally break. It would be the end of me.

I sat there as the seconds ticked by and the fear grew bigger and bigger. I watched my panic grow until it was a big, shiny bubble, like the ones I used to blow when I was a kid. A big rainbow bubble of soapy water and childhood dreams. And then it popped.

It was all over, just like that. The bubble was gone, the fear exploding into the vast nothingness of the park.

I got to my feet. The counting I'd been doing trickled into nothing until all the numbers blended together and I was alone with nothing but one wish, one deepest, darkest desire in my heart – to have Bebe, no matter how selfish, how fucked-up, how evil of me that was.

My legs were quick to carry me back to the apartment and I watched the sunrise over the city as I made my way back. I was freezing cold, my skin like cool marble as I made my way to the building. I glanced up, but there were no lights on in my apartment. Bebe must have been fast asleep, and the thought of her hair fanned out over my pillow made my cock grow thick and hard. Desperate to sink myself inside her, I raced past the doorman who wasn't even trying to conceal his shock anymore, and up the stairs. Two at a time.

Stumbling into my own apartment, I held onto the door handle for dear life, the speed I'd ran towards my home had taken it out of me. I was out of breath, not even my vigorous workouts at home preparing me for the brutal outside. But there was nothing that would dissuade me from the only thing I wanted. From holding her in my strong arms, making her promise she would never do anything like this again. Making her swear she'd be a good girl for me.

I walked into the bedroom, and my heart sank when I found it empty. The sheets were rumpled, and I noticed one thing right away.

Bebe had taken the white frame off the wall. She'd taken out the white paper and written a note on it in lipstick.

thank you.
xoxo bebe

I stared at the words, picturing her scribbling them down and then disappearing back into her own apartment. I wanted to be angry, but I couldn't find it in my heart to hold it against her. I understood, in the end, what this had meant to Bebe. Why she had run away.

Grinning to myself, I put the now ruined white canvas back into the frame, and put it back up on the wall. Her bright pink lipstick was now the focal point of my whole room, and I grinned as I stared at it adorning my wall.

It would have been so easy to despair in that moment, knowing Bebe had left me. But I couldn't bring myself to do it, couldn't make myself get upset about it. Because now, I had defeated the biggest fear of all.

I laughed to myself and shook my head as I climbed back into my bed, the sheets still warm from her body being wrapped up in them. I inhaled her scent, filling my nostrils with everything that made her so very unique, so fucking special to me. My beautiful girl, my stunning Bebe.

Things would be different from now on, because she made me defeat the monster that separated me from her. From now on, I would not be the man she wanted.

I would be the man she deserved.

Chapter 19

·BEBE·

NEGATIVE SPACE, PHRASE
*Helps to define the boundaries of positive space
and brings balance to a composition.*

I lay in my bed, staring at the ceiling above me. There was a small crack above my head, and for a second, my heart pounded with worry at the thought of the ceiling coming crashing down on me, just like my life had crashed the previous night.

Shaking my head to get the thought out, I pulled myself up and set on the edge of the bed. My phone was ringing incessantly, Arden's number flashing on the screen like crazy. I knew I needed to pick up, but answering her call meant owning up to my actions, and I was too scared to do that just yet.

Dragging myself off the bed made my head explode in white noise and pain. I managed to get myself to the kitchen, drawing myself a large glass of ice-cold tap water. I drank it hungrily, gulping down the calming liquid before I picked up my phone. It was time to face the music.

But before I got the chance to, there was a sharp, angry knock on my front door. I knew it was her.

That was the thing about Arden. She cared. She cared even when I was being a bitch to her. She cared when I didn't. She cared when nobody else did.

"Bebe, I know you're in there," she called out angrily. "If you don't open this door right the hell now, I'm going to knock it down."

I groaned inwardly and moved towards the door. She was pissed, and she had every right to be. Still, I was terrified of her anger and of finally accepting all the mistakes I'd made the previous night. It meant remembering… and to remember was the worst part of the whole thing.

I opened the door and Arden stormed into the room, her eyes shooting daggers at me.

"How could you do that?" she snarled at me.

Her voice was pure anger, and her body was overflowing with signs of betrayal. I felt guilty then, really fucking guilty, for having let her down the previous night. Arden only wanted the best for me, and I'd known that all along. But I could never accept it, her kindness and the sweetness she exhibited with me, even though I didn't deserve any of it.

Forget. Forget. Forget. And then move the fuck on.

It was an eternal motto, but it felt that as long as I kept Arden around, I'd never be able to move away fully from Posy's death. It had always been the three of us, and existing with just Arden by my side felt wrong, like we were missing our queen bee. Arden turned to me now, as if I was supposed to lead the broken mess of our friendship to the finish line. But I couldn't handle it.

Hell, I couldn't even handle looking at myself in the mirror. My eyes spoke of what I had been through, and I couldn't take it.

"Arden," I started, my voice raspy and apologetic. "I'm sorry. I know I've fucked up."

"Sorry?" she barked at me. "You're fucking sorry? Well, guess what Bebe, sorry just won't do anymore. Sorry won't fucking cut it."

I felt the pain then, so sharp and intense it made me gasp and recoil in surprise. It felt like I was being severed, like a leg being cut off and the phantom limb was still kicking, even when it was long gone.

"Arden," I pleaded with her. "Please. Just give me one more chance, and I'll make it up to you, I swear to God."

"I don't care who you swear to," she laughed, shaking her head. "I'm done believing your lies. You want to destroy yourself that badly, Bebe?"

She thrust something into my hands and my fingers trembled as they wrapped around it.

"Here. Knock yourself out."

She didn't even touch me as she handed it over, and I watched her storm out of my apartment, slamming the front door behind her so hard it wouldn't even close, probably throwing it off the damn hinges. I felt hot tears prickling my eyes, but I refused to acknowledge them. Instead, I stepped into the hallway and glared at a curious neighbor staring at me through a crack in her front door.

"Mind your own business!" I barked at her, the tears threatening to fall.

"We only get one family," she said in response, then closed the door.

No one had mistaken Arden and me as sisters before.

But as I closed the door, I tried to tell myself meaningless little lies that would make the whole situation better, diffuse some of the tension left in the air from her abrupt departure.

It didn't matter anyway, did it? If she wanted to blow me off, so be it. I had a ton of other friends who weren't as judgmental or as demanding as she was.

But if that was the case, why was I crying already? Finally, I was unable to hold it all in and I let the tears slide down my cheeks. There one second, and gone the next, just like Posy had been. And now I was finally, mercifully all alone.

I knew Arden would never forgive me for what I'd done. In her mind, I was heading down the same destructive path as Posy, trying to ruin myself the exact same way our queen bee had. And I was doing a damn fine job of it, too.

The previous night had been a mistake.

The night I'd spent in Miles' apartment was blurry and hard to remember, but I could still feel his stubble beneath my fingertips, almost as if I'd just brushed my skin against his. Miles mattered even more now, but I wouldn't admit that to myself – no, not just yet. It was too soon to admit there was only one person left who cared about me.

Instead, my eyes focused on the locket in my hand, my fingers clutching at it desperately.

Posy's infamous silver locket. She never opened it. Never showed the picture inside to anyone. But she wore the necklace with the heart-shaped locket every single day I'd known her.

Posy's parents wanted Arden to have it because they'd been friends the longest. I suspected they never liked me, anyway, but seeing my friend get Posy's most prized possession still fucking hurt. And now here it was, the snake-like silver chain cold to the touch and slippery between my fingers.

I opened the locket. I had to see.

I'd seen Posy toy with it a thousand times, staring inside the silver heart.

Peep Show

And now, I was finally about to find out what she'd smiled at so often. There was a picture inside, just like I'd suspected.

I recognized the picture of us right away. It had been taken the summer we met, when we were all thin from too much booze and not enough food and wearing ridiculously short dresses with no underwear. I remembered the way we had posed for the camera. Arden smiling wide, her mouth half-open and revealing a pink piece of gum between her rows of perfect teeth. She used to chew gum all the time, said it helped her with the hunger pangs.

And then there was me, in a white dress that emphasized my tan, and eyes were so innocent I could barely recognize them. I had to remind myself this was when I was just starting to fit in with Arden and Posy's crowd. Maybe it was even the exact night when I finally realized I'd made it, and I was part of their stupid clique.

My eyes were turned to Posy, staring adoringly at her like she was my damn idol or something.

And Posy, Posy had one of her tits out, with her fingers covering the nipple, and a big grin for the camera. Her hair was wild and her eyes were hazy.

Posy had cut Arden out of the original picture. Now, it was just the two of us. Me, looking at her like a love-drunk teenager, and her, madness and passion wrapped into one hot little firecracker that changed our lives forever.

My fingers clasped around the locket, closing the picture shut. I couldn't bear to look at it. I couldn't bear to think of what it meant.

Poor Arden. Posy's parents had insisted she keep the locket, but neither of us knew what Posy had done to the photo inside. My heart swelled at the thought of Arden discovering it on her own, and I hated myself for putting her through that. I should have been there for her. I should have been a friend. I wasn't the only one who felt alone after Posy dying. We were two peas in a pod, except Arden had tried desperately to help me, and I'd done nothing but push her away.

I collapsed in the hallway, my back against the front door and the locket feeling like a cold, hard piece of betrayal in the palm of my hand.

I'd been a bad friend. And now it was too late.

The urge to throw that damn necklace through the window was so strong I had to force it to drop from my fingers, landing in a pool of silver on the hardwood floor. I couldn't even look at it anymore. All it symbolized was the end of an era, a time when I was foolish and young, stupid and happy. A time when I was in love.

That's what it was all about in the end.

The jealousy.

The anger.

The need to join Posy wherever she was now that she wasn't terrorizing the city's best nightclubs and sneaking onto the red carpet, flashing her tits to the paps and pretending she was someone. It was never enough that she was someone to me and Arden. Posy had always wanted so much more, and in the end, we weren't able to give it to her. I'd never stop blaming myself for not trying enough.

Yes, all of it was because of one little reason, the nagging thought in the back of my head, the tiny voice screaming at me that this was the answer all along, I'd just been too fucking blind to see it.

I'd been head over heels in love with Posy, and now, I finally had a hint – in the shape of a locket – that she had felt the same way.

Maybe Posy felt something for me too.

Maybe all those times we kissed and I felt sparks flying between us, the same fire was burning in the pit of her stomach.

Maybe, when we looked at each other and understood the other person to the last sliver of shame, regret and unfulfilled desires, she saw me for who I was.

And maybe, just maybe, she loved me for my brokenness just like I loved hers.

Since the moment the locket ended up in my hands, I wasn't mourning a friend anymore.

I was mourning a lover.

Chapter 20

·MILES·

SELCOUTH, ADJECTIVE
Unfamiliar, rare, strange, and yet marvelous.

Whatever I tried to do that day failed.

I couldn't stop thinking about her, couldn't stop going back into my bedroom to touch the sheets that still held the shape of her body. I stroked the spot where her ass had flattened the mattress until it disappeared and then berated myself for letting go of it so quickly. I wanted more. I wanted Bebe Hall back in my bed, and I wanted to watch her sleep sweetly and soundly.

Her scent was still heady and fragrant in my bedroom, almost too overwhelming to stay in it. But I couldn't walk away. I filled my nostrils with her perfume and my head with images of her, of us, together. I was well and truly hooked, addicted to her scent and the way she made me feel.

There was no going back now. I wouldn't stop until I had her. I was more determined than ever.

The thing that puzzled me was the raw need for her, the desperate, primal urge to make her mine. I'd never felt like that before when it wasn't all about sex, like a fucking caveman, wanting to make every inch of her mine and hearing her admit that she belonged to me completely. I realized as the day dawned in my Bebe-scented bedroom, that I wouldn't be able to stop the itch anymore. Bebe Hall had fucking arrived, and she was the obsession I didn't ever want to get rid of.

What would Dr. Halen make of this? I wondered briefly, but instead of dealing with the issue at hand, I wrapped it up in a big bow and put it in the darkest corner of my mind, where I didn't have to deal with it just yet. Not until everything imploded. And judging by Bebe's short fuse, that wasn't going to be long in coming, anyway.

The hours passed and before I knew it, it was evening, past seven p.m.

I'd eaten something but mostly just hung around the apartment listlessly, unsure of what I should be doing, until eventually I collapsed into bed. When my phone rang, I was grateful for the distraction. That is until I saw Bebe's name flashing across the screen.

Things would be different now. Now, Bebe would know how I really felt. And the weight of those three little words she'd whispered to me was heavy, almost too heavy to bear.

I answered with a slight tremble in my voice, as desperately as I tried to hide it.

"Hello."

"Hi… Miles."

Her voice was small and scared, like a little girl's.

"Are you okay?" I asked roughly, ready to knock out the teeth of whoever had upset her.

"Yeah," she whispered back. "Can we talk for a while?"

"Just talk?" My words were soft.

"Yeah," she said again. "I just want to hear your voice."

My heart ached with hurt. I wanted this, God, I really fucking did. But it was dangerous territory. It meant Bebe was in charge of me, at least judging by the way my heart was pounding for her, desperate to tell her how I really felt. To have her back in my arms where she belonged… But it was too soon for that. I would have to keep my distance a little while longer.

"Where are you?" I wanted to know.

"Lying in bed."

I could hear the mattress moving under her.

"Where are you, Miles?"

"In my bed," I admitted, my hands ruffling the sheets.

"The bed I slept in?"

"Yes."

A long pause.

"Does it still smell like me?"

Another pause to make my heart nearly explode out of my chest before I opened my mouth and confessed the truth. "Yeah."

"Do you like it?"

"I do."

"Do you wish I was there?"

A loaded question, bursting with promise and desperation.

What was the right answer? Of course I wanted her to be there with me. But the mere thought of Bebe so close terrified me. I'd never let anyone in, not anyone that mattered like she did. It had been years since I'd had someone in my corner. Years since I'd been anything but alone.

"I do," I finally said, and I heard her exhale slowly, then giggle.

"You like me," she teased.

"You like me too," I reminded.

"I guess we're even then."

We settled into a companionable silence, and I listened to the rhythmic, calming sound of her breaths. She was addictive, fucking incredible and scary as shit. I was terrified of a girl a foot shorter than me with fists so tiny they fit easily inside my own. She was the scariest person I'd encountered in my whole life. And I'd never wanted anyone more than her.

"Can we keep talking?" she asked softly. "I need to speak to someone."

"What's wrong?" I tried to find out, and I could hear the hesitation in her voice.

I wanted to break her. Force the truth out of her and make her admit exactly what had happened. It had to come from her, though, not from me forcing it to leave her lips.

"You can tell me anything," I added lamely, wondering whether that was true, even as the words left my mouth.

Would I really understand anything she'd tell me? I could barely picture her life, all fizzy champagne and loud music, pills and booze and drugs and rock 'n' roll.

"I had a fight," she finally murmured back. "An argument."

"With your friend?" I asked on instinct.

"Yeah," she replied after a short pause. "Arden."

"Do you want to talk about it?" I asked, feeling awkward as fuck. I wasn't a great mediator, and I had no idea what to do. Surely all girlfriends fought, right? But from Bebe's tone, I could tell this particular argument was more serious than the spats I'd seen girls have before.

"No," she replied sharply, and I exhaled with relief. "I really, really don't. Can you distract me? Just talk about anything, anything in the world."

My mind whirred and tried to come up with a question.

"What are you wearing?" I asked, and I could feel the hurt from her silence. "I'm sorry. I… I wasn't sure if that was what you wanted."

"No," she said sadly. "It's okay. I guess that's what we do, after all."

"Come stand next to the window," I asked her. "I want to see you."

I got off the bed, and the sounds from my phone told me she was doing the same thing. I stood in front of the tall window in the bedroom, my eyes finding her body on the other side of the street.

She was naked. Completely naked, her body exposed to my eyes.

I was still wearing boxers, and I was grateful for it. If I'd been naked, Bebe would have seen my dick jerk in response.

I raised a hand and placed it on the window, my other hand holding the phone. I motioned for Bebe to do the same, and she did.

"You're beautiful," I told her.

"You keep saying that." Her voice was low, sad.

"It's true. You're the most beautiful woman I've ever seen."

"So why won't you…" Her unfinished sentence hung in the air, and I watched her look down at the floor.

"Why won't I what?" I asked softly, because I was a stickler for self-punishment.

"Why won't you touch me?" she asked. "Why won't you fuck me, Miles?"

How could I explain it?

How could I convince her that suddenly, she was the only person in my life I gave a shit about, the only person I cared about, the only one I wanted to make an impression on? She would think I was insane, developing a connection to her she might not have even felt herself.

"I'm scared," I finally replied. "Do you understand why?"

Our eyes locked across the street. I could see the shadow her body threw behind, on the floor. It was small and shaking, like a child. I wanted to hold her. Tell her it was going to be okay.

"Bebe." Her name came out rushed, desperate, but I was too far gone to worry about how I sounded. "Can I…" I took a deep breath, "Can I come over?"

She stared at me, wide-eyed, her lips moving soundlessly as she answered.

"Now?"

"Yeah."

"Why?"

"I want to hold you."

"Will you? Do you promise?"

"Yeah."

I watched her chew her bottom lip, her eyes locked on mine, begging me not to break my promise.

"Come," she said. "I'll leave the front door open."

She cut the call and stepped away from the window.

My hands shook as I pulled on some jeans and a Henley. If I stopped for one second to think about this, I would change my mind, and I couldn't afford that. I needed to get over there and finally hold her. I needed to know what her body felt like against mine before I lost my fucking mind.

I looked at the front door that had taunted me so many times before.

Leaving the apartment had gotten harder and harder as the days turned into weeks, months and years. Until I was so secluded, so absorbed in my own fear, I couldn't even leave the apartment to go downstairs and get my mail. But now, I was going to risk it all for her.

The germs.

The fear.

The madness of going out there, to her apartment, to hold her in my arms. It wouldn't end well, none of this would.

Yet for once, I didn't give a shit.

I locked the door on my way out and slipped the key in the pocket of my jeans. Every movement felt like a losing battle, but I fought through it. Every step took effort I didn't know I had in me. Every fucking foot away from my apartment was like walking on pins and needles.

The doorman smiled at me as I entered the lobby.

"Looking good, Mr. Reilly," he said, and I managed a weak smile.

I forced myself to step outside, look up at her window to find a faint glow behind the glass. She was waiting for me.

For the first time in years, my existence had a purpose. For the first time in years, I gave a shit about someone other than me, and it was cutting me deep.

My next step was confident. My posture perfect. Suddenly, I wasn't doing this for Bebe anymore.

I was doing it for myself, and I couldn't fucking wait to have my fill of Bebe Hall. And I wouldn't fucking stop until her sweet juices were running down my thighs. Until I could taste her essence on my very soul. I wouldn't fucking stop, and she had no idea what was coming.

Chapter 21

·BEBE·

COUP DE FOUDRE, PHRASE
Love at first sight.

I left the front door open, and it let in a cold breeze from the hallway. Shivering in the sudden cold, I threw on a silk robe. I hesitated in front of the full-length window in my bedroom, debating between tying it loosely or so tightly it nearly cut off my circulation. The idea of Miles seeing me in the revealing outfit made me as excited as it did scared.

Then, I felt his electrifying presence like a punch to the gut. I turned around, my eyes finding his as he made his way to the bedroom.

He stood in the doorway, his knuckles painfully white as he stared at me, my robe falling slightly open in the front.

I felt the breeze from the hallway on my skin, causing goosebumps to erupt all over the surface that was now so plainly visible to him, only a few feet away. His eyes bore into mine, drinking me in like I was a piece of candy and he was trying to work out how many licks it would take to get to my molten center. It was a good thing Miles didn't know he'd reached it already.

Being vulnerable for him was the easiest thing in the world. Opening myself up to him was easier than spreading my legs every night for a different man. It came naturally, as if I was meant to be doing this and nothing else my whole life. Baring myself to him. Letting him see every flaw, every scar, every bit of baggage that made me who I was as I stood in front of him.

He took a sharp breath, his eyes angrily finding mine. He was so fucking close I could smell him, and it drove me crazy.

"Hi," I said softly, and the corners of his sullen mouth tugged upwards.

"Hello, Bebe," he said simply.

I reached for the belt of my robe, but he stepped closer, his hand lingering above my own, never quite touching my skin.

"No," he rasped. "Don't."

I let the silky material fall from my fingers, baring myself for him. There was nothing between us but some flimsy fabric and a lot of restraint that I wanted to get rid of, right then and there.

But I knew his limits, and a part of me understood why we couldn't act on this attraction yet, even though it was pulling us forcibly together.

I stared right into his eyes as the robe fell open between my tits, revealing a sliver of my pussy and the spot where my tits were divided by a little gap. He stared at me for what felt like a lifetime, his eyes heavy with emotion as he drank in my body. Finally, he managed to tear them away and glanced up, smirking at me.

"Tie it," he said roughly. "Quickly, before I change my mind."

I blushed and looked away, tying the robe firmly in place. I stepped towards my closet, my fingers shaking as I opened it and took a pair of lacy black panties from a drawer. I slipped them on, Miles' eyes following every little movement I made. I loved his eyes on me, the way they burned making me feel warmer than ever.

"Get on the bed," he said, and I climbed between the pillows and sheets obediently.

He paced in front of the bed, his steps impatient but filled with purpose while I lay back and giggled at him.

"Aren't you going to join me?" I asked him playfully, and he stared me down so hard I thought his eyes would start a fire in my own.

"No," he said roughly. "Not yet. First, I'm going to help you."

I furrowed my brow and turned away from him. This was something I didn't want to hear.

Knowing what he was going to say, I groaned and pulled a pillow over my head. But he was next to me in seconds, and I stared up at his handsome, chiseled face as he lifted the pillow from my arms, never quite touching me as he bared me to his demanding eyes.

"Tell me, Bebe," he said roughly, tossing the pillow to the floor. "Why do you fucking insist on avoiding the problem when it's staring you straight in the face?"

I raised myself to my knees, standing upon them. My face was mere inches away from his, and I watched him take a sharp intake of breath as we stared at one another.

"You being the problem?" I purred, my lips lingering so close to his I could taste his minty breath on them. "You are right in front of me…"

"Don't be a smartass," he said, and on an impulse, I reached for him, my hands desperately trying to wrap around his neck.

Miles snapped them up in one hand. We both gasped the second we made contact, his skin so hot it felt sizzling against my ice-cold wrists. He stared into my eyes as he stroked the tender skin on my wrist, the very spot I used to cut up, once, twice, three times.

Then, he let me go, as if he'd burned himself by touching me for the mere few seconds it took him to ignite the fire I knew would never die in the pit of my stomach. My body reacted to him intensely, desperate to please him, needy to find his approval. I would have done anything for the man in front of me, and I felt pathetic for it.

"What happened last night, Bebe?" His voice was laden with things left unsaid.

"I got drunk," I shrugged, smiling at him. "You know how it goes. A little too much booze, a little less control than I should've had. No big deal. Right?"

"Not right," he snapped, and I scowled at him as he paced the room again.

"Why do you care, anyway?" I spoke up, the self-preservation instinct I knew so well kicking back into play.

My whole life, I'd learned to deal with moments like this.

The second someone got too close for comfort, I would start pushing. I would push and push and push until I forced them out of my life.

It worked every single time.

But something was telling me it wouldn't work on Miles Reilly.

"I care," he snarled at me. "Because I give a shit about you. Because I'm not some meaningless fling you find at the club. Because I don't want to watch you breaking yourself into tiny pieces... and because I'd rather avoid having to help you put it all back together."

"You wouldn't help me," I laughed bitterly. "You would never help me."

"No?"

He reached me in two quick steps, and I took a sharp breath when his face lingered above mine, his expression fierce.

"What have I been doing this whole time then, Bebe?" he asked, and I turned my face away, tightly shutting my eyes. I couldn't even look at him.

"Look at me, sugar."

I shook my head no.

I felt his fingers before they even made contact, at first just ghosting over my skin, the phantom feeling of him holding my chin so strong I could swear it was real. But nothing could prepare me for the moment when he actually did it, wrapped his fingers around my jaw and made me look at him with a sharp, decisive tug.

"Open. Your. Eyes," he ordered, and my eyelids trembled as I lifted them. "Good girl."

"Don't," I said uncomfortably, wiggling under his watchful gaze.

"Don't what?" His voice was so soft. Not a whisper, though. It was too rough, too filled with raw need to be a whisper.

"Don't call me that."

"Look at me."

"No."

"Bebe..."

My eyes flew open again, and I stared at him.

Up close, he was so painfully handsome I wanted to scream. The dimple in his cheek, still visible even though he wasn't smiling. Only one, not two like other people had. His stubble, his hair. His beautiful eyes. Miles Reilly was going to break my heart, he just didn't know it yet.

He grinned at me, his finger touching my bottom lip. On instinct, I opened my mouth for him and he groaned at the sight of my tongue flicking out to wet his finger.

"Don't," he said with restraint.

"Don't what?" I whispered.

"Don't tempt me."

"Touch me," I begged, and he closed his eyes firmly.

"I can't."

"Miles, touch me."

He opened his eyes. They'd never looked clearer than that night in my bedroom, filled with so much pain and desire I wanted to scream for him.

"I won't be able to stop," he admitted.

I leaned forward, my lips a second away from touching his.

"Then don't…"

He let out a groan so painful I stopped, and the next second, he'd taken step after step backward until his shoulder blades hit the wall behind him.

"Stop," he said, and I sat back on the bed, my legs crossed and my eyes desperate as we stared at each other.

"Why?" I demanded. "Why the fuck should I stop? We both want this."

He suppressed a growl and looked away from me, rubbing his temples roughly.

"Bebe," he said again. "You can't keep doing this. Your friend was so worried the other night. *I* was worried! You could have fucking died."

"But I was fine," I said with a bright smile. "See? I'm totally, perfectly alright. Not a thing amiss."

I gave him my best fake smile, but I knew he saw right through it. It was no use hiding things from him.

"Look." Now my voice was sharp. "I don't meddle in your business, so stay the hell out of mine."

"Oh, you don't?" he laughed bitterly, reaching for his phone and showing me the pictures of Lana and me in that club.

I blushed at the sight of our tongues down each other's throat. The way our hands groped each other's flesh in a desperate attempt to get Miles off. I'd used Lana, just like I used everyone else. What a cheap shot.

"Whatever," I replied weakly.

"Not whatever," he shook his head. "You're hurting yourself. Why?"

"Because," I snarled, giving him an ugly look. "Because I'm hurting. Okay?"

"Okay." He stared me down. "Why are you hurting, Bebe?"

"My friend," I said lamely. "My friend died."

Miles kept looking when he asked, "When?"

"A year ago now, I guess," I shrugged. "I don't really remember the exact date."

February 17th. It was fucking burned into my mind. I couldn't forget it even if I got my memory wiped.

"Who was she?" he asked. Was I imagining it, or was his voice a little gentler now?

"Posy O'Neill," I said in a soft voice. "She was my best friend. Mine and Arden's."

"How did she die?"

I looked up at him, feeling the pressure of his stare.

"Drug overdose."

It felt like a guilty confession.

"I see," he muttered.

He saw alright. He was judging me just like every-body-fucking else who found out. Poor little rich girl, lost her bestie and decided to go down the same path as her. Feeling sorry for me, no doubt, feeling like I deserved his pity.

I jumped up on the bed and threw a pillow at his head on impulse. I roared when he dodged it and kept throwing things, pillows, sheets, a stuffed teddy, anything I could get my hands on.

"Fuck you!" I snarled at him. "You don't know me! You don't know her! You don't understand, you don't know anything, anything!"

He closed the distance between us with two steps, and his hands wrapped around my wrists once again. He pulled me down and I collapsed on my bed, my chest heaving and my breaths desperate, choking, ready to break me down.

"Breathe," he told me gently. "Breathe deeply, Bebe. Breathing is everything. Breathing is control."

Something told me he knew what he was talking about.

I focused on my breaths. On the way my chest rose and fell as he held me down and breathed with me, teaching me how to do it. I did it until it didn't feel like a chore anymore. Until it felt completely natural.

"That's a good girl," he murmured, and I smiled up at him on impulse.

"Miles," I said softly, and his eyes locked onto mine.

Something passed between us in that moment of looking at one another, a feeling I didn't quite understand because I'd never felt it with anyone else, not even Posy. It was sweet, and sad, yet full of promise.

"What is it?"

His voice was just as soft, and I could feel the words against my lips. I hummed and closed my eyes, my body arching on an impulse to be closer to his. I felt his body stiffen, and I let my eyes fly open again, staring into his own.

"Miles, will you help me?"

It was the first time in my life that I had asked for help.

Before, it had been forced on me. Given to me. Offered to me. But never like this, never after I humiliated myself completely like I just had. Hot tears burned the backs of my eyes, and I wasn't sure whether it was because I was embarrassed, or because I felt so very emotional.

He stared down at me, his mouth opening wordlessly.

"Yes," he groaned after what felt like an eternity, and my body sagged with relief. "I'll help you, sugar."

Chapter 22

·MILES·

ESPOIR, NOUN
Hope.

She was taking hold of me, and I'd stopped fighting it.
There was no use in denying her electrifying effect on me anymore. I saw it mirrored in her own eyes.
"I would really, really like to fucking kiss you right now," she said, smiling up at me.
I just then realized the position I'd gotten her into. Her body was underneath mine, her wrists were held down by my own strong fingers. She was trapped, captured. And I couldn't get enough of the sight of Bebe Hall losing control. It felt like a momentous occasion.
"Except I feel like you might kill me if I do," Bebe went on, and I grinned at her dangerously close face. "Am I right?"

"Probably," I said back, my voice rough.

She bit her bottom lip, dragging her teeth across it. The way she drove me crazy was so intense I knew I wouldn't be able to hold back for long. I needed to taste that gorgeous mouth.

Why was I holding back? Why wasn't I letting myself do this? I'd kissed so many girls before, fucked women whose names and faces I forgot the second they walked out my front door. But for some reason, I couldn't bring myself to do it with Bebe. *To* Bebe. I would never be able to let go of her the way I had the other girls. I'd cling to her, and she'd be sick of it in a matter of weeks. She'd toss me aside, and I'd be left broken and more bitter than ever.

So it was self-preservation that kept me from taking that final, fateful step. Holding back was hard, but it had to be done.

"How can I convince you?" she asked with a wicked little smile. "I know you really want to."

"You do?" I asked, lowering my head as I laughed, and realizing just what a mistake that was when I caught the scent of her throat.

It was her perfume mixed with the sweet scent of her skin, so overwhelming I wanted to double over and weep for what I would never have.

"Miles," she said, her voice barely above a whisper. "Miles, kiss me. You have to kiss me. I've been waiting so long for this…"

I stopped staring at the hollow of her throat and raised my eyes to hers, a monumental mistake. Now, I could barely fight the instinct and the rush of adrenaline going through my body, telling me to do it. Succumb. Take my chance. Taste her. Take her. Have her. Forever.

If only it were so easy.

"Please." Her voice was throaty, raspy. It was turning me the fuck on. "Please, Miles. It's all I want. I just want to feel your lips on mine. I just want to feel your breath on my lips. I just really, really need to taste you. To feel your tongue. To let you have me. Please, Miles. Please."

Her eyes were burning, her mouth barely moving, the words coming slowly, softly.

"Please," she begged one last time, and I leaned down and pressed my lips to hers, as simple as that.

Sweetness, such overwhelming sweetness. It took over, fighting the bitter taste of panic in my mouth and winning victoriously. I tasted her like a man possessed, like I'd never been hungrier for anything than I was for that oh so sweet mouth. I would never have enough, and I deepened the kiss because I couldn't help myself, exploring her mouth and claiming every last inch of her beautiful body as my own pressed down against her.

I felt her inhale beneath me, her heart pounding against my chest as I got on top of her, suddenly so needy, so desperate I was clawing at her, trying to tear her robe off, trying to get to her skin. It was all I needed. More of her. Not fucking fabric, lace or silk be damned. I wanted *her*. My Bebe. *Mine*.

"Slow down," she said desperately against my lips, but I shook my head no and ripped her robe wide open.

Claiming her. Letting her know I wouldn't let go, no matter who else had, no matter what she thought. I was in it for the long haul. Every lick of her convinced me that this was what I needed. My salvation and my damnation.

"Open wider," I growled at her, and her lips parted in a soundless gasp.

I couldn't help myself. I took more and more from her until she was a moaning, dripping little fuckdoll ready to be used. She was begging for me, my name a constant prayer on her lips, her hands clammy as her long nails clawed at me. Whether she was trying to push me off or get closer I wasn't sure, but I couldn't stop. With every touch and every moan from her lips, I grew more and more addicted. Like a pathetic fucking fool.

"Wider," I snapped, and she moaned tearfully as my tongue slipped into her throat.

I fucked her with it and she squirmed beautifully beneath me. My tongue claimed her mouth with desperate, needy motions to tell her who she belonged to. And she knew. It was obvious, from the way she wriggled under me to the way she screamed my name against me, either begging me to stop or keep going. It didn't matter at that moment because I wouldn't have been able to stop anyway.

I stared down at her, her eyes closed and her chest heaving as I took her, my hard cock pressing between her legs as my body assaulted hers. And suddenly, I felt like shit, like I was taking advantage. Making her do something she wasn't sure she wanted, forcing myself on her because I was stronger, not giving her a choice.

My body forced itself back, and my mind and dick both roared in protest as I made myself get off the bed and take several steps away. Once again my back bumped against the wall and I took a deep, sharp breath, my head pounding and my eyes finding Bebe's on that fucking bed, rumpled from our kissing and so fucking inviting I could barely resist its call.

"Come back," she rasped, kneeling, crawling towards me on the bed, her tits hanging so perfectly. "Come back, now."

I shook my head no.

"Miles," she hissed. "I want you NOW!"

I felt my shoulders go back. My jaw set. My hands forming fists, my knuckles turning white.

Bebe saw the change too, and she got off the bed abruptly, coming towards me, a sheet wrapped around her now bared body. I was so distracted by her curves I could barely look into her eyes, but I did my damn best.

"Miles," she repeated and came closer, each step she took sealing her fate. "Why are you fighting this? I want it. I want you."

She reached for me. An inch away.

My body reacted the only way it knew how.

I grabbed her outstretched hand with one hand and her hips with the other. She gasped as I turned her around, pushing her against the wall. I let go, my fist connecting with the wall, slamming into brick and paint, smashing a hole in it. Bebe shrieked.

"You. Don't. Want. This!" I yelled at her, and she whimpered before grabbing my hand.

I didn't understand.

Why wasn't she running?

If she knew what was good for her, she should fucking run.

She stared at my fist, my knuckles bloodied and the hole in her wall gaping, not that she gave it a second thought.

"We n-need to clean this," she muttered. "Fast. I have a first aid kit in–"

"Shut the fuck up," I groaned, snatching my fist from her. "Just shut up for a second."

She didn't even hesitate before stepping on her tiptoes and kissing me. Gently this time. Sweetly. Like an inexperienced little virgin. It drove me fucking wild.

"You won't scare me off," she whispered against my lips. "Never ever, Miles."

"You don't know that." My voice was shaky, unsure. I hated myself for it. I felt ashamed.

"I do," she promised. "I know."

She spread the fingers on my hands with hers, and her long nails dug into the backs of my hands when she intertwined them. I shivered, the touch so oddly intimate yet satisfying it sent sparks shooting down my spine. I wanted her like this, convincing me that she'd stay, telling me she wanted nothing but me. I was obsessed with the idea, holding onto her without trying to show it and desperate to have more of sweet Bebe Hall.

"I can't touch you, Bebe," I admitted, my voice broken.

"You're touching me right now." She brushed her lips against my own and I growled into her mouth. "See, it's not so hard. Your hands on mine… Your lips on mine. One thing at a time."

I'd never told her the extent of my brokenness, but standing there, in the room alone with her, she seemed to understand me to my very core. She knew why I was hesitating, she got that I was scared. She was understanding, and sweet, and so fucking irresistible it drove me wild. I wanted nothing more than to drive my cock into her pussy. Bare, no condom, make her understand who she belonged to.

She reached down, took the zipper of my jeans in her hand and I froze as it slowly came down. Froze as her hand slipped inside. Almost cried out as her warm fingers wrapped around my cock. I hissed and took a step back, shoving my cock back in my jeans. My heart was pounding like crazy.

"No," I grunted. "Not yet. I need to watch you. Watching is safer."

Her face fell, and I swallowed the lump in my throat.

"For now," I muttered, and just like that, her pretty smile was back. "Get a toy."

She rushed to her bedside table and I watched her rummage in it as I sat down on the plush bench in front of her bed. In seconds, she was back, kneeling in front of me with her eyes big and hopeful, full of promises I desperately wanted her to keep. Her eyes found mine as she placed a big purple dildo on my lap.

"Tell me what to do," she said, and my cock swelled from the pressure of her words, the promise of what she'd do to herself for me thick on her tongue.

"Strip," I growled.

She didn't move for a second. She still had a sheet wrapped around her in a makeshift dress, but now I was desperate for it to be off. I wasn't going to touch her, not yet. But that didn't mean I couldn't enjoy the fucking perfection of her naked body.

Slowly, she untied the sheet around her tits, and let it fall down to the floor. Her body was bared to me now, beautiful in its nakedness and so enticing I had to grip the bench to keep my hands to myself.

"It has a suction cup," I smiled widely. "That's good."

She blushed and looked away. The urge to wrap my fingers around her chin again was strong, but I fought against it, knowing that the second I touched her, I wouldn't be able to stop.

"What do you want me to do, Miles?" she asked sweetly, and I grinned at her, my eyes holding a promise she didn't understand yet.

"Your mirror," I rasped. "Put it on, high enough that you can suck it on all fours."

She shook as she crawled to the mirror. My skin prickled at the view. She was so naturally submissive, not even thinking about getting up to her feet to do as I'd told her. The dildo went up, and she pressed it against the immaculate surface of the silver mirror until it stuck to it.

She looked at me over her shoulder, her eyes holding a question on what to do next.

"Suck it," I said simply. "Ass towards me."

Her body was shaking, but she did it. Got on all fours and got to work on the purple monster, her pouty lips wrapping around it, taking in the tip and then the first notch.

"Spread your ass for me," I breathed, and her hands went behind her, parting herself, baring her cunt and her tight little asshole for me. I groaned at the sight.

"So fucking beautiful," I muttered. "Such tight little holes you have, sugar."

She mewled around the dildo, sucking it deeper.

"Come on, let me see how deep you can get it," I groaned.

The thing was huge, at least six notches, and I knew she couldn't get the whole thing down her throat. But goddamn, I wanted to watch her try.

She struggled with it, forcing it down her throat, her fingers digging into her butt as she choked herself for me. The sight was fucking incredible, intoxicating. I'd never wanted anything more than I did Bebe in that moment, but I forced myself to stay seated, and rearranged the throbbing dick in my jeans. I was painfully hard, my cock begging to be thrust into her, to feel how her silky pussy wrapped itself around me. But I made myself stay in place, forced myself to wait until she retched, quickly withdrawing from the dildo and staring at me over her shoulder with tears in her eyes. Two strings of saliva hung from her bottom lip, and when her bottom lip trembled, it dripped down her tits.

"Goddamn, Bebe," I muttered, the struggle not to touch her getting harder by the second. "Goddamn."

"Please, Miles," she said, crawling closer. "I so need to fuck."

"You can fuck," I growled, and she desperately came closer, but before she could touch me, I held a hand out. "The dildo."

"Fuck you," she snarled, and I laughed in her face.

"I want to watch, sugar," I said roughly. "Let me watch you take it."

"The whole thing?" she asked needily, and I shook my head with a wicked smile.

"The tip and the first three notches," I said. "That's how much you took down your throat, so that's how much you get to fuck."

I could see the protest in her eyes, but she bit it back and glared at me for another second before crawling back to the mirror. She positioned herself in front of it, her angry eyes connecting with mine as she pushed onto it, moaning as her pussy wrapped around the purple dildo.

"Watch me," she ordered, and I grinned.

"No one could stop me right now," I muttered, and I loved the faint hint of a smile on her face before it broke out into a needy moan.

She fucked the dildo, her tight little cunt making a wet, sucking sound as it took it.

"Fuck it," I growled. "Fuck it for me, Bebe."

She bent right over and her nails dug into the hardwood floor and she started slowly riding the dildo until her mouth opened in a surprised little 'o'. She loved it, just like I knew she would. It was plainly obvious from the tremble in her knees, from the way she licked her lips and the expression in her eyes, devouring me.

I leaned forward, my elbows on my knees and my hands clasped in front of my face. And I watched her put on a show for me. It was what Bebe did best, after all.

Chapter 23

·BEBE·

AMOUR SANS FIN, PHRASE
Endless love.

The toy felt cold and slippery inside me. I rode it while I stared into Miles' eyes, so hungry for more of him I would have done anything just to see that look on his face. Desperation mixing with need, and so much lust it was clouding his vision. It was everything I wanted, and I'd ride myself to tears if it meant getting more of it.

I felt myself drawing close to orgasm, his eyes encouraging me to let go of everything and let my body convulse on the dildo.

"Do… do you want me to?" I managed to get out, and his eyes glinted with need.

"Want you to what, sugar?" he asked.

"Want me to come?" I rasped, my voice reflecting the restraint I was forced to place on myself, because I wouldn't do it without his permission.

"Of course I want you to come," he growled, and I let out a sigh of relief, but then he was up on his feet and in one stride his finger was on my lips and he was tilting my chin back, making me look into his eyes. "Not yet, Bebe. You only come with me from now on. No more toys."

I wanted to scream.

"Let me stop then," I begged, my ass moving on top of the toy. "Let me stop, Miles."

"Stop," he said simply, and I fell forward on my elbows, groaning when the toy slipped out of my pussy with an embarrassing wet sound.

I crawled to his feet, lying in a heap on top of his gleaming boots. I had the overwhelming urge to lick the smooth black leather, but I fought against it. He'd already humiliated me enough.

"I want to take photos of you," he muttered, and I looked up at him. "Like this. When you're a mess. When you're playing. When you're mine."

"Take them," I whispered, and he reached for his pocket instinctively.

"I don't have my camera," he said.

"Take them with your phone," I whispered.

"I…" He hesitated, staring down at me. For some reason, he didn't want to do it. He was looking for excuses. I didn't understand why, but now I was desperate for him to make this moment eternal.

"Please, Miles?" I asked sweetly, getting up on my knees and placing my palms on his thighs. My eyes connected with his, and I watched his Adam's apple bob when he swallowed thickly. "Please. I want you to have this. Have me. Have everything."

He brought his phone out of his pocket with shaky fingers and pointed it at me. I sat at his feet demurely, but I couldn't help the smile making its way on my face as I stared up at him. I heard him chuckle when he took the picture.

"Aren't you worried I'll show someone?" he asked, and I gave him a devilish look.

"I know you won't," I said. "You're too jealous."

He stared me down as I laughed and put my head against his leg.

It was hard to understand Miles completely. Now that he was in my bedroom, though, I was starting to see more and more glimpses into who he actually was. He'd been a different person on the other side of the street. Untouchable, unknown. But he was real now, and it was heart-meltingly sweet and sad at the same time.

His weaknesses were splayed out plainly for me to see. I didn't know the term for it, but I could see what he struggled with. I now understood why I'd never seen him in a club, or out in the city. He had trouble leaving his home, and he was even restless and shaky in my apartment. He was sensitive. Somehow, I could tell being this close to him was as exciting as it was hurtful for him. But I couldn't leave, make it easier on him. Not now. I was already too far gone.

"What makes you think I'm jealous?" he finally asked me, and I looked up at him.

"Aren't you?" I asked softly.

He groaned, and his hand lingered above my face before he let it touch me, gently caressing my cheek. His touch was electric.

"I am," he said. "I'm jealous of every single person who so much as looks at you. I want to lock you up, so I'm the only one that gets to see you."

Why did my skin prickle at the disturbing thought? Half of me wished he'd go through with it, while the other half shook with fear.

Instead, I snatched his phone out of his hand and giggled as I made my way across the room.

"Don't run from me, Bebe," he drawled, and our eyes connected with his simple request.

I didn't want to run. The only place left for me to go was in his arms, and I wasn't sure whether I ever wanted to leave them.

"I'm not running," I said, holding the phone up.

His hand flew in front of his face when I snapped the picture. The photographer didn't want any evidence of himself being involved. He was the man behind the camera, behind the scenes. I understood now that I was his subject, his muse. In the end, he was only there to take the photograph.

I placed the phone on a side table and approached him slowly.

"I Googled you," I said, and his eyes widened, his pupils dilating. "Lana told me your last name."

"You..." For once, he didn't know what to say. I could almost hear the erratic beat of his heart, his panicked gaze meeting mine across the room.

"I know who you are," I nodded with a wicked little mile. "I know what you do."

He didn't say a word. Just kept staring at me, eyes wide and imploring me to go on.

"You're a photographer," I said simply. "A very elusive one, I might add. You never go to any gallery openings. Half the people who follow you don't even know what you look like. Not many photos of you online. I guess the only ones who know for sure are your subjects."

I moved closer and noticed he was shaking.

"The girls," I went on, my voice more than a little bitter. "Girl after girl after girl. Their tits. Nipples. Asses. Pussies. Erotic photos. Meant to get you off, meant to confuse you. Overlaid with images that you think represent them. Churches. Empty, cold, derelict buildings. That was a mean one. Flowers. A closed rose. A daisy in bloom. I was jealous of that one."

"You don't…" he started, but his voice trailed off into nothing. I had him. I knew everything. And he hated me for it, just as much as I hated myself.

"Sometimes I wonder," I said softly. "What you'd choose for me. Maybe a heart-shaped pill. Maybe a bottle of champagne. Maybe you know me better than I know myself. Or maybe you don't know anything at all."

His strong, muscular body was shaking as I reached for him. I was torturing him, making him hurt. It had to be done. My fingers wrapped around his own and he clung to me desperately, like a lost child. It was heart-breaking. My anger, my jealousy dissipated. Vanished into thin air. He was just a man. A man who was hurting. A man I could try to fix…

"I don't care," I whispered. "About any of it. I'm the one that's jealous. I don't want you to do it anymore. I want you to take photos of me. Only me."

"I…" Yet another unfinished sentence. I was desperate for him to go on, but he wouldn't.

"Pick me," I said softly, a replay of the conversation we'd had once already. "Just me, Miles. Why not? I'll be good for you. The best girl you could want; the best you could wish for. You know I will be."

"I…" He was at a loss for words. And I was grasping at straws, feeding my own desperation when he wouldn't.

"Please," I whispered, and he let out a slow exhale.

Then, his hands were on my shoulders. He pushed my naked body down to my knees and I gasped when he did it. My eyes were on his, straining to see through the haze that was now between us. He tugged down his zipper and his palm closed over his cock and he groaned at the sight of me on the floor like that. I wanted more, and I wasn't afraid of reaching out to get it.

I hooked my thumbs in his jeans, tugging them down desperately. Miles didn't try to stop me. I pulled them all the way down and then I got to work on his boxers. His fingers gripped the underwear but I begged him with my eyes to let me do it, let me get him naked and start working him. Finally, he let go, and his boxers fell away.

His cock was a monster, huge and thick, the veins throbbing right in my face and filling my mouth with water.

"Come on," he groaned. "Don't stare. It's not polite, sugar."

I leaned closer. My lips could barely wrap around his tip. He was so thick, bulging at the sight of me. When I tasted his precum I mewled helplessly, and he let out a sound so animalistic, I thought he would just succumb to his urges and take me like I wanted him to all along. But no, his hands were in fists and he was holding back, just like Miles always did. Too bad I wouldn't do him the courtesy of acting the same prim and proper way. I had a reputation for a reason.

As my mouth wrapped around him, my eyes were glued to his and I started to suck. His taste filled my mouth, but I longed for so much more. I'd never get it like this, but I would sure as hell try and give him a taste of what I could do. Miles groaned when I went deeper, at first shyly, but my courage picked up with each lick and stroke of his throbbing cock. He tasted like power, and I was addicted to the way it made me feel. His height, his massiveness, made me think I was nothing but a doll, and I couldn't get enough of it, knowing he could pick me up easily and do anything he wanted to my body.

"Jesus, Bebe," he muttered when I choked myself on his length.

I looked up in time to see his hand linger above my head, his fingers touching a single strand of hair and testing its softness between their tips.

He groaned at the feeling and it gave me the courage to be better, to show him what he'd been missing all along. I sucked harder, deeper, scraped his cock with my teeth.

The game we were playing would never have a winner. He kept pushing me away, and I kept crawling back, desperate for more. But I couldn't stop myself. I wanted him more badly than anything else in my life, and I wouldn't stop until he gave me what I wanted.

I licked the underside of his cock hungrily, from his balls all the way to the glistening tip, and he wrapped his fingers in my hair. I was getting sloppy, my mouth dripping, leaving a wet trail all over him. His cock dripped with my spit and he moved one of his hands under it, catching some and making me take it back in my mouth. It only served to encourage me, and I kept bobbing my head, desperate to get more of him inside me even when it was plainly obvious he would never fit.

I caught my breath and stared up at him, daring him to make me go on.

"Oh, Bebe," he growled, a warning in his voice.

"Tell me you don't want me," I challenged him. "Walk away now, and I'll leave you alone."

The sight of such a big and powerful man trembling in front of me was bone-chilling. He wanted to move, his whole body screaming at him to get away, but he couldn't move a step away from me. I watched his fists fall down next to his body and his eyes close in defeat, and then my mouth was back on him, taking more from him, taking everything I wanted to have.

This time, I didn't show any mercy. I sucked him like the only thing left to do in the world was to make him come. Show him my talents, convince him I was worth it, even when it meant humiliating myself.

Stopping wasn't an option. There was only the promise that he would stay if he thought I was good enough, but I would have to work hard for it. Harder than I'd worked for anything else in my life.

"Stop," he breathed, and I could tell he was close.

I shook my head no and kept working, teasing him, his cock throbbing in my mouth, his veins close to exploding. I licked his balls and he shivered. He was so close I thought he'd pop if I licked him one more time.

The need to come up for air was strong, but not as strong as the urge to tell him how I felt. I let his cock fall from my mouth and looked up desperately.

"Miles," I whispered. "Stop running."

His hands grabbed my throat and I choked in surprise. He fucked my mouth. Carelessly. His cock filled me to the brim and I felt the tears coming, but I wouldn't look away from his eyes.

Look at me.

You're doing this to me.

But I'll take it if it means getting you.

I'll take it, Miles.

I felt a trickle of warmth down my throat and swallowed greedily when he let out a groan and let go of me, his cock slipping from my mouth with a wet pop as he stumbled backward. I coughed and sputtered as he reached for his jeans and pulled them up, his eyes desperately looking for an escape from the room. I saw the panic, recognized the fear in his gaze.

"Please," I begged him. "Stay, calm down."

"No." His movements were feverish. "I need to get away. Right now."

He moved past me, and my fingers tried to catch his but gripped at nothing instead. I crawled after him, but he was already at the front door, his steps so much longer than mine. Our eyes connected one last time, and

I licked my lips, trying to soundlessly beg him to stay.

"I'm sorry," he muttered, the little words so fucking broken it killed me inside.

He closed the door firmly on the way out and I let out a wail of frustration, the sound mixing in with his booming footsteps on the stairs.

Chapter 24

·MILES·

LA DOULEUR EXQUISE, PHRASE
The heart-wrenching pain of wanting the affection of someone unattainable.

I could barely remember getting home. All I knew was, suddenly I was in my own bathroom, splashing ice-cold water on my face and trying desperately to regain my focus.

My cock was still wet from her mouth, and my hands shook as I tried to wake myself up. I couldn't let myself do this. Fall completely in love with her. She would end up breaking me worse than I'd ever broken myself.

"Focus," I muttered to myself, my hand bracing the wall and my eyes finding my reflection in the mirror.

I looked like shit. My eyes were wide and panicked, the vein in my forehead painfully throbbing and my cock doing the same thing. I'd started coming when I'd pulled away from her, letting her taste only a bit before I left her on the floor like that. I hated myself for it, for leaving her as if she meant nothing when really she was all that mattered. But my self-preservation instincts were screaming at me to get away, to run. I couldn't let her hurt me. I knew that if she did, I'd never come out of it alive.

Somehow, I managed to stumble into the bedroom. I stared at the sheets, at the lipstick message she'd written in the frame.

There was no way I could sleep in there tonight.

It felt all too natural to take the other route, walk towards the small room and open the door to the trash, the smell, the fucking putrid reality of what my life was in the sensory overload of the room.

There was a sleeping bag on the floor. I didn't use it too often. Just on nights when it was especially bad.

I half-walked, half-crawled inside, inhaling the scent of the trash like a sweet welcome home. I crawled on the floor, my body rigid against the silky sleeping bag. I didn't even deserve that. Any kind of comfort was too much for me, almost like a punishment instead of being a reward.

The stench was almost too much, so I cracked the tiny window open. It was barred, thick iron rods protruding from the windowsill to the top of the dirty glass. It was a prison of my own making.

I laid down, refusing to cover up, even when my teeth chattered in the cold. I fell into a dreamless sleep, disturbed by horrible images of what would happen if I let Bebe get closer. I woke up in a sweat what felt like every ten minutes, but I still didn't leave the small room. I owed this to myself, to remind me of what a fuck-up I was, of how I'd never be anyone but the man from my past.

It felt like years had passed by the time dawn came, and I was convinced I'd aged a decade that night alone. My body felt broken and tired when I opened my eyes one final time, shivering in the cold and drenched in sweat from the dreamless terrors in my mind.

Somehow, I managed to drag myself out of the room. I shut the door firmly behind me and braced my back against the wood. I needed a bath like never before.

The walk to the bathroom was excruciating. I half-fell into the bath, clothes still on, and started pouring scalding hot water over my body. I had a bottle of bleach next to the bath, and I dumped what was left of it in the water. I'd never hated myself more than in that moment when I let my weakness cheat me of happiness yet again.

Heat and stinging greeted me as my clothes filled with water. My hands trembled and shook as I reached into the bathroom cabinet. A cigarette. I would kill for one now, but there were none left. I'd chain-smoked them all the last time I did this. Because try as I might to forget, this was my reality. No matter whether I had Bebe or not. And last night had just sealed my fate with her.

I knew what I had to do. Finally, it was becoming obvious just how dangerous my relationship with Bebe was, fucking me up in more ways than I cared to admit.

The only thing I could do was to distance myself.

And I knew exactly how to do that.

I mixed the bleach with bubble bath and sank into the warm, stinging comfort. The urge to breathe in the water and fill my lungs with it wasn't as strong as it usually was, and I knew it was because of Bebe. I would just have to learn how to handle it after I pushed her away. It would be hard to keep the feeling of liveliness she put in my blood when she wasn't around anymore.

I scrolled through my phone in the bath and put some arrangements into place. The only way to get over Bebe Hall was to let someone else have her. And what better distraction could I offer her but not one man, two instead, so she could pick and choose. Maybe it would ease the loneliness in my heart, and ease hers, too. I doubted the pain of letting her go would ever truly go away, but I didn't have a choice. To condemn her to a life with me would be selfish, and so painful for both of us. I couldn't ever see Bebe and me together in the long run. She'd get sick of me, and she'd leave, breaking my heart in the process.

A small voice in the back of my head was insisting that I was wrong. That I had to give her a chance, give *us* a chance, to see what came of it. But I was too scared to listen to it. I took the easy, painful way out.

Once I was done with my bath, I dried my burning skin and wrapped myself in a pristine bathrobe. T minus twelve hours and Bebe would be in the hands of two strangers. I would be watching them fuck her, my heart breaking, all the while knowing it was the right thing to do. I needed to push her far, far away – while I still could.

My phone rang shrilly as I got out of the bath, and I was surprised to find the name of Dr. Halen written across my screen.

I hadn't talked to her since our encounter in my apartment.

"Hello?" I answered the phone stiffly, unsure why she was calling me at 8 in the morning.

"Miles," she said, her voice streaked with worry. "I've been trying to reach you."

I thought of my forgotten laptop. The Skype meetings I'd missed. I felt ashamed.

"I'm sorry," I muttered.

"Miles, are you alright?" Her voice showed genuine concern. The brief flirtation from her in my apartment was now gone, replaced by professional worry. "I haven't heard from you in a while. I can tell something's off. Do you need anything?"

My mouth and mind fought over what to tell her.

"There's a girl," I finally managed to get out.

"Another one?"

"A special one," I clarified. "One I… care for."

"I see," she said simply. "Is there a problem with her?"

I thought about her question for a second, unsure on how to answer her.

"I'm scared," I finally confessed. It was so easy to tell her, even easier now that I didn't have the video option on my phone. It was just our voices, and her soothing, calming soprano was lulling me into a sense of safety. "I'm scared she's getting under my skin."

"Well, do you want her there?" Dr. Halen asked, and I hesitated again. "Miles," she went on. "Don't push her away. This could be good for you. Does she understand?"

A simple question, but loaded with so many other implications, secrets, and lies.

Did Bebe understand that I was broken? Sheltered? Vulnerable? That I was a shell of a man, my darkest secrets hidden underneath a shiny veneer of fake bravado and charm?

Maybe. But would she stick around if she knew the truth, that I could break any moment? I doubted it.

"I have to go," I said in a low voice. "Don't worry about me."

"Miles," she pleaded. "Please, let me–"

I didn't wait around to hear her concern. I just cut the call and sat down at my dining room table, finally risking a look across the street and into

Bebe's apartment. Her curtains were drawn, and I couldn't see a thing. I couldn't imagine how she was feeling. Maybe she was mad at me, or maybe she was trying desperately to understand. Maybe she would forgive me for this. But she most fucking definitely wouldn't forgive me for what I was going to do that night.

I sat at the table for hours, my mind whirring around the problems I was facing and my body unable to keep up. I felt crippled with worry, derailed by my thoughts of Bebe. Nothing could save us now. I'd already doomed us both.

When the clock indicated it was noon, I sent Bebe a text message.

Surprise for you tonight. Be ready at 9 p.m. sharp. There will be a knock on your door.

The reply came back so fast I was convinced she'd been waiting with her phone in her hand. It only sealed my belief that this had to be done. We were both in too deep, better to get out before either of us got hurt permanently.

I'll be ready. Can't wait to see you. xoxo

My heart broke for both of us this time. She was so naive, so fucking clueless of all the ways I was going to break her to make sure she didn't see me this way anymore. I'd already let things go too far. Now it was time to distance myself, detach myself from Bebe Hall. After tonight, I would no longer be in the equation. I would give her the night of her life without ever laying a finger on her, and then I'd wash my hands and move on. Back to my routine, back to regularly scheduled programming.

I couldn't bear to think of what would happen to me after Bebe. But I knew she could handle losing me. She wasn't as invested as I was yet.

What was going to happen after she moved on? Would we still be neighbors, or would the pain of seeing her apartment across the street from mine be too much to bear? Would I pretend it wasn't before I finally moved out, endured the annoyance of moving all my shit to a new place just so I could ease the pain of seeing her in the window and never getting to hold her? Was I being a selfish prick, looking out for myself by doing this, or was I trying to protect us both?

Only time would tell, but I knew it was what had to be done. Bebe would be better off without me, and I'd only have myself to blame for the pain I'd be in, not an innocent woman.

I wasn't looking forward to that night, but I knew it had to happen. And once it was over and done with, I'd finally be able to move the fuck on.

I would be a closed chapter in Bebe Hall's life, and she would be the girl that got away.

It was always supposed to be this way.

Because the monster never ends up with the princess.

Chapter 25

·BEBE·

ECCEDENTESIAST, NOUN
A person who fakes a smile.

The initial disappointment of Miles leaving my apartment was quelled the moment I got his text message. I'd been grinning to myself the entire day, getting ready and primping for whatever he had in store.

As it always happened, the minutes ticked by painfully slowly, and I was more impatient than ever waiting for the time to come.

What would he make me do? Would he finally sleep with me? Excitement made me shiver and adrenaline pumped through my veins when I thought about it. I was desperate for it, desperate for him.

By the time seven rolled around, I was ready. I'd taken special effort in every bit of my appearance, and I'd opened all the curtains to let Miles watch me as I waited for him. But I didn't even see a glimpse of him by the window. If he was at home, he was hiding from me.

I'd waxed, plucked and shaved everything below the eyebrows. My hair was a shiny, thick dark mane falling in perfect waves down my shoulders, and my eyes looked especially bright. Thankfully I still had a leftover tan from my last visit to the tanning salon, and I decided to wear a bright white babydoll to complement my complexion. On my feet, I wore sky-high pink heels. I looked innocent. Like the girl I used to be.

For the last two hours, I paced the room, hoping he would show up early. No such luck. The minutes ticked by even slower, painfully moving to the arranged time.

And then there it was, a single ring of my doorbell.

I ran to the front door and buzzed him in without checking to hear his voice. I was too nervous, my whole body trembling with fear as I waited to hear the sound of his footsteps on the stairway.

My legs barely managed to hold me up, and I shivered in front of the door, trying to prepare myself for whatever lay on the other side. Footsteps approaching. Fast, angry footsteps. There was an impatient knock, and then a man cleared his throat and it didn't sound like Miles.

Fuck. Fuck. Fuck.

Had he sent a guy over to fuck me?

I grabbed the door handle trying to steady myself. My heart was hammering in my chest and I felt dizzy.

Anger pumped through my veins, incomprehensible anger because he was fucking doing this to me. I wanted to be his, I wanted him to fuck me. Miles and nobody else. So what was he doing sending someone else over?

I yanked the door open and glared.

Two men.

Two men, one in a suit, one in jeans and a leather jacket. Both taller than me, both with arms that looked like they were going to hurt me like I'd never been hurt before, make me come so much I'd pass out from the feeling. I mewled when I saw them, a desperate little moan escaping my lips, but neither of them gave a shit.

The one that was suited up stepped inside while the other one closed the door.

And then they were on me, their hands all over me in what seemed like seconds, making me submit until I was a mess of moans and whispered begging, forced to my knees in the entryway, the men stripping before my eyes. I already felt the hot tears prickling, but I would never, ever let them fall. I wouldn't let Miles see how disappointed and hurt I was by what he was making me do. I would never let him know much this betrayal hurt. How badly I wished the two men were him.

"Up," the suited man barked at me, and I stood up, my knees nearly giving out.

"You call me *Sir*," the guy with the jacket said, taking a step closer to me and wrapping a hand around my throat. "You call *him* Daddy. Nod if you understand."

I nodded, barely able to make my head move before a little sob tore its way from my lips. Only now did I notice what they looked like, the sharp differences between them aside from the way they were dressed.

They were both only wearing boxers now. The guy I was supposed to call Daddy was older, around forty or so, but so in shape, he put me to shame. His body was covered with a thin layer of dark hair mixing with gray, and he had salt and pepper hair that made me go wild. He was handsome, in an old movie star kind of way, and I bit my lip as I stared at him before shifting my attention to the younger guy.

He was taller, though not as tall as Miles. His hair was light and he had a faint hint of stubble whereas his older friend had a beard. The younger guy, the Sir, was toned and lean but didn't have a six-pack like the other one. But he was still delicious, and what should've frightened me the most was the detached, almost sadistic look in his eyes. But it didn't. In fact, it only served to make me wetter.

"Pretty little girl," Sir smiled at me while Daddy grabbed a handful of my hair.

I struggled, but it was futile. Between them, they did an easy job of dragging me into the living room and pressing my naked, shaking body against the window.

I could see Miles in his apartment, shirtless, his expression rigid.

You're fucking hurting me, I wanted to scream, but I couldn't bear the words, so I kept my mouth shut in a pout, just glaring at Miles as the two men handled me.

They treated me like a little fuckdoll, doing to me as they pleased and tossing me between them like I was a toy. I felt the tears hotter than ever, threatening to fall any second now and humiliate me in front of the three of them. God, I wanted to fucking scream with the injustice of it all, with how badly I wanted it to be Miles instead. But I didn't have a chance to complain because Daddy approached me with a little pink ball gag and easily fastened it around my cheeks while Sir held my arms behind my back.

I fought back, but not as hard as I could have, which made me blush fiercely. But it got me so wet, having them there, putting the ball gag on me while Miles watched, I was dripping down my legs like a desperate little whore fucked up on God knows what, just desperate for another dose of dick inside her slutty holes.

I mumbled around the gag, and the men laughed in my face, making the first tear slip down my cheek.

"Awwww," Sir said, making me arch my back and grabbing my neck with one hand, forcing me to look over my back and up at him. "Already crying, whore? There's so much more you have to go through before we'll let you go… Maybe you're not as fucked-up as we've been told."

I whimpered in protest as Daddy went behind my back. They manhandled me onto the couch, and one held me down while the other tied my wrists together with silk ties. I was crying now, fresh tears falling freely as I glared at Miles through the window. He was going to pay for this. When I next saw him, I would hurt him. Physically and emotionally. I would fuck him up. It was already decided. Miles was going to hurt just as much as I was hurting now.

But looking into his eyes across the street didn't show any regret in his gaze at all. In fact, the bastard looked damn well pleased with himself, his face full-on concentration, his fist probably working his dick desperately while he watched me get treated like nothing but a fucktoy, three holes to dump cum in and nothing else.

"We heard you've never had two cocks," Daddy whispered in my ear, and my skin erupted in goosebumps.

"Look at her needy fucking cunt," Sir laughed. "Look at her. She's going to squirt all over us if you don't stop."

One of them reached between my legs and toyed with my clit, and I howled like I was in physical pain. And I fucking was, torn between reacting to their tormenting and keeping my eyes on Miles to punish him for what he was doing to me, let him know exactly how much it hurt that he would do this to me, right now, right on this fucking day that was supposed to be special. And he kept staring back, those eyes focused and strained, his cock probably close to fucking dripping. I wanted to fucking kill him. I wanted to fucking end him.

I watched them both put on condoms, jerking their cocks in front of me, teasing me endlessly.

Thank you, God, thank you, thank you, I prayed in my mind. *Don't let them fuck me bare, don't let them, I want Miles, only Miles God, please only Miles bare like that.*

And then, just like that, a cock was forcing its way into my cunt, one inch at a time. I moaned around the ball gag as Sir came in front of me, grabbing me by the cheeks and slapping me across the face so hard I saw stars.

"You better start moaning like the whore you are," he said. "Because I want to get off to you moaning first, crying second, and screaming third."

I cried. Fuck, how I cried.

Sir got on the couch below me, and I felt Daddy pull out with a popping sound so embarrassing they both laughed in my face.

"Come on, slut," Sir said. "Get her on top of me, I want to feel that cunt milking my cock. Wonder if you're as tight as I pictured you, or if you've already been properly stretched out for me..."

Daddy lowered me, whispering sweet things in my ear as my pussy sank onto the stranger's cock, filling me up so fast I bit into the ball gag and tried to get away. But Daddy grabbed me by the shoulders and made me sit on Sir's cock, all the way down until I felt him go past my cervix and I couldn't let out another muffled scream, just barely audible whimpers, and little sobs because it hurt so fucking good.

I couldn't keep eye contact with Miles, my eyes were too filled with tears, so I just kept glancing at him every once in a while, trying to see him through the mess in my eyes.

Daddy was behind me, and I felt the tip of his dick pressing urgently against my asshole, forcing its way in even if I didn't want to let him. I hoped he would be gentler, that maybe he would take mercy on me and stop this torture, stop me from coming all over them. But he showed no intention of doing that. He pushed so hard it fucking hurt. Fucking burned as he filled me, and I bit down on the gag, tears spilling down my cheeks.

And then they were both inside me, and I couldn't stop gasping from the overwhelming sensation of having both holes filled, my mouth stretched open by the ball gag, stretched so much I was sure at least one hole would tear if they pushed it farther.

"Good girl," Daddy murmured in my ear. "Aren't you a good little girl…"

They started moving, two bodies I didn't know, pushing inside me and forcing their cocks all the way. I tried to stop the orgasm that was brewing in my center, but I didn't last long. In a few minutes, my whimpers turned into cries and I was coming, my pussy spurting juice all over Sir, my ass working Daddy's cock while my mouth drooled all over that fucking ball gag. I cried not just because it hurt, but because it was fucking humiliating being used like that. Because for once, I'd let myself believe a man actually gave a shit about me, wanted me for who I was and not for my body. But Miles had proved exactly the opposite by sending these two men into my apartment. And now, I was going to prove to him just what a whore I was. I couldn't wait for him to see, and I fucking hoped he was glued to his window.

I let them fuck me. Not just that, I let them take advantage of me like that was the only thing I was good for.

They ravaged my body, not giving a shit whether I couldn't walk once they were done, because why would they? They'd get to leave the second they were done with me, and I'd be left to pick up the pieces by myself, just like I always was. So I just let them do it, coming all over them, part of me hoping they'd be done soon, and the other part, the fucked up one, hoping they'd take their sweet time with my holes.

And they did. They never stopped once, twisting me this way and that and just fucking, fucking, fucking me into a sorry, wet mess.

I stopped counting the seconds when I couldn't lift my head up anymore, too messed up to see whether Miles was still watching. I didn't even care anymore. He'd gotten what he wanted, and now he was probably done with me, just like everybody else.

They kept going and going and going, my body starting to hurt and crumble under their weight. I wanted to scream, but my mouth wouldn't let me.

They hauled me to my feet and pressed me against the window, and the glass fogged up when I breathed on it. I managed to look across the street. But Miles was gone.

Chapter 26

·MILES·

POSSESS, VERB
To have and to hold as property.

I couldn't stand the sight of her with another man for one more second. Pulling up my tracksuit, I didn't even pause to grab my keys or my phone on my way out, leaving the front door wide open. I took the steps two at a time, rushing so much I didn't even have time to glance at the doorman on my way out. I stormed down the street and barged past the doorman in her building. The stairs made me breathe angrily, rage seeping through every pore of my body.

Fuck. No. Bebe was mine. No way was I letting anyone touch her. Never again. Never. Ever.

Her front door was unlocked, but I still opened it with my shoulder, the wood bumping into the wall, plaster falling down in a thick, dusty cloud.

"Get the fuck OFF!" I screamed as I made my way into the living room, my hands shaking.

I felt every vein in my body throbbing. Anger making me an ugly, deranged monster that cared about nothing else but my woman. I needed her in my arms. *My* mouth on her. *My* cock in her tight little cunt. *My* hands all over that sweet little body. *Me*, fucking *me* tasting that sugar. Nobody else. Never fucking EVER again.

My eyes locked with Bebe's the second I walked into the room. She looked like hell and sex in that fucking outfit. Her eyes were red-rimmed and accusatory, and her mouth was trembling.

I went for the older guy first because I wanted to take my fucking time with the other prick.

My fist smashed into his face and I heard the sickening crunch of bone as the guy screamed.

"What the fuck," he roared, while the younger dude only laughed, still fucking my girl.

I saw red. Not just a mist, I saw their fucking thick, dark blood spilling all over the floor. I wanted to kill, maim, hurt, torture. I wanted to rip their sorry dicks off and stuff them in each other's mouths. My legs kept kicking, and my arms kept on punching with all the rage I had in my body. I heard Bebe's screams and saw the blood pool under the guy.

Turning to the other one, I knew I'd wipe that smirk off his face for good. He was a prick, fucking enjoying this, loving that Bebe was hurting. But I couldn't even look at her, too disgusted with myself to face her just yet. I was going to pay her back though, and I'd kill the two men for what they'd done to her.

My fists pummeled the guy against the wall. He put up a fight, but his punches landed on rock-hard abs and thick muscle throbbing with the need for revenge.

"Now you die," I growled in his face, and kept on punching.

His blood sprayed my skin, but it wasn't enough. I wanted him to understand suffering like he never had before. I kept punching, hitting, snarling, screaming. I beat him to a pulp until his nose was broken and his forehead bore a big red gash.

"Miles!"

I heard Bebe calling my name from afar, but I couldn't break out of it. All I knew was pain, hurting, hurting, fucking hurting *him* until it stopped hurting *me*. I held the bastard against the wall with one hand gripped around his throat and punched the fucker until his teeth broke and he gargled his own blood.

"Miles, please, Miles, I love you, Miles, don't, Miles, don't baby, don't…"

I dropped my hands and stumbled back, and heard the front door opening as the other prick ran outside. I watched the mess that used to be a man groan and sigh and cry out in pain, but I felt no fucking mercy for him. I'd seen the way he treated my girl and the moment I locked eyes with him I understood what he was. A deranged, damaged man just like me, but so different, so much more dangerous. He was a sick as fuck sociopath, who would've come back and hurt her when I wasn't looking. I saw it from the glint in his eyes, a look I remembered from the last time I'd been in an institution. I saw the darkness and the pain, but whereas mine turned inward, his was angry, vengeful, and thirsty for the pain of others.

"You're never coming back here," I snarled at the bloody mess on the floor. "I never want to see you again, you worthless piece of shit."

He stood up and his knees buckled as he grabbed his jacket.

"You're a fucking psychopath," he growled at me, and I stared him down until he stumbled out of Bebe's apartment, wishing I'd kicked his ass out myself.

And then it was just us, and I couldn't even look at her.

Couldn't bear the thought of her being angry with me, of not understanding why I'd done this. And most of all, I couldn't bear to think that maybe, just maybe, my Bebe had enjoyed it.

Because the jealousy would eat me up alive.

I heard it what felt like minutes after. The soft sound of sobs, of her crying like a little girl, so vulnerable, so fucking sweet it threatened to tear me in half. I was next to her in seconds, my arms wrapping around her shoulders as I held her, murmuring into her hair, trying to calm her down. All my fears of germs, of the unknown, were forgotten. All that mattered was the scared little girl in my embrace, shaking, trembling like a fucking leaf because of something I'd put her through. I'd never hated myself more than in that moment, but I also knew I had to help her before I started to worry about myself.

"Bebe," I whispered into her hair. "I'm so sorry. I'm so fucking sorry."

She started grasping at the fabric of my shirt between her little fingers, practically climbing on top of me in an effort to get closer. Her breaths were uneven and raspy, and she was still crying. For every tear that fell down her smooth cheeks, I hated myself a little bit more.

"Talk to me," I begged her as she settled on my lap. "Just talk to me, Bebe, I'm begging you."

She grabbed my chin with purpose and twisted my face towards her own. I shut my eyes tightly, still unable to look her in the eye.

"Look at me," she got out, hiccuping through the tears.

I forced my eyes open and looked into hers. She was so painfully beautiful, innocent of everything my sick mind had accused her of. I hated myself for it, and I knew it would be a long time before I could forgive myself for what I'd put her through.

"I'm sorry," I said, and she shook her head, swallowing tears. Biting back the pain. Just for me.

"Get it out of me," she whispered, and I stared at her, trying to understand what she meant.

"What, sugar?" I asked her roughly. "Get what out?"

"The..." She swallowed thickly, looking so completely broken I felt my devastation to my core. "The cum. They fucked me, both of them. I feel d-dirty."

I let go of her and punched a wall repeatedly. Once, twice, three times until the wall was sprayed with my blood and I groaned at the pain in my knuckles.

"Miles!" Bebe's screams finally got to me, and I walked over to her with fast, angry steps.

She shrank away from me, but I grabbed her gently, pulling her into my lap and walking down the hallway. She sobbed against my chest, her arms wrapping around my neck in relief when she realized I wasn't going to hurt her. Fucking shit, she really thought I could've done that. I was madly in love with her, and she thought I wanted to get her hurt. It was all my fucking fault.

When I finally found it, I walked into the bathroom, a beautiful room with white and mother of pearl tiles. I walked her into the huge shower and didn't let go as I turned on the water above us. It came in a luxurious warm spray, making my clothes stick to my body and stopping Bebe's naked body from shivering against me.

"It's okay," I whispered into her ear, water falling all over us. "It's okay, sugar."

I kneeled with her in my arms and let her down gently on the tile. She sobbed softly as I let the water rain on us.

"Open your legs," I whispered, and she let her legs fall open lifelessly like she was nothing but a doll following instructions now.

My heart broke for her, and I cursed myself a thousand times inside my raging head.

I reached for a loofah, lathering it thick with soap that smelled like strawberries and Bebe. Placing my hand between her legs, I started washing her slowly, my motions soothing and sweet. I focused my eyes on her because I couldn't bear looking down. Couldn't fucking think of anything but her eyes, those beautiful, beautiful eyes blinking back tears and smiling into mine.

"It's okay," I promised her again, and she nodded, sniffing a little. "I'll make it all okay, Bebe."

I was going to kill them both for fucking her bare. I didn't even dare ask her whether she was on protection. I knew I'd have to, but I swallowed the question every single time it came up.

The water was nice and hot as it washed over us, soothing away the pain and the worst of Bebe's weeping. I washed her so carefully, like she was made of porcelain and one wrong move would shatter her to pieces. I knew just how close to the truth that was.

"Bebe," I said gently, tipping her chin back and smoothing the loofah over her toned stomach, to her tits and her aching neck. The fingerprints of one of the jerks were still on her throat, red and angry. They would probably bruise, and every time I looked at them, I'd hate myself a little bit more. "Bebe, look at me. Let me see those eyes."

She raised a weary, tired look up into my gaze. I smiled at her, and she returned a faint, tired smile.

"I'm sorry, Bebe," I told her roughly. "I'm sorry for what I put you through, I should never have done that, I just…"

"Just what?" she whispered.

Her eyes looked at me with accusations flying. I knew she was angry, and she had every right to be. I just sacrificed her body to my own insecurities, like she was a cheap fucking whore.

"Just know I…" I swallowed. Couldn't get the words out. "I was ashamed. Scared of our… connection. Scared of you. I wanted to detach myself."

"How did that work out?" she sounded bitter and tired, and I couldn't blame her.

"It didn't," I admitted. "Because I fucked you up when all I wanted to do was push you away."

"Why?" she sniffled. "Why did you try to get rid of me? You're just like everybody else. Every single person who doesn't even want me…"

"I'm not," I said, grabbing her gently and pulling her closer. "I'm not, Bebe, I…"

"Say it then," she taunted me, her eyes boring into mine. "Say it, you fucking coward."

"I just… I…" I gasped for air.

The walls were closing in. The water switched between being boiling hot and ice cold, at first burning my back and then freezing the wounds. I could barely breathe. Could barely keep my eyes open. It was limbo, horrible, hellish limbo and I was caught without a way out, the only solution so unbelievably hard I couldn't physically imagine doing it.

"I do," I whispered. "You know, Bebe…"

"Say it!" She smashed her little fist into my shoulder and I was suddenly glad the shower was running because I was crying like a pussy. "Say it, you fucking jackass!"

I couldn't.

She tore out of my hands and stormed out of the shower, leaving me in there broken. I stumbled after her, my wet clothes running everywhere, puddles gathering around my feet.

"Bebe!" I snarled, grabbing her waist and pulling her against me.

"What?" she growled. "What the fuck do you want? You won't even admit it, you selfish bastard…"

"I…" Once again, my words froze in my throat. "Bebe, please."

My lips sought out hers, but she pushed me away.

"Bebe," I growled back. "Stop. Fucking. Fighting. Me. You're mine."

"I'm not!" she screamed.

"You are!" I yelled. "Mine. Mine. Fucking. MINE!"

She howled and I bit her lips, kissing her so fiercely she crumpled in my arms, desperately pressing her lips to mine, offering herself to me.

"Tell me," I ordered her. "Tell me you're mine."

"Yours," she whispered hoarsely.

"All mine," I corrected her. "I don't fucking share you."

"But you–"

"I. Don't…" I bit her throat and she cried out. Her body spasmed. She was fucking coming. My fingers fought their way to her pussy and I pulled the orgasm out of her trembling cunt. "…Share. YOU!"

Chapter 27

·BEBE·

PROTÉGÉ-MOI, FRENCH
Protect me.

His eyes on mine were so savage it sent icy shivers down my spine. He was poised like an animal, his arms wrapped around me in that one tense moment before he attacked. Our eyes danced over one another, caught in a dance I didn't try to understand. It was a battle now, but it was futile because we both wanted the same thing. I wanted him inside me, and he wanted to own me. It was inevitable.

"Do it," I growled at him, my voice raspy with need as my eyes zeroed in on his. "Just fucking do it, Miles."

He let out a low groan before he dipped his head, making his lips meet my own. I opened up in anticipation, desperate for another taste of him. He kissed me like I belonged to him completely. Like I didn't have a choice in the world about it. I was his property, and I would be, as long as he wanted me to stay in his arms.

My body responded to his with wildness I didn't know I possessed. My arms were raised in seconds, my fingers twining their way into his hair, and I yanked him down against my neck, making him kiss me savagely and leaving bruises in his wake.

"Harder," I bit into his neck. "Fucking do it harder."

His teeth sank into my skin and I howled underneath him, my body thrashing and trying to get him off me instinctively. The second I could, I clung to him again, desperate hands moving against him, clawing, grasping, claiming Miles Reilly for myself.

I felt him grazing my skin, but he wouldn't do what I wanted, and I yelped in frustration as I was picked up from the floor and carried into the bedroom.

We were both soaking wet, our bodies dripping with water from our shower together. I wanted desperately to pull him on top of me, but he had all the control in his hands. He tossed me on the bed, and I landed with a desperate moan, the bed molding to fit my body. I grabbed the sheets behind me, crawling away from him.

"T-take your clothes o-o-ff," I managed to get out, my teeth chattering against the sudden cold of the room on my naked, wet body. "M-Miles. Off. N-now."

He reached for his shirt and ripped it across his chest, my pupils dilating to black holes as I watched. His pants were next, and he got rid of them angrily like they were personally offending him for still separating us. I watched his body, the ink mixing with water, muscles bleeding into bones. He was incredible, magnificent. He was a wet dream, but he was also the salvation, the angel I'd prayed for every night. I stared at him like he was a god. My mind didn't understand what my body knew, and I panicked as I arched my back for him, desperate for him to grab me.

He did, his fingers bruising my ribs as he wrapped them around me, holding me up like he'd been the whole time. His thumbs caressed the skin under my breasts, and one slipped upwards to tease my nipple into a point. I exhaled in exhaustion, the simple touch almost too much for me to take.

"Miles," I breathed, realizing he hadn't said a word in what felt like hours. "Miles, talk to me."

"Talk to you?" he growled, letting go of me with one hand.

I gasped in fear of falling but he held me easily with one arm, raising me to him and inhaling the scent of my skin above my navel. He was an addict, a man possessed, free at last with his obsession. And I couldn't get enough of it, of him. I wanted things so cruel and twisted I couldn't even admit them to myself. He made me want the danger, the darkness. He made it so fucking clear what was out there.

Dragons. Fire-breathing, ash-inducing, flying fucking beasts who would destroy my life if I took a single step off the beaten path.

No, I had to keep doing this, one foot in front of the other, walking to my goal, slowly, slowly. Forget Posy, move on. Forget Posy, move on.

And suddenly I was only on the second step, an infinite number of others leading upwards, and I was falling, falling...

But Miles caught me. Easily. Like it was the simplest thing in the world.

"Tell me I'm yours," I begged him, breathless from the dreamlike thought. "Tell me I'm yours again."

"You are," he groaned, and then his hands were on his cock, and he was holding me above the bed, pushing me down on his hardness.

"Let go," I whispered, fighting him for show. "I wanna do it."

"No," he whispered, his voice almost in a trance. "Need to watch."

We both looked between our legs, and I squirmed when he placed his cock at my entrance. I spasmed away, and a thick string of precum clung to me as he slipped away. I cried out at the sight, the lust I was feeling overwhelming every other emotion in my body. I was a desperate, needy little fuck-doll and I didn't care about anything else but what the man before me had between his legs.

"Fuck," I begged. "Fuck it."

He did.

I sank on his cock with a shiver of relief and Miles' filthy mouth spewing curse words as he lowered me down, all the way down until I felt him in my belly.

"Miles!" I cried out, my fists slamming his chest. "Miles, too deep!"

"Shut up," he groaned, his free hand grabbing both of my wrists. "Shut the fuck up, sugar. Look at me, look right the fuck at me."

Our eyes connected, so intense I felt tears slipping down my face. His eyes were glassy, and in that one moment, I understood what it meant to be him, to be this broken, to be this hurt, and I wept for him.

"It's okay," he whispered, pulling out of me so suddenly I could barely catch my breath. "It's okay, sugar, it's okay baby, don't worry, it's okay…"

"Don't," I mumbled. "Don't stop."

"Never," he promised and started thrusting inside me.

I thought the pain would split me open, and I thought his groans would make me squirt before he spurted inside me.

I felt myself coming as he fucked me so absolutely relentlessly I left bloody trails down his back.

I felt myself coming again when he laid me down so gently. He grabbed my throat and I was already close, but when he held me, the pure insanity of it took over my body. His grip was firm, his fingers just a little too tight, but his thumb gently traced my bottom lip as he punished my pussy. His eyes were on mine, in my head, in my soul. He fucked me like he'd known me for centuries.

The tears were spilling but Miles kept fucking, and I kept letting go for him until my body started going limp, my eyes threatening to shut completely and my legs kicking aimlessly at the bedsheets.

"Oh my God," I whispered, my words jumbled and delirious. "Please, enough."

"Not enough," he growled. "Not enough!"

"When?" I begged tearfully. "When?"

"When. It's. All. Gone."

He looked possessed. Obsessed. He looked crazy, and I was more in love with him than I'd ever been with myself, with Posy, with God, with anyone alive or dead.

"Miles," I whispered. "It's gone. It's gone. I'm yours."

"Not until you take it," he groaned, licking my throat.

"So do it," I begged. "Come inside me, fuck me full Miles, please…"

He stopped thrusting, his body a statue above mine. I felt his hair, wet from the shower, dripping on my heated skin. He only seemed to just realize he was really fucking doing this, after what those two jerks had done to me.

A smile lit up his face, big, fucking cocky.

"Mine," he growled again, and then his body gave into mine, and he braced the headboard as he filled me up, my body reacting to his with such intensity he had to hold me down so I wouldn't climb all over him.

I felt him coming, not spraying me but leaking, fucking leaking into me so painfully slowly I wanted to scream. But I took it, and a laugh escaped my lips when I came as he did, making him bite my throat in a possessive rage like a filthy fucking animal.

He rolled to the side, taking my body with his, and I whimpered when I landed on top of him, my lips finding his for comfort. He kissed me with his hands clasped on the small of my back, and he told me what I so desperately needed to hear.

"I'm in fucking love with you, sugar."

Whispered words, a lover's promise so sweet in my ear I melted to his touch, kissed him all over as he laughed, and I felt his essence running out between my legs, all over him. I was in love, so fucking in love I couldn't see anything but him, my Miles, my perfect, beautifully broken Miles. He was all I'd ever wanted.

"Hold me," I begged him, and he pressed me closer to himself, his still hard, dripping cock a firm wedge between us.

He laughed nervously and I settled into his embrace, wild happiness making my mind and my heart race. Lying in his arms felt incredible, as amazing as I had known it would be all along, but the surprise was what came after.

The fact that I didn't want to move, not a single inch, not a fraction of one. I couldn't leave now, not like every other time when I was done the second they were. Now, I wanted to stay. Now, I couldn't do another thing than settle in his arms. Let him hold me. Let him take care of the husk that was left of the body he'd used, fucked and loved like nobody else before him.

I put my hands under my chin and he toyed with them as we stared at one another.

"Aren't you scared?" I whispered, still a little out of breath.

"Yeah," he muttered, and only then, I noticed the light tremble of his capable fingers. "Of course I'm scared."

"Don't let go," I muttered before I could stop myself, my fingers wrapping around his, my eyes begging him to understand what I needed so badly. "Don't let go of me now, please."

He stroked my hair, his smile so much gentler than his thrusts had been.

"Never," he promised me, the word as ominous and menacing as it was erotic.

Maybe that was when I should have been the most afraid.

Because the moment I fell in love with him, I knew he was a stranger. A dangerous creature I barely understood and who would never bare himself to me completely, leaving me guessing for the rest of the time I spent with him.

And now, he felt the same for me. And just like he'd said, he wasn't going to let go anytime soon. I just wasn't sure how dangerous that made him.

But in that moment, I didn't care, either.

All that mattered was his heartbeat underneath my ear. The way he held onto me like I mattered more than anything else in his life. More than he did. He'd protect me from the dragons.

But would he protect me from himself?

Chapter 28

·MILES·

CAIM, NOUN
Sanctuary.

Lying in bed together felt like the most natural thing in the world. The shape of Bebe's body against mine felt familiar yet strange, and I loved the way her tight, supple skin felt against my own. It was a revelation, one I'd spent years upon years walking away from, but now I couldn't get enough.

I wanted to inhale her scent like a drug. Fill my nostrils with the sweetness of my girl. Fill my mouth with her syrupy taste and taste the sweetness of her full, pouty lips until I was punch-drunk on them.

"Don't leave," she whispered to me, settling into my embrace. "Please, I… I know you have to go, but try and stay with me, please."

"I'm not leaving," I promised. "Not a chance in fucking hell, sugar. I'm going to sleep with you tonight."

Somehow, I even believed myself, knowing that I was telling her the truth. I pulled her in closer and she arched her back, her ass against my crotch making me hard as a rock like so many times before. She giggled when she felt it, wiggling her ass all over my lap while I groaned and pulled her even closer.

"Bebe," I said softly. "I want to know more."

"What do you want to know?"

"You…" I sighed. "I just want to know so much more about you."

"You think I've been hiding things?" Her breath was soft, sweet against my fingers.

I turned her around, so she was facing me, her naked body molding mine as perfectly as a piece of the same puzzle. She held onto me, and I let my shaky fingers loose in her hair, tangling in the strands and tugging gently on her beautiful locks. I never wanted to leave. Didn't even give a shit about all the usual stuff that should've been worrying me at that point. All that mattered was Bebe, and this moment, and as many more stolen ones as I could fit into my day – and night. I'd stay awake if it meant watching her, being near her.

"No," I exhaled.

"You're lying," she accused, trying to pull away.

My brow furrowed, and I didn't let go as I leaned closer, whispering in her ear, "Haven't you been hiding things, sugar? All those things you thought were too much for me?"

"I guess," she whispered.

"So, tell me. Tell me everything."

"I don't know where to start," she said weakly.

"Start at the beginning," I said. "Tell me about your childhood."

She smiled shyly at me, but it took her several moments before she could go on. Her eyes were red-rimmed before she even started speaking.

"I was happy," she confessed. "Really, really happy. I had an amazing childhood. I was such a happy little girl."

"Your parents, were they together?" I asked her.

"Yeah," she nodded. "They've been together for over twenty-five years now. My mom had me quite young, but her family didn't really agree. My mom's Tricia Wellstone."

I gave her a blank stare and she got up on her elbows and laughed incredulously.

"Don't tell me you don't know her?" she asked, and I shrugged apologetically.

"I'm sorry if I should, I guess I prefer to keep myself out of the public eye," I admitted. "And I'm not really the type to read tabloids, either."

"So, you're just assuming she's some kind of rich socialite?" Bebe asked, her eyes sparkling.

I fiddled with the duvet uncomfortably when she giggled and fell back into my arms, playfully pulling me down and kissing me deeply. I got lost in her sweetness once again, letting myself fall for everything she stood for, so very uniquely Bebe. I couldn't get enough of her, but she wouldn't let me hold her back after we'd kissed.

"Am I wrong?" I asked her cheekily, and she stuck her tongue out at me.

"No," she admitted. "She was a socialite. She was an it girl in the eighties, and she'd be more than proud to tell you that as well. Her family is super, super wealthy… it's old money. The Wellstone family are one of the founders of their city. Our lineage goes way back."

"Impressive," I told her. "But I get the feeling you're not really in touch with them?"

"No," she winced, a barely visible sign of uncomfortableness that I almost missed in the dimly lit room.

It was now fully dark outside. I couldn't remember the last time I'd spent the night in someone else's room, slept over in an apartment other than mine. It seemed almost incomprehensible that I was really doing it, being here in Bebe's bed and not giving it a second thought. There was nowhere I would've rather been.

"What about your dad?" I asked, and she gave me a bright smile.

"Dad is a lot like me," she told me, a hint of love in her voice. She was obviously a daddy's girl, and it brought a smile to my lips when I thought of her as a young girl with her father. I wondered whether I'd ever get to meet him.

"He started his company from nothing," she went on. "He used some of Mom's savings… She invested in him, like she always says, but her family never forgave her for using her trust fund, not even though Dad's company turns over seventeen million yearly."

My eyes widened at the size of the huge sum, but I didn't comment on it. Of course, I should have known Bebe was well off. She didn't just get an apartment like this from nothing, and she was always wearing expensive clothes – and lingerie. The money had to be coming from somewhere, though I didn't want to be rude and assume.

"Dad's family was really small." She twirled a strand of hair around her finger. "My last grandma died a few years ago, but we were never really close. So it was mostly just my parents and me."

I was itching to ask about them, but I made myself change the subject. I wondered if I'd ever get to meet the people who had Bebe, who made her into the amazing girl she was now.

"What happened later? When you were older?"

"I got bullied," she shrugged. "Like, a lot. Throughout primary school and high school."

"What?" I was genuinely surprised. "How could anyone bully you?"

I let out a small chuckle, but she glared at me and the laughter caught in my throat.

"I... I wasn't always like this," she admitted in a shaky voice. "I was a different girl back then. Vulnerable. I had braces, ratty hair, acne... No friends. Absolutely no one but my parents."

"And then?" I asked.

"And then they came along," she winced at the next part of her story. "Arden and Posy."

My heart pounded at the mention of those names. One of the girls, I already knew – the other remained a mystery.

"They were totally different, but from wealthy families just like me," she explained. "I'd gotten rid of my braces and breakouts, gotten a bit of a makeover thanks to Dad's publicist. I still don't know whether it was the worst or the best thing to happen to me. But it was enough for them to notice me at the university."

"What did you study?" I asked. I had Art History in mind for her, or maybe English Literature.

"Undeclared," she shrugged, giving me a shy smile. "I didn't really finish. I went for three years but barely passed a few exams. All I did was go out with the girls... It was all that mattered. Being *someone*, you know? Feeling like I belonged."

"With Arden and... Posy?" I asked, and she nodded.

"They were so glamorous. A year older, living off their trust funds, so I took advantage of my own too. My parents trusted me, there was no reason for them not to, so I just…" She swallowed the lump in her throat. "I just got this apartment and moved in. Posy died three months afterward."

I stared at her, my fingers gently caressing her cheek. I didn't know what to say. I couldn't deal with my own pain, let alone someone else's. But still, I hoped my gentle touch was enough to show Bebe that I felt for her, cared for her, maybe even…

"I loved her," she admitted, her eyes misty as she looked away from me. "I really did, she was such a special girl."

"I'm sorry, sugar," I whispered, leaving a fleeting kiss against her lips. "Did she…"

"She overdosed," Bebe choked out. "It was too much for her body, the pill she took."

All of it made sense then. Bebe's need to drink, to take stuff to drown her sorrows. I got it now, got the self-punishment and the hatred she felt for herself. She was punishing herself for what had happened with her best friend. But she would never replace Posy. She had earned her wings, and my girl was here to stay. The decision had been made without her help.

"Bebe," I said gently. "Please… What about your parents? Do they know?"

She shut her eyes tightly as a tear made its way down her cheek. I smoothed it away with my thumb, trailing it over her lips. She licked at it, tasting the saltiness of her own tears.

"They know," she said. "They called me when it happened, tried to come here, they were so sad. They loved Posy… they love Arden too. I wouldn't let them come."

"Have you…" I tried to make my words gentle, careful. "Have you seen them since it happened?"

"No," she shook her head weakly. "I think they've stopped trying, but the money is still coming... They must want to get rid of me so badly."

"No," I growled. "No, Bebe, you have it all wrong."

The shrill melody of a ringing phone interrupted us, and she sniffled before jumping out of bed like a flash and walking over to the coffee table. Her phone was flashing, and her brow furrowed as she picked it up and pressed it to her ear.

"What?" she asked stiffly. "I don't understand. I am listed? No one else?"

A long pause followed, but I was already out of bed and pulling my jeans on. I felt an emergency brewing, and I knew I'd want to help her.

"I'll be there," she muttered softly, cutting the call.

"What is it?" I asked, stepping closer to her.

She was shaking, her whole body trembling as I pulled her into my arms. I held her close, her sweet, tender body so fragile against mine it felt like a gust of wind would blow her over. I felt so fucking responsible in that moment, and my entire life, I'd been running from exactly that feeling – being responsible for someone other than myself.

But not with Bebe. I didn't feel the dread, the fear this time around. I just felt this overwhelming, crazy need to protect her. To make sure she was always okay and taken care of. There was nothing else I wanted anymore. Nothing in the world.

"Arden," she whispered.

"What?" I asked roughly, looking down into her scared eyes that looked like pools of darkness in the night. "Is she alright?"

Bebe shook her head, her bottom lip trembling.

"She's in the hospital," she choked out, and I held her closer, trying to hold in her sobs.

"We need to go," I told her roughly. "Do you know where?"

"St Paul's Memorial," she said, but pulled on my arm when I started walking. "But, Miles… You can't just leave. Right?"

I stepped closer to her. In her eyes, I recognized a person who had connected with me on the same level I'd connected with her. She'd been the one telling me her story, but through my actions that night, I had already revealed mine.

"I will go any-fucking-where for you," I told her roughly. "And no one in the fucking world will stop me."

Chapter 29

· BEBE ·

MOONSTRUCK, ADJECTIVE
Unable to think or act normally, especially because of being in love.

We managed to hail a cab in the street, a rare occurrence since it was Friday night and the city was littered with hammered students looking for a ride.

Miles looked enormous in the car, squashed in the backseat with me. The driver looked at us curiously as I barked the name of the hospital at him, but thankfully he didn't have any further questions. Seemingly sensing the urgency of the situation, he put his foot on the pedal and we were off.

I stared out of the window, my heart beating nervously as we wound our way through the busy streets. I felt Miles reach for me, but my hand remained limp and lifeless in my lap. The nurse I'd spoken to on the phone hadn't given me much information, just saying Arden had collapsed at home, and her boyfriend called 911. I was listed as her emergency contact, so they called me, not her parents.

I knew why. Arden's parents were older and quite traditional. They wanted to be heavily involved in her life, but Arden didn't want that, and she'd been pushing them away since before I'd met her. Her eating disorder had only managed to alienate them further, and I knew Arden had listed me as an emergency contact when this had happened before. She hadn't eaten, and she collapsed in a club while we were out once. It was fucking terrifying and I could still remember the crushing fear of not knowing whether she'd be alright.

The doctors chalked it up to dehydration and malnutrition, but Posy and I had talked them out of scheduling her a meeting with a therapist, saying she'd just gotten drunk on an empty stomach. But ever since that day, I regretted not telling the truth, and I'd asked myself countless times whether we'd made a mistake by keeping Arden's secret from the hospital staff – and her parents.

Just like me, Arden had almost completely cut off her parents, but after Posy passed away, she'd been in touch with them regularly. I resented the fact, still unsure whether it was because of my own insecurities or the deeply rooted jealousy I still had for both my friends.

When I'd been younger, I looked up to them like so many other girls at our university. They felt so untouchable, so incredibly out of reach that I didn't even bother trying to get closer. But when they approached me, it felt like the sky was lower that night and I was a part of the starry map. They'd put me on the horizon, and they could take me off it just as easily.

I did my best to imitate them, with Posy being the ringleader and shepherding us all into the life so many girls dreamed of. Starving ourselves so we were bone thin, and could drink on empty stomachs to get smashed easily, we dressed in expensive clothes and got paid to appear in the new nightclubs dotted around the city. As soon as word got out about us being there, the club was the new it place to be.

And now, there were only two of us left, and we were both in a fucking state.

I squeezed Miles' hand and risked a look at him. He had a smile on his face, encouraging but not insensitive, and he was so painfully handsome it made my heart beat a little bit faster. I was still terrified, so very afraid of him just walking out on me or finally coming to his senses and realizing I was not the girl he wanted me to be. But as the seconds and the minutes passed, he convinced me that he cared about the real me, and that was the reason he stayed.

Imagining how difficult the trip must've been for him felt impossible, but I felt the faint tremor of his hand as he wrapped his fingers around mine. Trying to comfort him, I let my own hand touch his, my fingers sliding along his knuckles gently. The events of the past day were a whirlwind in my mind, and it felt almost impossible to think about everything that had happened. I couldn't even do it, my head aching at the thought of those two men, and what they'd done to me.

Pulling my hand away sharply, I looked away, through the mirror. I felt Miles' searing gaze, but I refused to look back, instead focusing my attention on our surroundings. It was raining now, thick raindrops splattering against the windshield as we made our way downtown. The journey was agonizingly slow, and when the taxi driver turned around and proudly pointed at the clock, I couldn't believe we'd made it there in record time. It felt like a century had passed since I'd sat down in the car.

Miles paid for the ride and I gave him a grateful smile before we raced up the steps and into the hospital. We were messily dressed, Miles in his jeans and T-shirt and me in a hastily-thrown on outfit and his hoodie on top. He must have been freezing, but he didn't say a word about it, just held my hand as we made our way into the building.

The ER waiting room was filled with people that only served to make my anxiety worse. People who were bleeding, screaming, shouting and complaining. People that scared me, because surely Arden couldn't belong here? She'd been almost better when I'd last seen her. Surely, she couldn't have relapsed so fast?

"Bebe!"

I turned in the direction of the voice. "Nick," I muttered, pulling Miles behind me as I rushed toward him.

Arden's would-be boyfriend looked completely different than I remembered him. I'd met him a bunch of times, purposely embarrassing him by pretending not to remember him and making him shake hands with me awkwardly while Posy erupted into a fit of giggles. But now, he looked much different than the guy I remembered, and the sight of him in the hospital made me think about how different my life was to Arden's now. She was starting to settle down, slowly easing herself off the party lifestyle and beginning to build a life of her own. And here I was, still stuck in the same old lifestyle, just with new people and a new flavor in my mouth every day.

Nick was tall, not as tall as Miles, but handsome nonetheless. He'd lost some weight since I'd last seen him, and it had done wonders for his confidence. He didn't even look away from my eyes as he came closer.

We finally met in the middle of the hallway, and Miles lingered awkwardly behind me while Nick and I stared each other down.

"Well?" I said. "She's okay, right?"

My heart pounded in fear.

"She's ok for now," he replied. "They're running some tests still. She asked for you."

"But she's ok?" I asked roughly, and he nodded, urging us to walk with him.

But I couldn't. I was frozen to the spot. "Ok," I whispered. "I guess... I guess we'll be going, then."

"What?" both Miles and Nick said at once, and I looked at the wall, at the ceiling, at the floor. At anything but their faces.

I didn't know how to tell them. How to admit that I wanted to be anywhere in the world but stuck in that hospital, with both of them judging me. That I wanted to bolt for the door and run as fast as I possibly could just to get away from this whole damn mess. Because I was a selfish mess myself, and I didn't deserve Arden. I never had. I'd always been a terrible friend.

"I really should go," I said again, turning around abruptly and making my way to the door.

Before I could take another step, a wall of muscle and ink blocked my way, and I looked up fearfully into Miles' eyes.

"No," he said sternly, and I choked out a gasp, trying to get past him. His hands were on mine and he pulled me in, holding me close. "Baby, no. I'll come with you. Please, she needs you."

"She was f-fine the last time," I said brokenly. "It was just d-dehydration..."

He took my hand and I followed him meekly back to where Nick was standing.

"Are we ready?" he asked, completely ignoring my meltdown. I was grateful to him for that.

Miles nodded, and we followed and made our way down the white hall, into a wing of the hospital that seemed nicer, better equipped. I had a sinking feeling that Arden's parents would be there, and the urge to get away was so strong I dug my nails into my palms to stop myself from running.

Finally, Nick stopped in front of a hospital room and gave me an encouraging smile.

"She's in there, her parents aren't here yet."

My heart sank in relief, but at the same time, I was scared about seeing my friend in this position. Alone. Vulnerable.

"Should I…" My words trailed off into nothing, but both Miles and Nick gave me encouraging smiles, urging me to step inside.

I swallowed my pride along with every instinct screaming in my head to get away, and I walked inside the room.

Arden's bed was the only one in the beautiful white room. It looked more like a hotel room than a hospital, the bed thick and plush with too many pillows to count, and pretty, calming artwork on the walls. My friend looked small amidst the sheets. She was pale, almost ghastly so, and she looked thin, like she hadn't looked in months.

"Arden," I croaked, and she turned her head to look at me.

Whatever I was expecting to find in her eyes wasn't there. Her gaze cut through me like a knife, but it softened the next second. We were just two lost girls in that moment, both struggling with the path we were supposed to take after what had happened to Posy – or rather, what she'd done to herself.

"H-how are you?" I asked, awkwardly approaching the bed laden with pillows.

There were already flowers on the little table by the window. Nick had obviously done a good job, better than me.

"I'm sorry I d-didn't bring anything," I said, and Arden smiled softly.

"You're stuttering," she pointed out the obvious and I blushed deeply, still under their influence. They were the cool girls and I was just an impostor, a girl trying to worm her way into their clique. "I used to be just like you, you know."

"You used to st-stutter?" I asked lamely, and she shook her head. Her hands looked so small in the hospital bed.

"Before Posy found me," she said. "I was just a wallflower. I often wondered whether that's what I was always meant to be."

"Arden..." I approached the bed, pulling up a chair and staring at her. I swallowed the lump in my throat, which wouldn't let me ask the next question but I forced it out nonetheless. "Why did this happen, Arden?"

"I didn't eat enough," she shrugged. "Just these past few days, I swear. I've been good otherwise."

"You know how much I care about y-you," I said.

"Do you?" Her gaze was searing. "Because lately, I don't feel like you do, Bee."

"I do," I said desperately. "I've just... I've been too preoccupied with myself. Not seeing anyone other than me. And I'm... I-I'm really s-s-sorry."

It was the hardest part to get out, the actual apology. It turned my mouth to sandpaper.

A silence fell upon the room and I struggled to make sense of things.

"I really want to make th-things right," I said. "I want to make sure you're okay. Th-that we both are. This c-can't fuck us over forever."

"I know," Arden sighed. "But we've been doing a damn fine job of letting it."

She looked away, and suddenly the sight of her in that hospital bed was too much – I wanted to be in there with her.

I kicked off my trainers and climbed into bed beside her. She didn't fight it, making space for me in the sheets, and we hugged each other close.

It felt so oddly familiar I let myself remember the old times just for once.

Entangled limbs. Loud music. Whispered words, dirty as fuck.

I shook my head. Posy was fucking gone. And now it was just the two of us – survivors of the hurricane she put us through.

"Arden," I whispered, and she turned her head towards mine.

She was so beautiful it made me wonder how she never saw it when she looked in the mirror. Honey-kissed bronze hair, beautiful, big blue eyes. She was thin, too thin, medium height. She had killer style and a collection of heels I'd die for. We used to joke about whether Posy or I would inherit it, before… before it happened. Now, we were just two floating balloons, losing each other in the air. We had nothing to hold us together.

I tucked a strand of her hair behind her ear, and she let out a soft sigh when I did it.

"I miss you," I said softly. "I'm sorry I've pushed you away. You're so important to me… you're so special. I've been h-horrible. So self-involved. I've been trying to move past it, but…"

"I know," she admitted. "It's the same for me. Except I turned against myself… maybe you understand that too?"

We gave each other a knowing look. Of course she'd noticed my decisions getting worse and worse while her health deteriorated. We were both on our own path of self-destruction, and it needed to stop then and there.

"I'll be a better friend," I promised her. "I'll make sure you're okay."

"Okay," she whispered, her eyes flicking to the door.

It had a frosted glass panel, the shapes of the two men outside plain to see.

"Is that?" she asked, and I nodded, making her giggle. "He looks hot."

"Yeah," I muttered, biting my lip. "He's… something."

"Special," she finished for me, and I glared at her beaming face.

My fingers touched the tube going into her arm.

"Just some liquids," she promised me. "I'm dehydrated, and my blood sugar's low."

"Okay," I muttered. "But I'm not leaving until you do."

"Okay." Her eyelids were heavy.

"Do you want to sleep?" I asked softly, and she nodded, squeezing my hand.

"Bebe," she muttered, and I leaned closer, my lips an inch away from hers.

"Yeah?"

"Don't go," she begged, and I left a soft kiss on her mouth.

"I won't," I whispered, and heard her falling asleep the next second.

I pulled a sheet over her and stayed curled up next to her until I was sure she was fast asleep. Then, I got out of bed and lingered in the room. I had truly been a bad friend, the last thing either of us needed. I vowed to myself to be a better person and make sure Arden was alright.

I blew her a kiss before leaving the hospital room.

"Bebe," Nick greeted me, two steaming Styrofoam cups in his hands.

I pressed a finger to my lips and closed the door softly.

"She fell asleep," I told him.

"Her parents are almost here," he said. "Here's some coffee."

I accepted the cup gratefully when I heard Miles laughing. I looked at Nick for an explanation and he grinned.

"You'll have to see it to believe it," he told me, and I furrowed my brow, moving around the corner to see what all the fuss was about.

When my eyes took in the scene before me, I was sure I was dreaming.

"What on earth," I muttered under my breath, my chest rising quickly, my body already panicking.

"Bebe," Miles said confidently, turning towards me with a wide grin. "We've been waiting. Come join us."

Chapter 30

·MILES·

MERAKI, VERB
*To do something with soul, creativity and love,
to put something of yourself in your work.*

I noticed the change in her expression the second she saw who I was with. The tension in the room was palpable, so thick you could cut it with a knife.

I was next to her in seconds, my arm wrapping around her waist and pulling her against me like it was the easiest thing in the world.

"How is Arden?" I whispered in her ear, and she simply nodded once to acknowledge that her friend was okay.

I understood. Life was collapsing around her right now, every safety blanket she had was long gone. I was the only person left to make sure she was alright, the only one who knew how to help her, and I was desperate to make her better. I knew this was such an important milestone for her, and I was glad I was able to be there for her.

"Your parents dropped by," I told Bebe casually, treading carefully. "They heard about Arden."

It was like none of them were even listening to me, my words serving as nothing more but background chatter. They were staring at each other, Bebe's parents standing in the hallway, her mother clutching her bag, and her dad gripping Mom by the waist as if he were propping her up – the only thing holding her upright.

"Bebe," her mom breathed, and I felt Bebe tremble in my arms. "Bebe, oh God. We thought something happened to both of you."

"Arden's parents called them," I explained to my girl. "They tried to call you, but you didn't hear your phone, I guess."

I grinned at her widely, knowing full well what had been going on when she'd missed that phone call.

"Mom," Bebe choked out, and for a second I was sure she was going to collapse on the hospital floor.

But I held her up, gently ushering her towards her parents whose eyes were already misty as they locked with their daughter's gaze. I didn't have to hold her up for much longer, because her mom swept her up in a bear hug, sobbing when she finally had her daughter back in her arms. I stepped aside and watched the family reunion with a small smile on my face.

Bebe burrowed her face into her mother's shoulder, and her dad joined in, holding them both as they cried together. It was an intimate moment, and I wasn't sure whether they wanted me there or not. I felt awkward and out of place, the fear back in my veins, suddenly pumping with such force I thought I'd blow a coronary. I was panicking, hard, but I knew my job wasn't done just yet, and I needed to stick around for a little while longer to make sure Bebe was alright and would get home okay.

"Miles," her father finally spoke up, motioning for me to come closer.

The small family broke apart and now they were all staring at me, waiting for me to say something.

"I'm glad you've reunited," I finally managed to get out, my voice shaky and unsure.

"Are you ok?" Bebe was by my side in seconds, her hands all over me, fussing and worrying about me like nobody had done for my entire life. It was ridiculous how emotional it made me feel, waves of nausea mixing with overwhelming love for her as we stood in the hallway.

"I'm fine," I promised her with a weak smile. "I think I should get going."

She squeezed my hand, and I looked into her beautiful eyes.

"Do you have to?" she whispered, and I pulled her in for a hug, my arms tight around her as I held onto her for dear life.

"I want you to spend some time with your family," I said gently. "I would feel out of place here."

Excuses, fucking excuses because I was too weak to handle the hospital, and judging by the look in Bebe's eyes, she knew it, too.

"I want you to stay," she breathed softly, and I felt the curious gazes of her parents on us both. "But I'll understand if you really have to go."

I hesitated, trying my best to get the better of my demons, knowing I had already made an immeasurable step forward. Coming to the hospital had been a huge step. It was the very place of my nightmares, filled with germs and sickness and sadness, but I defeated every monster shouting obscenities in my head. Now though, I felt the tiredness coming on. The absolute exhaustion of facing my demons was making me weak, and I knew I needed to get home before it was too late.

"It's okay," I told Bebe. "Spend some time with your parents. Call me when you can, yeah?"

She gave me a sad little nod, but her smile told me she understood, and I loved her for it.

"I'll see you soon," I nodded at her, finally tearing my eyes away from her magnetic gaze and focusing on her parents. "I'm so glad I met you today, Mr. and Mrs. Hall. I hope I'll see you again soon."

"Likewise, son," Bebe's father told me, heartily slapping my back. "We're so thankful to you for taking care of our Bebe."

"We can't even tell you how much," her mom chimed in, pulling me in for a bear hug, which I was starting to think was a signature move of hers.

We broke away and promised to keep in touch, and I walked down the hallway with heavy steps, the weight of the world resting on my shoulders. Just as I was about to leave, I heard them talking again, Bebe's parents complimenting her and fussing over her, saying she'd found a great guy, and that they were proud of her.

"He's amazing," Bebe's words floated back to me. "I'm so lucky to have him."

"So tell me, darling," her mom giggled. "Are you two an item?"

I looked over my shoulder. From my vantage point, I could only see Bebe's back, but she looked over her shoulder in that moment, grinning at me.

"Yeah," she whispered, and I laughed out loud before leaving the hospital.

Standing outside, the fresh air felt cooling and cleansing for my soul. I briefly thought about walking back home, but it would've taken over an hour, and my body was tired, exhausted. I managed to find a grossly overpriced cab in front of the hospital, and sat in the back, fucking shaking as the man drove me home.

I hated myself for being like this. Fucking fragile like I was going to break any second, too terrified to even stick around and meet my girl's parents. We'd had a short conversation, sure, but it wasn't enough. I wanted to know everything, question them about every aspect of Bebe's life and make sure I knew everything down to the last detail. My obsession was growing, my need to know everything that made Bebe who she was overwhelming.

The driver stopped in front of my building, and I paid him before walking inside. The doorman was there again, but this time, instead of racing past him, I approached with a smile on my face.

Up close, I realized he had a kind face, the kind you were inclined to trust without knowing anything about the person.

"Hello," I got out, managing to fight off the worst of my insecurities as he looked up at me with surprise.

"Hello, Mr. Reilly," he said with a shy smile. "Not in a rush tonight?"

"Not yet," I shook my head. "I just wanted to thank you."

"What for?" He looked genuinely confused as I grinned at him.

"For always knowing me," I said simply. "For having my back, making sure I was okay. I'm sorry I've been running around like a headless chicken lately. I appreciate what you do for me."

I slapped a hundred in his hand, but he shook his head vehemently.

"I can't accept that, Mr. Reilly," he said firmly.

"Why not?" I asked him, and he looked away guiltily. "As far as I know, all the other doormen accepted tips. And you deserve it."

"Wouldn't be right," he muttered.

"Look," I went on. "Do you have someone special in your life?"

He didn't answer, but the tell-tale reddening of his cheeks told me everything I needed to know.

"Take her to Saffron on Fifth," I told him. "My friend works there."

He looked at me with surprise, and I laughed out loud.

"What, is it so impossible to believe I have a friend?" I asked, and he laughed guiltily. "We were classmates in high school. I used to go there a lot, when I still… could. I will pick up the bill. See? You take your lady out for a nice meal, and I have to leave home, challenge myself to pay for it. Win-win."

"Okay," he finally said, a bright smile lighting up his face. "Thank you."

I nodded and left for the stairs, making a sharp turn when I thought of another fear I could face that day.

"Hey, what's your name?" I asked the doorman.

"Eric." He replied with his first name, and it made me grin. "I'm Eric. My friend's name is Layla."

"Eric and Layla," I repeated with a nod as I jammed my finger on the elevator button for up. "I highly recommend the seared scallops."

I waved him off and took a deep breath before entering the elevator. My breath hitched immediately, panic seeping out of my pores as my back settled against the mirrored wall. I didn't even look at myself, feeling too scared and distracted to give a shit about my appearance. Instead, I focused on the closing doors of the elevator. Panic rocked my body, adrenaline making my heart jump and fall with the force of a carnival free-fall ride.

And then it was moving, moving faster than I ever remembered, practically shooting up to my floor. It was over in what felt like seconds, and I held my breath the whole time. And then it dinged, and the doors opened again, showing me the comforting, familiar hallway where my apartment was.

I stumbled outside, my knees weak and my arms flailing to hold on to something. I gripped the wall as I made my way to my apartment, the front door still wide open.

Peep Show

Usually, the cool calmness of my apartment managed to make me better in a matter of seconds. That night, it felt sterile and frightening as I stood in the doorway. Too clean, too pristine. Like a fucking mausoleum.

I stepped inside, my skin adjusting to the heat of the apartment. It was a change from the freezing air outside, and I sat down at my computer with renewed vigor and ideas.

My fingers worked the keyboard and I opened an interior website and started tossing things into my basket. I'd learned Bebe's favorite colors through my time with her, not by asking, but by seeing it everywhere around her. She loved silver and purple, so I decided to order stuff in those colors. I was pretty fucking clueless about interiors, but I figured some pillows, a rug and some frames would work.

I wanted her to feel at home here, with me. I was already working towards my goal of having her live with me, as weird as the idea was.

I'd never had a roommate. I lived with my parents, and then my grandmother, but never a housemate or girlfriend. It would be a completely new experience, just like so many other things when it came to Bebe.

Once I was done with my order, I walked into the white room, and slowly started to take it apart.

I didn't stop until I'd stripped the bed of the sheets and pillowcases and carried in some of my photography books to break up the whiteness of the room. I threw some of my clothes on the bed, even though I would never sleep in there. It would be turned into Bebe's room, not so she could sleep alone, but so she could get away from me the second she needed to. She needed a safe haven, whether she lived with me or not.

Finally, I picked up my camera. I'd taken so many photos of Bebe without her knowing. All that was left to do was develop the film.

I had a special place where I liked to do that.

I walked down the hallway, the camera weighing heavy in my hands. I opened the window to the storage room. It was still just as small, the stench just as strong and the place just as claustrophobic as I remembered. I entered despite my body screaming, begging me not to take a step inside.

Immediately upon stepping into the room, I was transported back to my childhood. I held back the tears as I slowly prepared everything for the film, the single bulb above me burning bright red. I forced myself to do it slowly, as if I wanted to torture myself by staying in there longer. But it was my process, the way I did things, and I couldn't have changed anything.

The photos came to life in front of me, all of them taken from my apartment and peeking into Bebe's.

I grinned at them.

The curve of her shoulder. The thin line that imprinted itself on her skin when she'd worn fishnet tights. Her bright red nails. Her full lips. A twinkle in her eye as she caught me.

Yes, I was already in love. There was no way I'd be able to escape what she made me feel now.

So I might as well accept it, and prepare myself for the greatest fall of all.

Chapter 31

·BEBE·

MONO NO AWARE, NOUN
The pathos of things — the awareness of the impermanence or transience of all things and the gentle sadness and wistfulness at their passing.

The presence of my parents in the waiting room was scaring me. We hadn't talked or seen each other in so long, I felt awkward in front of them, nervously stepping from foot to foot and sneaking nervous glances at the both of them. What surprised me was they seemed to be doing the same thing, watching me out of the corner of their eyes as if they were the ones who had something to be embarrassed about.

My mom kept holding onto my hand, her fingers nervously caressing my skin as if she were afraid I'd drop into a run and get away from them any second now.

"Do you…" the words got stuck in my throat, and I swallowed thickly so I could finish my sentence. "Do you guys want to go for dinner or something?"

"Dinner?" Mom asked, just as Dad nodded.

"That would be wonderful, honey," he said, and I gave him a smile back before impulsively pulling them both in for another hug. I couldn't help myself. I'd missed them, even if I was too chicken to admit it.

"I know a great place that's close by," I said. "Do you want to say hi to Arden before we leave?"

"We did a little while earlier," Mom filled me in, turning towards Nick who was still standing in the hallway, looking a little bit awkward. "Nicholas, was it? Arden's boy?"

"Yeah," he said with a nervous chuckle. "That's me, I guess."

"Do you want to come with us?" Mom asked.

I knew she was just trying to be friendly, but the question still seemed a little weird, and Nick looked at me for confirmation. A smile lit up my face as I remembered something, and I grinned widely as I filled them in on the plan.

"How about we get takeout delivered to the hospital?" I asked. "We can go to Arden's room. Not for too long. I think most restaurants are closed by now, it would be hard to get a table anyway."

"I love that idea," my mom beamed. "I'll order the food."

"And I'll get some snacks from the cafeteria," Nick offered, and they nodded to one another enthusiastically before disappearing in opposite directions.

That only left my father and me in the hallway, and neither of us could look at the other.

I'd always been closer to Dad than Mom. Not that we hadn't had a good relationship – we had, before I tossed it all away. But I'd always been Daddy's girl, unashamedly so. I knew he was much more like me than my mother was and much more sensitive than he cared to admit. But the one person he cared about most in the world was… me. He never put anyone or anything above me. I was his little girl, and he was set on making my life as perfect as he possibly could.

"Dad," I whispered, but I still couldn't look at him.

It had been almost a year since I'd last seen them. I'd cut them out, and for what?

To be cool?

To pretend I was better than them?

To stop being ashamed?

"I'm sorry, Dad," I added uselessly, feeling the tears burning my eyes as I stared intently at the floor. "I'm sorry for what I've put you through."

Posy's death was making me question my own mortality and the life choices I'd made, which were less than stellar in most of the things I'd done.

"It's okay," he answered roughly, but I could hear the pain in his voice. He patted me on the shoulder, his hand heavy and awkward. "I understand, sweetie."

It wasn't right, what I'd done, but just hearing those words leaving his lips made me raise my eyes to his.

There was no hiding the fact that I'd hurt him, maybe irreparably so. I'd given him no reason for our sudden separation when we'd been thick as thieves up until I decided I was too good for them.

"I do understand," he repeated with a shadow of a smile on his face. "I was young once, too. I've been ashamed of my parents."

"Dad," I begged. "I wasn't…"

"I know," he said calmly. "I know, sweetheart. Come here."

He pulled me in for a hug, shocking me by the sudden need to hold me close. My father was a man of action. He didn't speak or show his affection otherwise, which made his change in behavior even more strange. But I needed it, and when I felt his strong arms close around me, I was transported back to my childhood when my father was Superman – someone I turned to with anything and everything, and who always had the answer to whatever was bothering me.

"I won't let it happen again," I muttered into his arm, and he patted my back, still silly and awkward like he always was.

"Let's put it behind us," he said simply, giving me a big smile. "Let's make sure both of you girls are alright, so I can sleep better at night."

Thirty minutes later, we'd all gathered in Arden's hospital room after a lot of convincing and some hundred-dollar bills being exchanged with the nurses. But now, we had the room all to ourselves, and Arden's face lit up the second we all walked in. Her parents were there as well. I'd always gotten on with them, unlike Posy's – they reminded me of my own, even though they were quite a bit older. But they were also fiercely protective of their daughter – something we had in common.

We had Chinese takeout, boxes upon boxes of crispy fried chicken from the fast food joint downstairs, and some questionable snacks from the cafeteria, courtesy of Nick. We were contemplating the edibleness of the purplish-gray jello, Arden laughing so hard she nearly doubled over in her bed. She'd even gotten the doctor's okay to have a snack, as long as it was something on her allowed list of foods, and they'd taken out her fluid injection, so she was a free woman.

I sat on the bed with her while our parents took up the chairs, and Nick perched on the edge of the windowsill.

I looked at the people around me, faced with the sharp realization that somebody was missing. Miles should've been there with us. He'd earned his place in my circle and now, the room felt empty without him.

The subject of Posy weighed heavily in the air. She'd been the one to bring us all together, and the longer I thought about it, the more I realized how true that was. She was even the one who'd encouraged Arden to hang out with Nick while both she and I had dismissed the idea as nonsensical. Posy didn't know how to take care of herself, but when it came to the people in her life, she knew exactly what was right.

I missed her, the pain a dull ache in my chest that I knew would never go away. It would fade, slowly, slowly, until I only felt pinpricks of it years after her death. Finally, I was starting to realize she really was gone. I'd been shutting my eyes from the truth for a long time, but it was time to face the facts.

"I miss Posy," I blurted out when there was a lull in the conversation, and everyone's eyes turned to find me, nervously chewing my bottom lip. "I'm sorry, I really do."

"I know," Arden said softly, fidgeting with the wrapper of a fortune cookie. "I miss her too."

"I do as well," Nick piped in, and we both gave him surprised looks.

"She wasn't very… nice to you," I said awkwardly, and he chuckled.

"Not to my face, no," he said, shrugging. His eyes were on the plastic cup of Coke in his hands. "But she always encouraged Arden to spend time with me, and I guess she finally listened."

Arden giggled and stuck her tongue out at him, and our parents exchanged meaningful looks.

"I'm glad I did," she finally said, and they grinned at each other like they were in on a secret I didn't know.

My jealousy spiked at the sight, but the voice in my head told me to calm down. Why should I be jealous? I had my own secrets with Miles, and I was only now coming to realize how perfectly normal it was. It didn't mean I'd have to be a different person around my friends and family, or that I had to act in a certain way. But just like I didn't share confessions and private moments with Arden with Miles, it was also perfectly normal not to share our intimate... *dates* with anyone in the room.

A little smile played on my lips as I thought about what they'd think of me if they knew what kind of things I'd been up to. My parents' jaws would probably hit the freaking floor. Better to keep it to myself, after all.

I caught my dad's eye across the room and smiled at him while my mom squeezed my palm. I felt so safe in that moment, more than I did with three locks on my front door. My mind kept escaping to Miles, thinking about him with a desperation that willed him to appear back in the hospital room. I knew how tough the day had been for him though, the way he'd rushed out of the apartment. I was hopeful that he'd get better with my help.

I made a mental note to ask him about his problems the next time I saw him. Lately, it seemed like every waking second I was with him revolved around me.

The faint ache between my legs was still there, and I looked discreetly aside to wipe a stray tear from my face.

What he'd done hadn't been right, not in the slightest. But I believed him when he said he needed to get away. That things were getting too intense. Maybe it was what both of us needed to know, that we belonged together, not apart. And maybe things would be better now. Different. Special.

"I wish I could have one last chance to speak to her," I finally said after a long, contemplative silence. "Posy. I want to ask her some stuff."

"Like what?" Arden asked gently, her fingers wrapping around mine.

I looked into her eyes and smiled weakly at the memories that were begging to be let out.

"I would ask…" I started, my sentence trailing off into nothing.

What would I ask?

Maybe if she liked Miles.

Maybe if she hated me for moving on.

Maybe if she wanted me to join her.

"I would ask," I went on. "If she was proud of me."

Arden kissed my cheek and I smiled at her.

"You know what?" I said. "I think she would say yes."

My dad stared at me across the room, and nodded.

"Me too," Mom piped up. "She'd be proud of both of you."

Arden's parents agreed, and we sat there, a bunch of emotional messes.

"Well," Nick piped up awkwardly. "I hope she'd be proud of me too."

He came to the bed, pressing a kiss to Arden's hair. She beamed.

"I finally got the girl," he winked at me, and I laughed out loud.

Chapter 32

·MILES·

LACUNA, NOUN
A blank space, a missing part.

Once I was done with the photographs, I hung them up and left them to dry. I walked out of the room feeling a bit better, though my heart was pounding with anxiety and my nose was filled with the stench of that tiny, trashed little room. I still didn't completely understand why I put myself through the ordeal of being in there. It wreaked havoc on me, and I fucking hated it, but I couldn't stay away. It was like my own fucking cross I had to carry for the rest of my life.

When I walked into the living room, I felt lightheaded and weak all of a sudden, and I clung to the doorframe. My head was spinning, the wheels turning faster than ever as I tried to focus on anything but my unsteadily beating heart.

I felt it coming before it happened, the wave of nausea and panic mixing together in a killer cocktail that threatened to make my head explode. I felt the fear coming in waves, washing over my body with nauseating speed and making me want to collapse on the floor.

But I held myself up, willing my body not to move, stay in place and obey my mind instead. I employed every trick Dr. Halen had ever taught me, trying desperately to do what she'd said and calm my body down, distract it from the meltdown it seemed intent on having.

I felt physically sick, bile rising in my throat and threatening to spill all over the immaculate floor in front of me.

Spacing out, I felt my soul leaving my body and floating above myself, watching what my body was doing as though I wasn't part of the actions that were happening in front of my very eyes.

I watched myself drop to my knees, my palms on the floor, and scared sobs left my lips as I dry-heaved, trying to calm down, trying to take deep breaths, remembering Dr. Halen's words. Just breathe. *Breathing is control. Air in, air out, over and over again, just focus on that for as long as you can.*

Except it wasn't working. I was panicking, my body overreacting to the stressors from outside, desperately fighting enemies that weren't even present. I heaved and sputtered and choked on my own desperate attempts to call for help, all the while watching it from just under the ceiling, my brow furrowed and my arms crossed in front of my body, angrily looking down at myself, unable to understand why my body wasn't following the simplest of instructions.

"Help!" I called out, but it didn't come out right, it was just a desperate little croak.

I felt panic seeping through my pores, making the room stink of desperation. I was all alone, something I'd worked hard for, but that now seemed like the most frightening thing of all.

Crawling on the floor, I dragged myself to the couch and attempted to pull myself upwards, but my motions were shaky, my legs barely able to support my weight. I crashed down on the couch and regretted it immediately, the soft white leather sticking to my skin and reminding me of just how vulnerable I was.

The panic and absolute resignation to my fear were the worst I'd ever experienced.

Yes, I'd had panic attacks before, but nothing like this. Nothing this crazy fucking intense, where I knew with absolutely no doubt it was going to be the end of me and I was going to fucking die like this, all alone, with nobody to remember me.

Her face appeared in my mind, the beautiful line of her stubborn jaw making me want to run my fingers over the bones, her skin, her plump lips. I couldn't remember her name, though. All that mattered was her face, and I did my very best to remember every single detail of her beauty, as if that alone could save me.

I remembered her lips. The bottom lip slightly exaggerated, full and plump. The way her perfect teeth dug into her bottom lip, making it lose the bright color, as if she was getting ready for me to sink into her. Anticipation in her beautiful eyes. The way her dark brown hair fell down her back so perfectly; the way her tan skin erupted in goosebumps every single time I was near her. The way it felt under my fingertips, tender and sweet and silky. I wanted to taste her. But she wasn't there. I was completely and utterly alone.

"Help!" I cried out again, and this time, my voice wasn't as quiet or broken.

My soul felt a magnetic pull back into my body, but I resisted it with all my might, preferring to watch from above. I was hallucinating, fucking seeing things that weren't even there, and I hated myself for it. Hated that I was so damn vulnerable, that I was crumbling by myself, that I couldn't even pick myself up from the couch and call for help. I was a fucking mess, and embarrassment flooded my body along with absolute, concrete shame because of what was happening.

You're a man, Miles, I remembered the bitter voice saying. *Act like one! Be better than your parents! Don't succumb! BE BETTER!*

Except I couldn't, because this shit had been placed in my crib when I was a fucking kid, like a fairy making fun of the man I could have been, and punishing me instead, dumping every fucked-up thing it could think of on me as a baby. Maybe there had been a chance for me to turn out alright, but it was a long time ago, and just like everybody else, I knew now that I was doomed. It was the reason everyone else had given up on me, after all. I was destined to die alone.

I dragged myself off the couch, suddenly unable to stand the heat of the leather and the light above me. I was back in my body, and I regretted it the second I realized how useless that truly was.

I steadied my feet as well as I could and I talked to myself encouragingly as I tried to drag myself into my bedroom.

One step, two steps, three steps, stay in your body, keep your mind strong, keep the demons at bay. and just… Keep. Fucking. Moving.

I needed to get my meds, the tranquilizers I took just in case things got as bad as they were in that moment. I distinctly remembered the bright orange-tinted, translucent bottle of the horse-sized meds on my nightstand. I just needed to get there. The second I took the pill, I would feel alright again. I would be safe. I would be okay. Even if just for a little while.

But putting one foot in front of the other was a fucking ordeal. A task so ridiculously hard it felt like I was trying to climb Mount Everest. My arms and legs were shaking, and I was terrified of everything, every sound and tremble magnified until my head was left ringing and pounding in their wake.

Finally, I reached the threshold of my bedroom. I stumbled inside, the rumpled sheets reminding me of the one in *her* room, *her* body pressed close to mine. I realized with a huff how badly I needed her. How much I wanted her to be there with me. I was desperate for it, clinging to the idea of her, the thought of her lashes on her cheeks, every single one pronounced, dark and thick against her skin. That image ingrained itself in my mind until I could think of nothing else, obsessed with the idea of her, the girl the only thing keeping me from falling into the precipice I was standing in front of.

"Please help me," I said.

But my legs refused to keep moving and I collapsed like a tree coming down, my limbs banging the floor. This was what I hated most about my condition, the bone-crippling anxiety and panic attacks that could happen at any minute. I'd felt this one coming, but sometimes they came completely out of the blue and made me feel like a perfectly capable man living in a body that just wouldn't fucking work.

I sat on the floor with my back against the hardwood and forced myself to keep breathing, knowing that if I stopped I'd start to lose consciousness. It was all I could do, the only thing I could focus on. There was nothing else but the rise and fall of my chest, the swelling of my heart and the panicked gasps of air as I struggled to stay in my body yet again.

I wanted to scream, but no sound came out, reminding me of the nightmarish dreams I'd had as a child. I was afraid, so fucking afraid now, and all I wanted was for the girl whose name I couldn't remember to come and help me.

In my mind, I convinced myself that it would all be alright as long as she reappeared, with her bright smile and bubblegum lips and her sparkling eyes. As long as she was around and looking out for me I would be perfectly alright. But she was gone, fucking gone, and I was on my own.

I couldn't move, my body refusing to do what my mind was trying to tell it to. I saw my life flash before my eyes, feeling like I was going to meet my end right there, on the floor of my own bedroom. It felt like I was dying and even smelled like death as I raised my eyes and realized I'd left the small room open, the stench and the trash spilling out into the hallway.

Groaning, I tried to focus on something, any-fucking-thing to take my mind of the horrible tightness in my chest. But it wouldn't work, and there was nothing left to do but wait for it to be over. I tried to remind myself that it would end, like these things usually did, in a couple of minutes. It didn't help the way I felt though, like a fucking failure.

What kind of man couldn't even go outside to help a woman out without collapsing back at home?

What kind of man was so afraid, such a fucking pussy, he couldn't even handle an everyday activity for every other person?

What kind of fucking man was I, if I was a man at all?

The deep hatred I felt for myself burned through me like a vicious fire, but I couldn't stop it. The flames spread, licking tentatively at my ankles before engulfing me in ash and smoke. I was a mess, a fucking mess, and Bebe didn't deserve me.

Bebe.

Bebe.

I remembered her name… Her sweet, beautiful name that fit her so perfectly. I felt tears in the corners of my eyes as I came to a realization.

The only thing for me to do was to get the fuck lost. Get as far away from her as possible before I fucked up her life in all the ways I'd fucked up my own. I needed to get away, needed to breathe. Needed to let her live her life so I could waste mine on bleach baths and throwaway sex.

I picked myself up with tremendous effort and walked to my closet. I got out a suitcase, one I'd bought years ago in the hopes that the purchase would encourage me to go on a vacation. Fat fucking chance of that happening.

One thing was still true though – Bebe would be better off without me. And for once, that suitcase would finally come in handy. I'd walk away from her, walk away from the mess I made her into.

Knowing I'd never forgive myself for it, I started packing. But a lifetime of hating myself was better than years of ruining Bebe's life, until she finally realized just how miserable she was with me. She may not have known it yet, but she didn't want me in her life. And I'd be the one responsible for cleansing her of my mess.

"I'm sorry," I muttered to myself as I started packing. "I'm sorry, Bebe, I'm sorry for hurting you."

My words renewed my energy and I packed with anger and vigor, hating myself every step of the way. Leaving her would break me completely, and I knew the moment I left the apartment I'd never be able to make a human connection again. Bebe had fucking ruined me, but I needed to get the hell away before I did the same to her.

I'd send someone for the rest of the stuff, but for now, I had enough. With trembling hands, I sent a text to Meyers, the PI, with instructions. I put my suitcase on the floor and filled a big glass with water, drinking it in long, shaky gulps.

It was time to say goodbye once and for all. And once she understood

– once some time had passed – Bebe would know I'd made the right call. Leaving her alone was the only option that made sense, the only way she'd have peace in her own life.

It was time to leave. Time to walk out of her life.

Grabbing my suitcase, I turned around to walk out the door, only then noticing the figure standing in the room.

"Bebe," I whispered, and she stared at me, her eyes blank and then filling with hurt as she watched me.

She took a step back, then another one.

"I'm sorry," I admitted brokenly, but she merely shook her head.

Chapter 33

·BEBE·

KILIG, NOUN
Butterflies in one's stomach.

It was impossible to believe what I was seeing.

The man who'd held me in his arms only hours ago was standing in his own apartment, his fingers gripping a suitcase, ready to fucking leave. It was clear as day this was about me, clear as my own fucking reflection in the mirror that he wanted to get the fuck away from me, and I hated him for it.

"Please," I said pathetically, my voice breaking. "Miles, please, what are you doing?"

He stood in the middle of the room, staring at me and unable to say a thing. I hated him for it, for not replying to me and for pretending like this wasn't the worst thing he'd ever done to me. Worse even than the two men he'd sent over to fuck me relentlessly, worse than the games he'd been playing with me for weeks. This was the moment he was going to break me, and he was going to make me handle it all on my own.

I raised my accusatory gaze to him, and we locked eyes. I saw so many things in his eyes, so many things I'd never seen before. But none of them made me understand what he was doing, and my blood boiled with anger and fear.

It took less than a second to reach him, and my fists pummeled into his chest, angrily smashing against him as I cursed him out, hating him for everything he'd put me through. It was plainly obvious now I should've walked away a long time ago, but as much as I wanted to hate myself for not doing it, I fucking couldn't. I was addicted to Miles, punch-drunk on my love for him, the love he so obviously didn't have for me.

"Bebe," he said brokenly.

He wasn't even fucking trying to defend himself, knowing full well how shitty this was.

"Were you just going to walk out?" I screamed in his face. "You were just going to leave me here, weren't you? Without explaining a single thing, you fucking bastard!"

I felt the tears slipping down my heated cheeks, but I refused to acknowledge them, instead just pummeling his chest again and again until he groaned, still not even attempting to stop me or touch me.

"Defend yourself!" I screamed at him, now feeling like a banshee, wanting to tear him to fucking pieces. "At least tell me why you're doing this, Miles! Why are you fucking doing this to me? *How* could you even do this to me?"

He didn't even try to deny it. Just swallowed thickly, his Adam's apple bobbing as he did, and glared at me with feelings in his eyes I couldn't explain.

To me, it felt like I'd just taken care of one broken aspect of my life, only to have the other one broken and shattered into pieces. Miles looked away from me as if he couldn't even handle looking into my eyes, and I hated him with every fiber of my body. I knew one thing though – I wasn't going to leave that building without an explanation.

I stared at him until he finally raised his eyes to mine, and when he did, I suddenly understood everything.

I'd never seen pain like that before. Obvious, fucking heart-breaking pain that threatened to pull us both apart with its intensity. I wanted to ask him why it was there, who'd made him feel that way, but I was too fucking scared to ask any questions. I just wanted to make sure he was alright.

His eyes spoke of a hurt I'd never known until we lost Posy. He'd lost someone too, and I was only seeing that now, only understanding in that moment that he was even more alone in the world than I was. He had no one but me, and now he was running from that too.

"Miles," I breathed, the word coming out jagged and scared. "Miles, don't go."

He let out something between a growl and a moan when I touched the side of his face, my fingers caressing his cheek and gently touching his brow, wiping away the hint of moisture at his eyes.

"I'm so sorry," I whispered. "I'm so sorry for what happened to you, Miles."

"You…" he started, but his words trailed off into nothing.

"I'm going to help," I promised him. "I'm going to make sure you're okay. And if you still feel like this, if you still want to leave by the time I make sure you're alright, I'll let you go. I promise I will, okay? Okay, Miles?"

He didn't react, his eyes going glassy and shining with a fear I didn't recognize.

"I love you," I told him, and then I kept repeating it.

As I pried the badly-packed suitcase from his fingers, gently letting it down on the floor and pushing it out of his view, I could see what was been in there, a random assortment of things that told me he hadn't planned this, that he'd let his own panic take over and pack anything and everything he could get his hands on in a mad rush.

I kissed the side of his mouth, my lips gentle and promising him it would all be alright as I led him to the couch, sat him down and poured him a big glass of water.

And finally, I kneeled down next to him and took his hand in my own, telling him I'd stay, no matter what.

But he wasn't there anymore, and I felt like I was alone in the room. His body was just an empty shell, his mind miles away.

"Is there anyone I can call?" I asked him. "Anyone who can help me... help us? To make sure you're alright?"

"Pills," he muttered. "Pills."

"Pills?" I repeated, my eyes confused, then finally realizing what he meant. "Are you meant to take a pill? I'll get them, just tell me where they are, okay?"

I squeezed his hand for comfort, and he nodded absently, unable to so much as look into my eyes.

"N-nightstand," he muttered.

I jumped to my feet and ran into his bedroom, rummaging through his nightstand. I found a bottle of meds and pried it open, my shaky fingers spilling the bright white pills all over the floor. I cried out in exasperation and dropped down my knees, picking up one of the pills and racing back into the living room.

For a second, I was deathly afraid he wouldn't be there anymore, thinking maybe he'd just grabbed his suitcase and walked the hell out of my life like he'd meant to do only a few minutes ago. But when I saw him sitting in the very same spot I'd left him in, my heart ached at the thought. I filled up his water again and brought the glass to him along with the pill. He looked at me helplessly, and I realized he was so messed up he probably couldn't even hold the glass by himself.

"Here," I muttered. "I'll help."

I tipped his head back, opened his mouth. He followed my motions robotically, and I placed the white pill on the tip of his tongue, being sharply reminded of the contrast between the pills I liked and the ones he was forced to take. It felt unfair to even think of the drugs I took when Miles was suffering through all of this.

He swallowed, and I tipped the glass into his mouth. I watched the stubble on his Adam's apple as he took a deep swig of the liquid, and smiled encouragingly at him.

"W-what now?" he asked with a jagged edge to his voice, and once again, my heart broke for him.

"Is there someone I could call?" I asked. "Is there someone to talk to? Like a family member?"

He shook his head no and I bit my bottom lip nervously.

"Maybe a friend?"

Another slight shake of his head. This was upsetting him, and now I felt even more nervous and scared.

"What about a doctor? Maybe a therapist you've been talking to? Anyone like that?"

"Y-yes," he managed to get out. "Dr. Halen. My phone. Her number... it-it's in there."

He handed me his phone with shaky fingers and I touched my own to his hand in what I hoped was a reassuring caress. Then, I scrolled through his contacts until I found the doctor's information. I dialed her number without hesitation, even though it was the middle of the night.

The doctor answered quickly, her tone filled with concern and something else I didn't very much like. It was hard to miss the affection in her voice. The fear that she felt something for Miles filled me with dread.

"Yes, Miles. Is everything alright?"

"Hello," I said awkwardly. "It's… My name is Bebe. I'm Miles'… He's not feeling well."

"What's wrong?" she asked promptly. "He hasn't overdosed?"

"No," I answered after a short pause, my heart filling with even more fear.

Surely that wasn't even an option. Surely my mountain of a man would never think of hurting himself in that way?

"He's not feeling well?" she went on, urging me to continue.

"He isn't," I said. "I gave him a pill – a large white one from an orange bottle. He said he uses them in emergencies."

"Yes," she confirmed. "Xanax. It should kick in soon. Are you with him?"

"I am," I said, sneaking a glance at him.

His face was panicked and etched with worry, but his breathing had eased a little, and I was grateful when the wheezing sound disappeared completely. I would do whatever it took to get him better, I decided on the spot. I couldn't handle him being in pain any longer.

"I want you to stay until he calms down," Dr. Halen went on. "Please, for my sake if no one else's. I need to know he's alright."

"I will, of course," I promised, jealousy cutting through me like a knife. "Would it help to get him into bed? Maybe a shower? A bath?"

"No," she said with sudden urgency in her voice. "No baths. You do know about his habit, don't you?"

My silence must've answered the question for her, and she sighed warily before going on.

"Who are you?" she asked, and I sat down next to Miles, putting her on speaker. "I need to know your relationship with my client. Will you be able to handle the situation, or would you like me to drive up to the city? I could be there in twenty minutes."

"I'm staying," I replied firmly. I wasn't going to back down now. "He's my responsibility tonight."

And as far as I was concerned, until my very last breath. I didn't say it, but I hoped it was obvious from the tone of my voice.

"Alright," she said. "But what is your relationship?"

A silence fell upon the room until Miles grunted as if waking up from a slumber.

"Mine," he growled. "She's mine."

His words made my heart ache. And I didn't confirm nor deny what he'd said, instead pulling him into my lap and settling his head between my knees. He looked up at me as I held the phone in one hand and stroked him with the other, gently easing him into a sense of security.

"Okay," Halen replied primly. "That's good. Please stay with him tonight. Make sure he's breathing well, and do not let him take another pill for eight hours. If anything goes wrong, call me. Will you be able to handle this, Bebe?"

My name on her lips felt like a strange little intimacy, but I gave Miles a brave smile as I nodded.

"I will," I promised. "I'll call you in the morning with an update."

"I'd appreciate that," she said. "Good luck, Bebe. Good luck, Miles."

She cut the call and we lay on the couch together.

"Just breathe," I told him gently. "And everything will be perfectly alright."

He turned his beautiful, soulful eyes onto mine, and nodded.

With a start, I realized he believed me.

Now it was up to me to stay true to my word.

Chapter 34

·MILES·

SAUDADE, NOUN
The love that remains after a person is gone.

The minutes were ticking by painfully slowly, and I was consumed with guilt for making Bebe go through this shit with me.

The shame after she'd found me with my packed suitcase was still there, painful whenever I thought of it and ever present in the back of my mind. I wished I'd never reached for that suitcase. I wished I'd never even thought of leaving her when she was what I needed most in the world. Even if it was a selfish decision, I wasn't going to let go of her that easily.

It was after five a.m. when I got the urge to take a bath.

But Bebe didn't know my shameful secret. She didn't know about the bleach I poured into my baths, the dirty cigarettes I sneaked while I was in the bath or even the occasional cigar, and I was scared beyond belief of her finding out just how fucked-up I really was.

I kept glancing at her. She'd made countless cups of tea, changed into a shirt of mine that barely covered her butt in the tiniest thong. She was fucking delectable and I couldn't wait to sink my teeth into her.

Both of us were wide awake, and there was no way we'd be able to fall asleep after the day we'd had. But Bebe seemed intent on staying, even though I'd told her a couple of times I'd be totally fine on my own.

She came over with another steaming cup, this time coffee. I accepted it gratefully and gave her a shy smile. I felt ashamed about showing her this side of me. About her seeing just how fucking vulnerable I was. I wanted her to know I could be strong for her, too. Wanted her to realize I'd always have her back… But now, she'd seen the absolute worst of me, and the shame was threatening to eat me alive.

"I want a bath," I told her easily as if it was the simplest thing in the world. "Would you mind if I took one?"

"Not at all," she replied with a smile, but then I saw the memory flicker through her eyes.

She'd remembered Dr. Halen's words, no doubt, remembered the doctor's warning about letting me in the bathroom. She seemed to hesitate, but I'd already gotten up.

"I'll leave the door ajar," I promised her. "I'm feeling so much better now, sugar, and I'm so fucking grateful."

She gave me a little smile and nodded, and I walked away from her. But instead of feeling relieved, it felt like the world's burdens had been placed directly on my shoulders. I was nervous, nervous and scared of what this meant for our relationship. I couldn't bear the thought of her walking out on me – not now, not ever.

I walked into the bathroom and drew a bath, the water so scalding hot it steamed up the whole room. Just like I'd promised, I left the door ajar, and I heard Bebe turning on some music as I got rid of my clothes.

I was a fucking mess, the whole evening leaving me in pieces. But mostly, I was just deeply fucking ashamed of Bebe catching me in that state of mind, of seeing me at my most vulnerable. I would've done anything to keep that side of me from her, but if I was being honest with myself, it was going to come out one way or another, and she'd know sooner rather than later about all my dirty little secrets.

She still didn't know the whole story, though. I wasn't sure when I'd be ready to share that.

I watched my reflection in the mirror. I'd lost some weight recently, my mind preoccupied with all things Bebe. But I still looked good, my muscles rippling and the ink stretching tautly across them.

I checked to make sure Bebe was still in the living room, and then dug in the cupboard until I found the nameless white plastic bottle. I turned it upside down above the bath, pouring in the entire contents and filling the bathroom with the stench of bleach.

Then, I climbed in.

The bleach made me hiss out loud, but I took it, just like I always fucking did. Sometimes, weeks went by without me taking one. Sometimes, I'd take three in a day. Either way, for years it had been the only real thing I felt, back before when I'd met Bebe. Now, the sting was still there, and so was the pain, but somehow, my bath was lacking what I wanted from it so badly.

To feel alive.

"What are you doing?"

I turned around abruptly, seeing Bebe standing in the doorway with a sweet little smile on her face. But it dissolved as she sniffed the air, making a face at the stench of the bleach.

"It stinks in here," she said, scrunching up her nose. "Want me to open a window?"

She strode inside before I could stop her, trying to reach the window but tripping on the white plastic bottle. My heart fucking stopped and I watched her lean down and pick it up as if it were in slow motion.

"What's this?" she asked softly, lifting it up to her nose and making a face when she smelled the remains. "It fucking stinks."

"Bebe," I said, sinking deeper into the bath, my heart pumping panicked blood through my body. "Please, just go."

"I'm not leaving," she said, a hint of surprise to her voice which soon turned into anger. "Why are you trying to get rid of me again, Miles? There's no fucking way I'm leaving."

"Go," I begged her, my voice fucking breaking. "Please, Bebe. I don't want you to watch…"

"What's in there?" she finally asked. "The bottle, Miles. Is it in the bathtub?"

Before I could protest, she'd reached me, sitting on the edge of the tub and smelling the water.

"Is it…" she whispered, her eyes finding mine. "Is it bleach?"

I didn't reply, just shut my eyes as tightly as I possibly could and willed the whole moment to go away.

But next thing I knew, she was sliding into the bath with me.

"No," I growled, my arms grabbing her as she gasped. The heat and the bleach were too fucking much for her. I hated myself for making her do this, for putting her through all this fucking embarrassing shit.

"Bebe," I begged her, trying to get out. "I'll stop, I swear, just get out… I don't want you getting hurt, sugar, please…"

"Too late," she growled in reply. "Now, every time you do this, I'm getting in with you. And you'll only have yourself to blame if I get hurt."

I howled in pain, but she climbed on top of me, my white shirt sticking to her skin as she sunk her body in the bath. She writhed in my lap, hissing at the sting of the bleach, her legs wrapping around my waist, that tiny fucking thong the only thing separating her from my engorged cock.

"Bebe, no," I begged her. "Please, get the fuck out."

"No," she said. "Kiss me, you fucking fool."

I kissed her. I kissed her with so much desperation it shocked me, and felt her gasp against my lips as she let the bleach eat away at her skin. I'd never hated myself more, but the passion I felt for her in that moment overcame anything else I could have possibly felt. I tore at her, my fingers twirling in her hair, desperate to pull, tug, get her fucking closer.

"Miles," she breathed desperately. "Miles, please…"

"Get out," I said roughly. "Last fucking warning, Bebe. You need to get the fucking shit out of here."

"NO!" she cried out, and I shut her complaint with a kiss, desperately claiming her mouth.

And then the sting from the bath was gone. The heat was gone too, my burning skin now on fire for different reasons than the horrible water we were in. She was igniting me. She was the fucking spark, she was the one lighting me up.

I kissed her with absolute desperation, not trying to hide a single bit of it anymore. She returned the kiss with the same passion, sinking her teeth into my lower lip so angrily she drew blood. She gasped when she felt it between us, but I wouldn't let her move away. I kept kissing her, claiming her pretty little mouth until she begged for more.

"Let me in," she said angrily. "Let me in your fucking head, Miles."

I was scared to. Who knew how she'd react when she saw all the terrible things that were inside my head? She'd never look at me the same way again, that was for fucking sure.

But for now, I couldn't fucking resist. I had a gorgeous woman rubbing herself all over my dick, and I was desperate to have her, claim her, teach her some fucking manners.

"Mine," I growled against her throat, my fingers finding her pussy and ripping the thong off under the water. She gasped when I did it, my wet shirt clinging to her skin and revealing her pretty, pert nipples beneath the wet cotton. "I'm not letting go, Bebe. I'm never. Fucking. Letting. Go."

She mimicked my desperate movements, getting up and then sinking herself fully on my cock, impaling herself on my thickness until I hissed at the contact her pussy made with my dick.

"Ride me," I growled at her, and she bounced up and down, splashing water everywhere. "Fucking ride me, sugar, don't you dare stop now. I'm too fucking desperate for you now."

She rose and fell, riding my cock into an orgasm that made her pussy twitch and spasm. I could tell how badly she needed it, how fucking desperate she was for my cum. She groaned and gasped as I filled her up, our skin burning together with the bleach.

I pulled her closer, her body hot and tight against my own, holding on for dear life as we spilled water all over the bathroom floor. She gripped me by the hair, her fingers digging into my scalp as she breathlessly fucked herself with my dick. It was an act of desperation, an attempt to get as close to me as possible. Did she want to be in my head? Then I'd let her see it all, as long as it meant having her in my arms for as long as I fucking wanted.

"Oh, Bebe," I grunted. "Ride me. Fucking ride me, I want to feel you."

She did. She rode me like it was all that mattered in the world, her hisses turning into desperate little cries and mewls until she crashed down on me, her orgasm taking her by surprise just like it had me. She was about to stop, but I couldn't let her do that, not there and not then.

"Keep fucking going," I growled at her. "Keep. Fucking. Going."

She let out a desperate little whimper, so I decided to take matters into my own hands. I grabbed her hips and fucked her burning cunt viciously, with every shred of emotion left in my body.

The anger.

The pain.

The love I felt for the innocent woman in my arms.

I showed her everything as I took her, and I never fucking let go. I fucked her relentlessly, and from that moment on, we both knew she belonged to me completely. She was mine.

"Don't let go," she hissed, just like she had the first time we'd made love. "Please, Miles, just don't let go of me."

I looked right into her eyes and pumped my cock into her and she mewled, biting her lip. We were both a fucking mess, and I'd never wanted anyone more than I did her. I was a man obsessed, possessed and overtaken by her beauty, grace and the fucking firecracker personality that made her shine.

"Will you stay?" I asked her, teetering on the edge of an orgasm, so fucking close to filling her up. "Will you stay with me, Bebe? Will you be fucking mine like I need you to, baby?"

"Yes," she replied breathlessly, and the world stood still for a second. "Yes, I will be yours. Only yours. All yours. Forever, Miles, forever..."

My orgasm was fucking brutal, ripping through the walls of the bathroom with its intensity, our grunts and screams echoing around the room and making me grateful I owned the whole fucking floor.

"My girl," I grunted, driving myself into her one last time. "My. Fucking. Girl!"

Chapter 35

·BEBE·

EUNOIA, NOUN
Beautiful thinking.

My teeth were chattering, even though my most intimate parts were stinging from the bleach and from the pounding he gave me.

Miles wrapped a towel around me, and his eyes lingered on mine for a long second before he moved away, smirking to himself. His cock hung between his legs, still semi-hard and dripping.

He was at his most vulnerable in that moment, and he'd let me see him. He'd let me see the side of him he was afraid of showing the most.

He drained the bath, and I tossed the white plastic container into the trash. He didn't comment on it, and I didn't say a word either. But I was absolutely determined I wouldn't let him close to it ever again. And if he did, I'd stay true to my word and get in the bath with him.

We settled on the sofa, and through the wall-to-ceiling windows of his apartment, we watched the sun rise over the city.

I had seen the sunrise many times before, but that day it felt especially significant. It was the dawn of a new day, the start of something special. And I was going to make sure this day was the first of many when both Miles and I would get better, slowly but surely on our path to recovery.

Me, from being a fucking mess, and him, from whatever inner demons he had haunting him all these years.

I was desperate to know more. I wanted to find out every little detail that made him the man I knew, eager to find out what had shaped him. But he didn't seem willing to share, not until that morning when I gasped as the sun colored his apartment in so many hues it felt like we were sitting inside a beautiful rainbow.

"It's stunning, isn't it," Miles said softly. "All the colors in the world in one fucking room."

"It's incredible," I admitted.

"The realtor told me about it," he said with a grin. "Said I was paying for the view. I complained for weeks until I fucking saw it. And now, I would be happy to pay double the price to see this every morning."

I settled into the crook of his arm, cuddling close as he held onto me.

"It's why the apartment is white," he said, and I looked up at him. "I wanted the sunrise to color it."

It was a small offering, a glimpse into the way his curious mind worked, and I loved him for letting me be a part of it.

"Thank you," I whispered, and he grinned down at me. "For telling me. For including me."

"I want you to know everything," he told me gently. "Everything that makes me... me."

"Really?" I asked eagerly, and he laughed at me, making me blush. "Sorry, it's just... You haven't seemed very eager to divulge any kind of information about yourself, and I'm so desperate to know more..."

"I'll tell you," he said softly. "You're the only person I'm willing to tell. Ask what you want to know, sugar. But please don't be disappointed by my answers, okay?"

I nodded and found a comfortable spot underneath his arm. We watched as the sun turned the room the most brilliant of colors, and I fell in love with his apartment, which I'd always thought was a little lifeless and impersonal. But now I understood it, from the stark, undecorated walls to the all-white furniture. He was an artist. An artist through and through. And he preferred the play of nature to whatever he could have done to the place himself. I loved that about him.

"Tell me," I asked softly. "I want to know everything there is to know about Miles Reilly."

"Where do I start?" he asked, and now, it was my turn to grin at him.

"Start at the beginning," I said simply. "Tell me about your childhood."

Immediately, I felt like I'd said something wrong. His face darkened, his expression fell, and the walls went back up.

"Or not," I was quick to say. "You could tell me about something else, anything. Tell me about your job. I'd love to know more about it."

"Okay," he said, seemingly perking up at the opportunity to speak about his work. "You know I'm a photographer."

"I could tell you were into it," I said cheekily and he tickled me under my chin, making me giggle. "But tell me more. What kind of stuff? What are you into? What kind of art do you like? Is it a hobby or do you make a living from it?"

He laughed and shook his head at my curiosity, and for a second I was worried his walls would go back up again. But then he started talking, his voice deep and kind as he filled me in on the details.

"I like watching people," he said, and I watched the sunrise through half-open eyes as I listened to him. "I like their expressions, the way I make them feel. Women, especially. I like their reactions to stimulation. Any kind. Music, sex, things that make them feel."

"Do you take photos of them?" I asked, trying to fight back the jealousy that was spiking my heart into a faster beat. "Of women?"

"You know I do," he said simply. Of course I knew. I'd Googled him, saw the photos of girls, overlaid with this and that. The very thought sent a wave of jealousy through my body, but confusing me further when he laughed lightly. "Maybe I should say I did. Before a certain someone came along."

I beamed up at him and he flicked my nipple with his long, strong fingers. I gripped his arm and made him wrap it around me, hugged into him.

"Go on," I whispered. "I want to know more. So much more. I want to know everything."

"Everything, huh?" he asked, chuckling. "There's a lot to tell. You sure you wanna stick around for it?"

"Yes," I whispered, giving him a vehement stare. "There's no place I'd rather be, actually."

"Good," he growled, an edge I couldn't interpret present in his voice. "Do you know what double exposure is?"

I nodded. "You overlaid their pictures with another picture."

"Yes, I take most of my photos on film and then develop them. After, I alter them digitally, creating a double exposure. It basically means joining together two photographs into one, overlaying one on top of the other. I pick whatever I think is fitting for the woman in the picture. I've done an innocent girl with church candles, her dad was a minister. I had a hippie chick with flowers blooming in a field. And so on and so on."

"What about me?" I asked impulsively. "What would you pair me with?"

He laughed and ruffled my hair and I made a show of sticking my tongue out at him.

"I guess you'll just have to wait and see," he said, and I furrowed my brow at him, prompting him to explain. "I have an exhibition at La Gallerie in about a month. I'd love for you to come and see the photos."

I stared at him, and wondered out loud, "Will you be there?"

"I hope so," he said simply. "I really would love to be. It's my first big exhibition. Most of my work is sold online as prints."

"Do you make good money?" I asked him, and he laughed at my honesty. "Sorry, I'm just curious. I don't know anything about this stuff."

"I do," he admitted. "Enough to live on. But I inherited some money, which made this apartment happen."

I looked around his place one more time. We lived on the same street, in an upscale part of town, but now that I was finally here, I knew his apartment must've cost at least half a million more than mine. It was truly exquisite. I would've loved sharing it with him...

I blushed at the thought, averting my eyes and burrowing my face into his shoulder.

As if sensing my discomfort, Miles tickled me and I giggled against his skin.

"What about your family?" I muttered, half mumbling because I wasn't sure whether he'd dodge the question or answer it truthfully.

"My family?" he repeated, and I nodded against him, still trying to hide my face. "Are you sure you want to know?"

"I do… please," I begged, and he sighed heavily before starting to talk again.

"I had a family," he said. "Parents. My father was an investment banker, my mom a housewife. We lived in a little suburban house until my father got laid off at work. Then, the rumors started spreading."

"What rumors?" I asked gently, looking up at him.

My fingers were exploring his face, the stubble on his chin, the firm line of his jaw. I was falling more and more in love with him as the minutes passed. I was falling for him so impossibly hard I could almost feel the impact physically.

"About my father," he replied stiffly, his eyes on the sun now fully above the horizon. "That he'd committed fraud, that he was the one who'd driven the whole bank into the ground. There was a whole bunch of layoffs after he left, and rumors like that spread quickly. Dad was fucking crucified. Blamed for everything. It made everything hellish. I was only three years old at the time."

"What happened?" I asked, my voice barely a whisper.

His story was building up to a crescendo, and I was starting to get nervous, even though all of it was in the past. I wanted him to be okay, I wanted his father to be alright. But a voice in the back of my mind was telling me this story didn't have a happy ending.

"He killed himself," Miles said simply, his voice barely even breaking. He held a hand up when I tried to speak. "Please don't worry, sugar. It was a long time ago, and I was just a kid. I barely remember him."

"But you still lost him," I protested. "You still lost a parent. A father. I'm so sorry, Miles. I'm so sorry you had to suffer through that."

He gave me a strange look, and in that moment we connected on a level we hadn't before, seeing the loss of our friends and family in each other's eyes and suddenly understanding we really did know what it was like, what it meant to lose someone like that, so suddenly, so final.

"Thank you," he said softly, then switched his gaze back to the window. "Would you like to know more, sugar?"

"Yes," I whispered without hesitation. "Please…"

Chapter 36

·MILES·

SERENDIPITY, NOUN
Finding something good without looking for it.

"What happened next?" she asked. Her voice was soft, not prying in the slightest, and I knew I could trust her. She was the first person I wanted to divulge the truth to, and it shocked me. But I should've known it would've been her in the end.

"Were you close with your mom?" she wanted to know.

"Used to be," I replied. "I guess when I was really, really little. I have a few nice memories of her. But after that shit went down with my dad, it was all downhill. Our house was taken away from us, and we moved in with my aunt. She had a house full of kids, and she didn't really care for having two extra people around. We didn't stay there long."

"What about your dad's company?" she asked. "Did they ever apologize for the wrongful accusation?"

I loved how she assumed it was wrongful, without me having to tell her. I loved her a little bit more for that alone.

"That came later," I shook my head. "But no, at the time it was a royal fucking mess. No one would employ Mom, not with my dad's last name. And she refused to get rid of that, saying she wasn't going to give up the last part of him. But I think it was really because she needed an excuse to feel sorry for herself."

Bebe touched my hand and I looked away as she stroked my skin, her touch so sweet, so fucking tender.

"Did she ever find a job?"

"Yeah, at this seedy bar," I explained with a grimace. "It was fucking awful. The guy there…. the owner. She started dating him, but he was bad news. She got herself high on dope, then stronger shit. She was an addict before I turned five years old."

I didn't want her pity, but her tender caress against my skin still felt so nice I could barely tell her to stop. And when I did, she ignored it, continuing to stroke me gently, as if she was trying to tell me it would all be alright. And I let her.

"My aunt kicked us out," I went on. "Around my birthday, too. So we moved into this seedy trailer park… My mom, me, and the guy. But it all went downhill from there."

"He didn't like you?" Bebe guessed, and I shook my head.

"No, he really fucking didn't," I confirmed. "And my mom and he both got deeper and deeper into the hole of addiction. The place we lived in… It wasn't fit for a child. It wasn't even fit for a fucking human being. It was a mess, a fucking junkyard. I used to wade through the trash just to get to my own bed, it was awful."

"Didn't they take care of you?" Bebe asked with a shaky, worried voice. "Didn't they care that you weren't being taken care of properly?"

"If they did," I went on, "they sure as fuck didn't show it. I lived in that shithole with them until I was twelve years old. Then, my mom got diagnosed with cancer."

Bebe gasped at my words, and I squeezed her hand reassuringly. It was all behind me now, but if it weren't for the ghosts of my past I would have well and truly moved on already.

"She died quickly," I said. "And her boyfriend only got more and more aggressive. It must have been two weeks after she died that he kicked me out. I was only twelve."

"Miles," Bebe breathed, her expression horrified.

I understood how heart-breaking the story was, in the back of my mind. I knew it wasn't any way to treat a child, or anyone, for that matter. But I'd never told this story. Never shared the pain of my past with anybody. And somehow, it felt like a fucking relief. Like I'd finally exhaled after years of holding my breath.

"It's okay," I said. "I only spent a few nights on the street. Then, I contacted my aunt and moved back in with her for a while. But already I was… fucked. Broken. What happened had shaped me and it was starting to show."

This was where the hard part came in, and I felt deeply embarrassed, having to tell her about my nasty habit. But I realized with a start I had left the trashed room open earlier when I'd had my panic attack. A quick look into the hallway revealed that it was now firmly closed, no sign of my weakness anywhere.

"I'd gotten so used to it," I said shakily. "The trash, the mess. When I lived in the trailer park it was perfectly normal to be surrounded by shit like that, and I... I guess a part of it stuck around. I felt weird if I wasn't surrounded by it... If I didn't have a corner to myself, a small corner where I could hide behind the filth, like I'd had in the trailer."

"Your own room?" Bebe asked, and I shrugged.

"Not really, there wasn't an option to have that in the overcrowded house," I explained. "But I had a small corner in the basement, and it turned from a storage room into a fucking... shrine to the life I'd lived before. I found comfort in it. Collecting used beer cans, dirty fucking pizza boxes, building forts with the stuff. I was a repressed kid, I didn't know how to interact with others."

"Did it make you feel safe?" she wanted to know, and I nodded, not trying to hide my surprise. She understood.

"My aunt found out," I finally managed to admit. "Not long after, maybe when I was sixteen or so. She called it my dirty little secret, made me feel really fucking ashamed of it. Threatened to throw me out if I didn't stop... But I couldn't. And she stayed true to her word."

Bebe's eyes were filling with tears now, but I was desperate to tell her that it wasn't as bad as it maybe sounded from the way I was telling the story. But of course, we both knew that would have been a blatant fucking lie. My life had been a mess.

"She sent me to live with my grandma," I finally said. "I barely knew her. She was Dad's mom, and she was really fucking strict."

I chuckled at the memory, remembering the woman who had shaped so much of my life. Her name was Delores and she was a former school teacher, strict and old school about everything she did.

"I lived with her until I was eighteen," I went on. "She was great but different. We weren't very affectionate to one another, but she supported me fully. She got me my first camera, helped me use a light room at school, pulling on some strings from her own teaching days."

"She was a teacher?" Bebe asked, and I nodded. "She sounds amazing."

"She was," I said simply, plainly revealing that she was gone.

When Bebe looked at me, I shrugged and swallowed thickly.

"She was much older. She died peacefully in her sleep when I was eighteen. But she did one thing before she left me, and I've always been grateful for it. Unlike Mom or my aunt, my grandma believed Dad had been innocent, and she spent most of her later years fighting to prove it."

Bebe settled into my arms and I pulled her close, inhaling her intoxicating scent as I went on, my voice a whisper in the shell of her ear.

"A few months after grandma died, I got an official post-mortem pardon for my father," I explained. "Along with a large settlement. I used it to buy this apartment and moved in about ten years ago. I had such high fucking hopes for this place."

She pulled my arm around her, urging me to go on with her eyes.

"I guess I just crumbled," I admitted. "Over the years, I got worse and worse. The only hobby I stuck with was photography. And I left the apartment less and less until I was fucking confined to it. Until it was too late."

"I'm so sorry," she breathed, her words barely discernible they were so soft.

But they meant the world to me. And what meant even more was that I'd told her my story, something I hadn't shared with anyone before Bebe. She'd been the right person to tell though, and I felt like I'd gotten rid of a huge burden. There was only one thing left, one dirty secret to share with my girl.

"I…" I started, my words breaking off painfully. "You know I'm messed up, right?"

She turned in my arms, directing her deep dark eyes into mine. She didn't say a word, just stared at me, and it felt like she was looking straight into my fucking soul.

"I have these panic attacks, and anxiety too," I went on. "I take meds – antidepressants, and antipsychotics. But there's another habit, something you don't know about."

"I think I know," she whispered, and it was my turn to stare at her. "I saw it… The little room."

My blood froze when I thought of it. The stench, the dirty little room, the epitome of my shame. But then I thought of something else, of the fact that Bebe was still there, right in my arms. She'd seen it and hadn't walked away. Hadn't judged me. She'd stuck around to hear my explanation, never stopping to ask me herself. She knew I'd trust her enough to fill her in eventually. My heart nearly burst with the love I felt for her in that moment.

"It's my secret," I admitted brokenly. "A dirty fucking secret. Because it reminds me of my childhood. Because it's the place where I feel safe. Surrounded by all this… fucking shit that used to be in the trailer. Sometimes it's the only place where I feel like myself."

Bebe squeezed my arm and I hugged her, my chest heaving.

"It's okay," she whispered, peppering my skin with kisses. "It's all going to be alright. I'm glad you told me. Do you like that room?"

"I fucking hate it," I admitted it. "I fucking hate what it is and what it stands for, and that I'm so dependent on it."

"I have an idea," Bebe said. "Do you want to come with me?"

"Yes," I nodded automatically, already trusting her with whatever she had in mind. "What are we going to do?"

"We," she said, jumping up from the sofa. "Are going to scrub that room clean and turn it into a proper dark room. And you'll never have to deal with your nightmares again. Do you think you're ready to let go of it?"

I stared at her in front of me, so small but so fucking full of life, overflowing with energy and enthusiasm, ready to help me in any way she possibly could. She was incredible, amazing. She was the missing piece I needed to feel whole again. She was the missing part of my fucked-up equation.

"You want me to get rid of the room?" I asked her, and she nodded with a shy smile.

"I want you to turn it into something positive," she explained. "Something that doesn't give you anxiety. A place where you feel safe without it being shameful for you. A place where you can be yourself, but you aren't afraid to show it to me, either."

The fear of her seeing my room was intense, making me shake.

"Are you sure you'll be able to help me?" I asked her in a desperate voice.

I realized now that I needed her so badly.

"Yes," she replied, sounding more sure of herself than ever. "We'll do it together. Our little project. Okay?"

I stared at her, my heart pounding. I wasn't sure whether I was ready for this, but she seemed so excited about it and so eager to help me. But what would happen if I crumbled under the pressure, if it was all too much for me?

With a start, I realized there was a smile on my face and that I didn't give a shit. I wanted to give it a try.

"Okay," I said.

Chapter 37

·BEBE·

WABI-SABI, NOUN
A way of living that focuses on finding beauty within the imperfections of life and accepting peacefully the natural cycle of growth and decay.

I could see the fear in his eyes as we approached the innocuous white door. He feared what lay behind, and I squeezed his hand to reassure him that it would all be alright. And then I opened the door.

Immediately, the stench was overwhelming. I fought the urge to raise a hand to my nose and hold it. I fought the urge to retch. Instead, I just offered Miles a bright smile and passed him the rubber gloves I'd found in his cupboards. We'd also gathered a whole bunch of cleaning supplies. I was starting to think this was Miles' only vice – apart from the tiny room, he kept everything else neat and tidy.

"Let's get to work, shall we?" I asked, and he merely nodded, giving me a second glance as if he was surprised by my lack of repulsion. "This place isn't going to clean itself!"

We stepped inside. The room was so tiny we had to maneuver so it would fit both of us. We were surrounded by trash, things I wasn't even sure Miles had used himself. There were pizza boxes with the rotting remains of the dish, takeout containers, bottles upon bottles of acidic drinks that smelled so disgusting my eyes watered. There were apple cores and vegetable peelings, there were dirty blankets, there was anything and everything that I could imagine, the odor of it all so overwhelming it was burning my lungs more than the bleach ever could.

I didn't let it faze me though, I just got to work, and Miles followed suit.

We worked for what felt like hours but must have been less than thirty minutes. The tension in the room was palpable, the fear and anxiety coming off Miles in waves. I stopped in the middle of picking up some trash and smiled brightly at him.

"Why don't we put some music on?" I suggested, and he nodded, his eyes nervously flitting around the trashed room. "What kind of stuff do you like?"

"Just… traditional old school rock," he said, and I made a face that made him chuckle. "What?"

"You're so old," I stuck my tongue out at him. "We're listening to my music today."

"Fine," he said with an exasperated sigh.

I tapped the app on my phone, and the tiny room filled with the sound of upbeat electronic music. Miles shot me a surprised look, but a few minutes later, I could tell the mood in the room had been lifted. We bantered and bickered as we cleaned the room, dragging out trash bag after trash bag. Then, we got to work with the cleaning supplies, and we scrubbed and scrubbed and scrubbed until the room started to resemble the storage place it should have been all along.

It took us five hours to clean the room, despite how small it was. I was surprised by the amount of residual gunk in there, but after all that time had passed, we stopped, exhausted but so pleased we smiled at one another.

"It looks amazing," I told Miles, and it really did.

The room was still just as tiny, but we'd cleaned the small barred window until it gleamed, and now it was filled with light. The hardwood floor was still intact, and the walls would need repainting, but the place was now spotless. I'd never done physical work like that, always relying on cleaners, but now I beamed with pride as I looked at the room.

"I'm so proud of us," I told Miles, but before I could get the full sentence out he was next to me, pulling me close, his hands rough on my own.

He kissed me with so much vigor, I knew right away how much this had meant to him. He kissed me like he was never letting go.

"Get the fuck in the living room," he growled at me, and I mewled, stumbling out of the small room and pulling off my rubber gloves as I approached the main living area.

Miles was close behind me, and I felt his minty fresh breath on my skin as he followed me outside. We'd been airing out the living room, and the windows were wide open. We were only on the sixth floor, so people could easily see us if they looked up.

I turned to face Miles and he was on me in seconds, rushing to tear my clothes off my body.

"Miles," I protested, but the word turned into a needy moan the second his hands made contact with my body.

I was desperate for this, desperate for him. I needed him so badly my whole body pounded with the need to feel him inside me again. I wanted nothing else but to submit to him completely, do everything he asked of me, kneel for him, crawl for him.

"Please," I begged as he tore into my clothes savagely. "Miles, please… Don't fucking stop."

He let out a low growl as he worked my body into a position he liked better, my ass against his crotch and my arms shivering as he held them above my head, pulling off my top and tugging my pants down until I was fully exposed to him. He got rid of my underwear by practically ripping it off me, and I mewled when the cold air hit my skin.

Then, he was tearing at his own clothes, desperate to get naked and join me. I stared at him, once again relishing in the beauty of his body, which was almost heart-breaking. He was a monster of a man, so fucking tall and strong, and it hurt to think of all the things he'd been through in his life. I wanted to personally hurt whoever was responsible for the shit he had to deal with on a daily basis.

"Touch me," I begged him, and he was on me in seconds, pushing me against the wall, my body helpless to his whims.

He raised my arms above my head again, pinning them above me as his mouth assaulted my throat, sucking at it as if he were trying to suck my damn soul out. His free hand was between my legs, his thick fingers roughly pushing into my pussy, fucking it into a state. I was dripping wet and ready, my mouth spitting words in a frenzy I was so desperate to have him hurt me more.

"More," I told him hungrily. "More, I want more."

And then he dragged me to the window and I was pressed up against it, my naked body on full display for anyone below on the street. It reminded me of the first time I'd seen him, and I found myself gloating, knowing I'd taken the previous girl's spot.

"Are you sure?" he asked roughly, and I nodded over and over again, desperate for him, desperate to have every bit of cruelty he had to offer.

"Hurt me," I begged him. "Fuck me hard and fucking hurt me."

In seconds, he'd pulled me to the next window. The one that was open, the breeze cold on my skin. I tried to shriek, but Miles slapped a palm over my mouth, holding me firmly in place.

"Don't scream," he ordered me, and I swallowed my fear as he held me out of the window, one hand over my mouth, the other in my hair.

The street was so far below me, but I didn't feel afraid. I let him have me completely and gave up every last vestige of control, packed it up all pretty, wrapped a bow around it and placed it in his care.

My eyes widened as I took in the street, my tits hanging heavily above it. This was it. This was the moment of madness I'd been waiting for.

I felt his cock entering me, the pure pleasure making me cry out for him. My hips bumped against the windowsill as he started to fuck me, relentlessly and showing absolutely no mercy for my poor flailing body.

Coming wasn't a decision, there was no option to back out of it. He fucked me so hard I was squirting over his cock in seconds, drenching him in my juices and begging helplessly for more as he dragged my hair back, making me look at the street, at my own apartment across from it, at everything I was willing to let go of so I could have my Miles.

His cock was punishing me, stabbing me so savagely I howled from the pain and pleasure combined. He fucked me like I was his property, and I fucking loved it.

I hoped he would never stop. His rough fingers were pulling my hair so tight I felt tears in my eyes, pricking and stinging and hurting me as he drove into my cunt again and again. And I couldn't get enough. Hooked on the feeling, the sensation, hooked on the way I felt every vein on his cock throb against the walls of my pussy as he took what he wanted.

My skin was covered in goosebumps, partly from the fear and partly from hanging out of the window, but I didn't give a sweet shit. I barely even noticed. All that mattered was this moment, where I belonged to him completely, and where I placed every last hope in his hands, letting him do whatever the fuck he wanted to with me – body, mind, and soul.

And right now, he was deciding to fuck it. Fuck it until I screamed for mercy but kept coming on his cock like a brazen whore, too far gone to stop myself and too drunk on my love for him to even want to try. I was an addict, and he was serving up exactly what I wanted, what I needed. I'd never have enough of him, of this.

"Come inside me," I begged him. "Fucking come inside me, right now."

"Fucking take it," he told me roughly. "You're going to take all of it, aren't you sugar?"

He turned me around in seconds, his cock slipping out and I mewled at the loss of him. Now, I was hanging outside as he held onto my waist, and he lowered me even farther out the window. I was terrified, my blood pumping, my heart and head screaming both from the fear and the pleasure. I never felt as free as I did in that moment, being completely dependent on him and reliant on his mercy.

"Do it," I said for the last time, but this time, the tip of his cock nudged at my asshole.

My eyes widened, and I whimpered, but he ignored it. He spat in his palm and lubed his cock for me, and then he was pushing inside, slowly, painfully slowly, but so relentlessly I knew he would be fully inside me in seconds.

I felt myself fighting him, felt the burn as my asshole tried to push him out, and he touched his fingers to my lips gently, giving me a crooked smile.

"Let it happen, sugar," he whispered. "Let it happen for me."

I exhaled, and he slipped inside me, making me gasp as he lowered me above the ground. I was terrified, so scared I was breaking out in a sweat. I looked into his eyes, feeling the absolute madness of the moment. Then, I threw my head back and laughed.

I laughed for him, for us, and for Posy. Because I was still here and damnit, I was going to live my life until the very last moment and enjoy every fucking second of it. I was going to love it, and make it worth it for every other person that didn't get to live theirs.

Miles chuckled and grabbed my tit, his other hand firmly supporting my back so I wouldn't fall. He drove into me one last time and it was enough. He grunted and came inside my ass, came so much I felt it spurting out of me as he kept fucking. I groaned for him and let go, letting my hands fall down and dangle above the ground.

"You're so fucking incredibly beautiful," Miles told me, letting me enjoy that special moment. "This is… it's incredible. I'm in love with you, sugar. I'm so fucking in love with you."

I opened my eyes slightly and blew him a kiss.

Epilogue

·MILES·

TOUJOURS, FRENCH
Always.

My nerves were getting the better of me.

I was breathing shallow, panicked breaths, my back pressed against the wall and my sweaty palms brushing against the metal of the coat rail. At least no one would find me here. At least people would think I didn't even show.

The doors opened a sliver, and my heartbeat quickened when I heard approaching footsteps. And then she was standing in front of me, a big bright smile on her lips and a cheeky expression in her eyes.

"There you are," she said, and I smiled guiltily at her. "Come on, I'll make sure everything's okay. I'll make sure you're okay."

"Promise?" I asked her shakily, and she nodded, a smile tugging up the corners of her lips. "Promise me, Bebe."

"Promise," she nodded. "I promise it will be okay. Now, will you come out with me?"

I gave a slight nod of my head, and my hand found hers in the cloakroom. It was dark and stuffy in there, but it was less frightening than the gallery outside, where people were waiting to meet me.

Bebe held my hand firmly but gently, and she tugged me out of the corner I'd gotten myself into.

"Come on," she said gently. "I'll be here every step of the way. You know I will. Have I ever let you down?"

I thought of the past few months. Of my girl by my side through doctor appointments, through meeting Dr. Halen in her office every week. I thought of her showing me all her favorite places in the city, and how patient she'd been when I broke down in the middle of a bookstore. How she'd helped me, taken care of me, how she'd made sure I was alright. And I knew I trusted her more than I'd trusted anyone else before. I was willing to put my life in her hands if it came down to that.

"No," I replied simply, a small grin on my face. "I trust you. Let's go."

She pulled me out of the cloakroom, and the light in the gallery was blinding, making me shield my eyes. But then I heard it, as we made our way front and center of the room. The applause. It was so fucking loud.

I looked up, my eyes focusing on the people around me.

The gallery was beautiful, modern and sleek, in monochromatic tones that ensured that the art stood out, not the furniture or the interior design of the room. It was a clean, open space and I loved it. It reminded me of my apartment in many ways.

There were countless people in the room, and as Bebe led me to the stage, I glanced at everyone in there. Men and women, of all sizes and colors

Peep Show

and beautiful fucking shapes. I would have been uncomfortable as fuck in this room a few months ago. In fact, I would probably never have come there. But now, with Bebe by my side, a surprised smile lit up my face. Maybe this was where I was meant to be after all.

She didn't stop until we reached the podium, and she handed me a microphone with a bright smile. She was wearing a tight little red dress with a flounce at the bottom, and black velvet heels. She looked so fucking stunning I wanted to make her drop down and spread her legs for me, so I could suck on her sweetness like a damn lollipop. I was head over heels in love with the girl. She awoke emotions inside me I didn't even know I was capable of. She was incredible, incredible, incredible. And I loved her with every cell in my body.

"Ladies and gentlemen," Bebe said into her own microphone. "Miles Reilly!"

Once again, applause. And this time it was deafening.

I looked into their eyes, their expectant smiles edging me on. And for once I didn't see demons, or monsters, or men out to get me. I saw the people, the stories, the personalities I was so desperate to catch in my own work. And I loved it.

I smiled wide and waved at the crowd and they cheered.

"I don't know what to s-say," I said shakily, my hand forming a fist.

This was hard. Fucking hard.

And then she was next to me, just like that, her hand wrapping around my own and her encouraging smile meant only for me. I fell in love again, every time I saw that sparkle in her eyes.

"I'm lucky enough to have my muse standing next to me," I said, my eyes now only on hers, as if I was speaking to her the way I usually did when we were home alone. Her legs on my lap, chucking popcorn in my face as we watched a movie. Parting those legs to let me see her tight, wet little cunt. Fucking her, the bowl of popcorn overturned, the mess forgotten. Yeah, I was craving that. But I also knew I'd have it that night because now, Bebe Hall was mine. And I wasn't letting go.

"I believe my next exhibition will be quite different," I went on. "Because if it was up to me, I'd only have photos of her. She's that incredible."

A collective 'aww' went through the room, but I wasn't done yet.

"So, in many ways," I said. "What you are seeing today signifies my past. And my future is standing beside me. Without further ado, I'd like to show you my work."

Everyone whooped, and several people in black outfits approached the canvases that were covered with sheets. On the count of three, they pulled the sheets down, revealing my work to the guests. There was complete silence, but the only reaction I cared about was Bebe's.

I looked right into her face as she glanced around the room, letting go of the microphone. I saw how crestfallen she was, how much she hated it. The images of those women, naked, overlaid with all the things that signified them. She turned her hurt gaze to me, her bottom lip trembling, and I took her hand in mine. She let me take it reluctantly, and I led her to the biggest canvas, my masterpiece.

She gasped when she saw it and I smiled to myself.

It was a portrait of Bebe, one I'd taken months earlier. She had her arms in front of her body, hiding her naked tits. Her middle was visible, her sleek, taut stomach so sexy I wanted to lick it. The rest of her was covered in a rumpled white sheet. She had some hair in her face and was trying to pull it back, laughing as she did it and looking straight into the camera.

Just like all my other work, this one was a double exposure as well.

Peep Show

I'd struggled for months on what to pair with Bebe, but I knew I'd hit the nail on the head.

Her picture's overlay was a photo she'd taken of me. Shirtless, with my hands extended protectively in front of me, shielding my face from everyone. Because she was a part of me. And I was a part of her. Together, we made a whole.

She looked at me, and her eyes were filled with tears.

"For you," I said brokenly, and she gasped, running into my arms.

No other words needed to be said. We simply hugged, and the crowd cheered and applauded, but for once in my life, I didn't give a shit. I wanted them all to see how much I loved this beautiful, stunning, exquisite girl. I wanted them to know how much I cared.

The next second, several people joined our hug and I laughed as I saw all the people joining us. Her parents, Arden's parents, Nick, and finally, her best friend, the girl who'd been her rock these past few months, and who'd become such a staple in my apartment I always joked around I should just give her a key.

"I'm so proud of you!" Arden told me with a bright smile. "What a beautiful collection, and the centerpiece… Wow."

We smiled at one another and I felt the genuine love coming from her. I liked this girl, a lot. She was as good for Bebe as she was for me. And her boyfriend was nice as well.

Bebe's mom was so excited her cheeks were blushing fiercely, and her father kept clapping me on the back as he congratulated me. In that moment, surrounded by friends and family and my girl's hand in mine, I felt complete.

For the first time in years, I didn't feel alone.

One look into Bebe's eyes… Those brown, beautiful pools of dirty little secrets and whispered promises.

And I was complete.

I pulled her against me, her body willingly bending against my own.

"You," I breathed against her lips, not giving a shit who was watching. "You've changed my fucking life. And I'm never letting you go."

"Miles," she breathed.

"You need to be mine," I said. "I want you to be mine completely. I want you to wear the sign of it. I want my baby in your fucking belly. I want my ring on your finger. I want you beside me. Now, and forever."

She blinked the tears away as I dropped down to one knee, bringing out a little box from my pocket. The ring inside was something I'd gotten three months ago after she'd helped me clean out the dirty room, a week after my last bleach bath. I hadn't taken one since.

It was platinum, with a big diamond because I knew my little magpie liked shiny things.

My anxiety was sky high. I could barely breathe. But I had to do this.

I popped the box open with shaky fingers and smiled at my girl.

"Will you make me the luckiest man alive?" I said.

"Yes," she whispered, and I slipped the ring on her finger while the whole damn place cheered.

And for once in my life, I wanted them to see every last bit of it.

Because there was nothing more beautiful than the girl in front of me, my ring glistening on her finger as she threw herself around my shoulders.

Nothing more beautiful than *us*.

THE END

Acknowledgements

It was a rainy evening when I looked across the street and saw him. He was just a half-naked figure in the window, and I tried not to look, but he sent my imagination on a chase for stories. Now, I'm pretty sure all he does is try on outfits and admire himself in the mirror, and yet, I'm still grateful for him, because he made me write Peep Show.

I have a number of people I'd like to thank.

First off, my boyfriend Tilen for being a part of me, for being the missing puzzle piece that makes me whole. Thank you for holding my hand. Thank you for leading the way.

I'd like to thank author besties Alessandra Hart and Jade West.

Alessa, you may not know it but sometimes, you're the reason I get up. Because I get to talk to you. Because you get me. Because you have my back, and you're the best friend a girl could wish for. Because you Photoshop my face onto camels and make me laugh even on the worst day. Because you're YOU, and I love you.

Jade, what can I even say? From the moment you saw Peep Show's cover, you've been supportive and kind, always knowing the right thing to say, always pushing me forward. I wouldn't be this far without you, and you are my rock. Thank you.

To my editor, John Hudspith – how do you do it? How do you make my words this good? I'm forever envious of your talents.

And to the incredible Letitia Hasser who designed this cover – GIRL! I want to frame it it's so beautiful.

OK, time to get mushy!

The stranger in the window made me touch a part of myself I don't feel comfortable sharing. The part that's afraid of anything and everyone. The voice in my head that tells me I'm too weak. Too fragile. The lonely girl I've kept hidden away because I'm afraid of her. With Peep Show, I've discovered her beauty. I've discovered her pain. And I've found a story inside it.

I've been emotionally invested in a book before, but I've never felt like this – like I'm pouring a piece of me, a piece I'm terrified of showing you, into words.

As I wrote Miles Reilly, I fell in love with him. And with it, I came to accept a part of me that I'd deemed damaged, broken. I came to realize it was something to battle, something to better, not something to be ashamed of.

Miles taught me to speak out. Miles taught me to help others. Miles told me to stop being fucking selfish, sugar, and see all the broken souls out there, and give them a piece of me that will make them feel less alone.

Miles and Bebe's story consumed me for four months, and I'm surprised I got it done in that time because it was a hard one to write. I couldn't be happier that I did it though, and I've let myself open up about things that are difficult to speak about.

I know we all have our demons, our secrets. I am hoping that Miles, Bebe and I have taught you it's okay to speak about them. It's okay to say you're hurting. There are people who will help you. There are people who care.

And you know what?

There is a happily ever after for you.

Now go chase it.

Isabella xx

Printed in Great Britain
by Amazon